CONTRA-ODESSA

Asteroid Publishing, Inc.

Library and Archives Canada Cataloguing in Publication

Markman, Alex
Contra-Odessa / by Alex Markman.

Issued also in electronic format.
ISBN 978-1-926720-16-6

I. Title.

PS8576.A677C66 2011 C813'.6 C2011-904485-4

Library and Archives Canada Cataloguing in Publication

Markman, Alex
Contra-Odessa [electronic resource] / by Alex Markman.

Electronic monograph in PDF format.
Issued also in print format.
ISBN 978-1-926720-19-7

I. Title.

PS8576.A677C66 2011a C813'.6 C2011-904486-2

Printed in Canada

Contra-ODESSA is a work of fiction. Names, characters and events are the products of the author's imagination. Any resemblance to real persons, organizations or events is coincidental and not intended by the author.

Book cover by Maryna Bzhezitska

Other novels by Alex Markman

Payback for Revenge

Messenger of Death

The Dark Days of Love

Table of Contents

Foreword

Inspired by a true story, this novel is about the activity of KGB and CIA agents in Argentina in 1960s. Enthused by success of the Cuban revolution, Soviet Union leaders stretched their resources to support communist and leftist radical groups in Argentina in their struggle for power. America was very active there as well, supporting political parties and movements that opposed the assault of communism. Interests of the two superpowers, as well as their secret services, collided in Latin America.

Shortage of foreign currency was one of serious obstacles for the Soviets. To solve this problem, at least in part, they sent to Argentina a group of its best operatives with the task to find Nazi criminals and high-ranking SS officers, who kept their fortunes in Swiss banks—fortunes obtained by looting during World War II—and extort from them their secret account numbers. This money was indeed used for support of the communist movement in Latin America. I happened to know about this operation by sheer chance.

Once, on a bright Saturday morning, my longtime friend Dr. Z visited me for a cup of coffee and a small talk. Before coming to Canada he lived in the former Soviet Union, where he was a reputable doctor in charge of elite sport teams. Among the best in the field, he was widely known in the privileged circles of the communist regime. He was regularly sought after to treat the privileged of all sorts: prominent party leaders, technocrats, and—another part of the human race susceptible to ills—high-ranking KGB and GRU officers. Many of those secret service bosses became alcoholics and drug addicts who, sensing the end of life approaching, were eager to share with someone trustworthy the intriguing secrets of their past. Perhaps, knowing that Dr. Z was friendly with many famous Soviet writers they had hoped that he would tell them the story, which, as they had thought, should belong to history. Or, it might have been the intelligence, quick wit, charisma, and excellent "miracle" medical service, which was Dr. Z's signature at every visit that loosened their tongues, leading them to spill the beans.

At the time of Dr. Z's visit, I was writing a novel about Stalin's time and needed access to open KGB archives. When our second cups of coffee arrived, I asked him if he still knew someone who could help me with this. He promised to make some calls.

"You know," he said, "some twenty years back, I had a few patients among top-ranking KGB people. One of them called me at one o'clock in the morning. 'Come to me at once,' he said. He begged me to save his life. Although I was still mostly asleep, I detected by the timbre of his voice that he was dying. Using words that were never a part of my vocabulary, I dressed up and went to him. When I arrived, I recognized that he was drunk, and obviously had one leg in the grave.

"'I have to take you to the hospital,' I said to him. 'I have neither proper medical instruments, nor the whole range of medication, to save your life.'

"'No, no,' he protested. 'Under no circumstances. This will ruin whatever remained of my carrier in KGB, and subsequently my whole life. I would rather die.'

"'But if you die in my hands, it would ruin my carrier,' I argued, 'and perhaps a lawsuit will follow.'

"Anyway, to make a long story short," Dr. Z

continued, “I did whatever I could. It took a few hours to bring him back to the land of living. In late morning, when he felt much better, I was about to leave but he begged me to stay.

“'I need your company, please,' he said. 'I want to tell you some stories of my life. You know, in the '60s, I was one of those who were in charge of organizing a heat team, whose task was to find former SS members and Nazis who kept their money in secret accounts in Swiss banks, and make them speak. Eventually the team got in quite a mess there. Four of them disappeared without a trace. But later I got a hint of what happened to them. They had plenty of professionally forged passports, connections in different parts of the globe, incredible skills.'

“Suddenly he was so weak that he fell asleep,” Dr. Z said. “At that time I was not interested in the story. I had so many encounters with people like him, heard so many no less intriguing stories, that another one wouldn’t bother me a bit in my state of exhaustion. All I wanted was to go to bed. I have never seen him afterward.”

Dr. Z said that he did not know the names of KGB operatives. Most likely, this was true, although even if he did know them, he wouldn’t have told me. In the middle or late 1960s, when they operated in Latin America, they were young, in their late twenties or early thirties, which means that as of now, in the year 2011, they may be still alive in their late sixties or early seventies.

Prologue

The KGB department responsible for intelligence and subversive operations in Latin America was always at the backyard of the Soviet leaders' political games. The region was too far from the hottest spots of the Cold War, such as Western Europe, Korea, and later China. After the Cuban crisis though reports were composed regularly, but they were delivered first to the chairman of the KGB, and only then, upon his discretion, were included in a presentation to the leadership of the Communist Party about the state of affairs in the places of marginal importance. That's why the head of this department, Oleg Kruglov, was rather puzzled when the chairman, Vladimir Semichastnyi, called him in June 1962, and invited him to the meeting in the Kremlin at 3:00 p.m., to the office of Nikita Khrushchev, the top party leader and head of the government. Kruglov was at a loss; should he rejoice or grieve? As the Russian proverb says, "Save us, Lord, from the Master's favours."

Feverishly arranging in his mind statistics of achievements and details of the most important events, he rushed to the Kremlin, where he was led to Khrushchev's office. In it, he saw the two, sitting imposingly in huge comfortable chairs, Khrushchev and Semichastnyi.

"Come in, Kruglov, don't be shy," Khrushchev invited him as if they were longtime friends. He stood up, shook hands with Kruglov, and gestured at the vacant chair. Kruglov did not detect even a trace of insincerity in his smile.

Semichastnyi also stood up and shook hands, and

then returned to his chair and crossed his legs. Kruglov looked around in search of a place for his thick binder, filled with most important intelligence reports from Latin America.

"Put it over there," Khrushchev said, stretching his hand at the table in the corner. "You won't need it anyway. We'll have just an informal chat."

"It's OK. I'll hold it, if you don't mind," Kruglov said, asking permission. Getting an approving nod from Semichastnyi, he took the vacant chair and put the binder on his lap. The friendly reception did not lull his vigilance and did not blunt his alert. There were too many falls into abysses, starting with the encouraging smile of a boss.

"I invited you to get information from the source, so to speak, about the state of affairs in Latin America," Khrushchev began, leaning back in the chair. His posture and manner conveyed the notion that the conversation was going to be friendly and lengthy. "The Cuban example convincingly demonstrates that a similar revolution may take place in other countries of the region. Right in America's backyard! I don't need to explain to you what it would mean for the global communist movement. What can you say about the political climate there?"

"The economies of these countries are getting worse by the day," began Kruglov, clearing his throat. His voice became husky from excitement and anxiety. "People get agitated and furious; socialist and communist ideas conquer their minds. Many take to arms, but at present they lack effective leadership, capable of uniting separate forces for the organized fight."

"What is your evaluation of our spy network there? Can we give them a meaningful support? For sure, Americans don't sleep. They understand the danger of progressive movements."

"Our agents' network there is not so strong as in other parts of the globe," said Kruglov. "It all boils down to money. Our enemies have big financial support, and not only from Americans."

"Who else?" Khrushchev raised his eyebrows.

"From Germans. From the former SS members, and all sorts of Hitler's high-ranking myrmidons. Mind you, they robbed all of Europe during the war, placed money into Swiss banks—their fortunes are beyond estimates, I guess. But they supply more than money to reactionary regimes. Some of them take part in military training of ultra right groups, and often participate in military operations."

"Yes, yes." Khrushchev nodded a few times. "Where is their largest concentration?"

"In Argentina, Paraguay, and Brazil."

"Why did they choose Argentina? Who laid the road for them there?"

"One of the reasons—before the war there was a large German community. Easy to dissolve among them. Most of them had money and enjoyed strong political influence. Some of them accepted newcomers from the Third Reich with a welcoming embrace."

"How did it actually happen? I guess, not without the help of Argentinean government."

"You are right, Nikita Sergeyevich. A lot did Eva, or Evita, as they call her, the wife of the former president Peron. She traveled Europe at the end of the forties, met with heads of governments, spoke with the Roman pope, and succeeded in obtaining support and understanding. Even worked with Otto Skorzeny. This Hitler's hero established an organization, whose task was to smuggle Nazis from Europe to Latin American countries and elsewhere. Its name is an irritant to the Russian ear: ODESSA."

"Why did they use the name of our city?" Khrushchev asked. "What is common between Odessa the city and this organization?"

"This is a coincidental occurrence of sounds and

letters," said Kruglov. "It is an abbreviation of its name's first letters." Kruglov pronounced it in German: "Organization Der Ehemaligen SS-Angehorigen. This means: Organization of the former SS members."

"I understand," Khrushchev grumbled. "I remember Skorzeny, of course. I was then on the South Front. Partisans captured Mussolini and wanted to bring him to justice. Well, we thought, he is done for, this fascist. But no, soon we got news: Otto Skorzeny made a raid with his team, and freed Mussolini. Not for long, actually."

"Skorzeny is not from a weak stock," remarked Semichastnyi. "Not for nothing was he Hitler's darling."

"He was arrested by the Allies, wasn't he?" said Khrushchev.

"Captured, put in jail, and escaped," said Semichastnyi, nodding for the emphasis. "We still don't know how he managed that."

"We can only guess." Kruglov shrugged his shoulders. "Money played the main role here. The former Hitler's band had enough of it to bribe a saint. Swiss banks safeguard their fortunes."

"Corrupted Western world," Khrushchev said with a grimace of contempt. "Money solves everything there."

"Exactly," agreed Semichastnyi with enthusiasm. "If this hero were in our prison, I'd love to see him attempting escape."

Khrushchev cackled, rocking his swelling belly. Semichastnyi joined him out of sheer subordinate's solidarity.

"After he escaped," Kruglov continued, "he became more than a hero, like an idol in the minds of Nazi criminals. No wonder he was the head of an organization busy with dispatching Nazis from Europe."

"What can you say about our spy network in Argentina?" Khrushchev directed his question to Kruglov

"Not large, but efficient," was the answer. He knew

that Khrushchev was not very strong in spy activity abroad, and even international affairs in general. Some of his orders caused nausea in top KGB commanders and those who executed them. Kruglov felt in his gut that something of that sort was going to happen now. "Our people are solidly implanted in Buenos Aires. Some are in business, others are professionals—engineers, teachers, whatever profession they had had before. They are mostly involved in gathering information, but some penetrated both progressive and reactionary movements, and even the government."

"All of them are local recruits?"

"No. Almost all of them are our people, sent there right after the war, when immigration to Argentina was pretty strong."

"At the same time when Eva helped the former SS members?" asked Khrushchev.

"Absolutely right, Nikita Sergeyevich. Often Nazis shared the same ship with the Jews, who escaped death in concentration camps, and different sort of other folks from all over Europe. Eva had hoped that they would bring to Argentina either money or professional and business skills. And that's what really happened. With SS money she managed to implement many social reforms, the most important of which were government pensions for seniors and free medical service for the population…"

"Of course," Khrushchev interrupted. "It is easy to spend stolen money."

"She did not forget herself either," said Semichastnyi. "Her husband, the former President Peron, now lives in Spain in luxury. No doubt on the money Eva got from Germans."

"Getting back to our network there," Khrushchev directed his question to Semichastnyi. "Can we expand it? Can they substantially assist progressive movements there?"

"It all boils down to money," Semichastnyi said.

"We have almost no foreign currency. Our people are self-sufficient there. But, on the other hand, they can't do much beyond gathering intelligence."

Khrushchev tightened his meaty hand into a large fist, and thought in silence for a minute. When he raised his head, his stare was heavy and grim.

"Do Nazis still have their money in Swiss banks?" he asked.

"Some of them do," Semichastnyi said. "We have reports from former SS people who changed allegiance and became our informants. However, to make even a rough estimate of what they have is beyond possibility. Information about their account numbers, as well as the amount of money in them is known only to owners of these accounts."

"Do you think that some money is still there?" Khrushchev kept asking. Kruglov wasn't able, in spite of all his feverish efforts, to understand why the top boss of the Soviet Union was so interested in the Nazis' money. "Wouldn't it be simpler for them to transfer it to Argentina?"

"It is simple, but rather risky," explained Kruglov. "This country lacks political and economic stability. At any moment left-wing parties may seize power there, and then anything may happen with their money. Even worse, they may start hunting these Nazis, and then these SS guys would have to be on the run. In such a case, the money in Swiss banks would be very handy. In general, comrade Khrushchev, rich people all around the globe prefer keeping their money in Swiss banks. Not only for themselves, but for their heirs as well."

"Any way to find out their secret accounts?"

"No chance. These are secret numbers. They are known only to the account holders. Bank officers would not share this information for any money, as the punishment is long years in jail."

Khrushchev stared at the wall, deep in thoughts. Then he turned to Semichastnyi.

"I have an idea I want to share with you," he said, turning his head from one to another. "What if we send to Argentina a team of reliable operatives, and ask them to find Nazis who have secret Swiss accounts. Ah? We can use this money to support progressive movements in Latin America. What do you think, comrades?"

Kruglov gasped, but put himself together just in time. He decided to speak only if Khrushchev demanded an answer specifically from him. Luckily, Semichastnyi saved him from trouble, at least in Khrushchev's office.

"It's a brilliant idea," he said, but Kruglov detected a great deal of anxiety in his voice. "Indeed, we are short of foreign currency. It is logical to take money from war criminals and spend it for a righteous cause."

"Good," Khrushchev said, rising. "Report to me about the progress regularly. Attend to the matter immediately."

"Absolutely. Our reports will be under the caption 'Contra-ODESSA.'"

Khrushchev laughed. "I like it. Good luck, comrades."

Chapter 1.

The jungle of Amazon basin in Bolivia was never quiet for long. Shrieks of giant parrots, alarming chirps of monkeys, growls of jaguars, or deafening yells of animals being killed or eaten alive by predators always disrupted brief stretches of silence, particularly at night. In this mess of flora, mosquitoes, and swamps, a special unit of the Bolivian army chased communist rebels, trying to advance with as little noise as possible.

Their commander and instructor was an American, Glenn Sheppard. Only twenty-nine years of age, he was already one of the best in the CIA crop fighting guerillas in Latin America. However, he realized only after getting into this legendary rain forest that it was hardly possible to prepare people for war in the jungle. Something unexpected always came up, forcing the commander, and soldiers, to make an instant decision and rush into action. The difference of right or wrong was usually a matter of life or death.

Maurizio, the second in command from locals, stayed about thirty steps away from him, holding his automatic rifle at the ready. When foliage was not too dense, Glenn glimpsed at his face. He smiled. Glenn could not help but admire him; this dark-skinned mestizo smiled most of the time, no matter what danger or hardship he was going through. Even before a battle, he remained in good mood, when all other soldiers were tense, if not scared.

"What is the secret of your happiness?" Glenn asked

him once.

"Death is inevitable," Maurizio answered. "I have no idea when it will strike. I don't know how to avoid it. That is why I don't want to spoil my life worrying about it."

Before coming to Bolivia, Glenn was convinced that all nonwhites belonged to inferior race. It was not a hostile feeling, not a racial theory, or some sort of conclusion based on experience. This was just a notion that needed no explanation or supporting arguments. That's how God creates things, he thought. In Bolivia, he had to work with them, live with them, and fight with them shoulder to shoulder against the common enemy. Most of them were illiterate, but smart nonetheless, eager to learn, reliable in hardships, and with sense of humour. Some of them became his friends.

Maurizio shortened the distance between them and said, "Hot, isn't it?"

"Terrible," Glenn agreed, wiping streams of sweat running from his forehead into his eyes. "I gather it' s about a hundred Fahrenheit, if not more."

He did not mention it was also 100 percent humidity, as a rain shower started, making his idle observation superfluous.

It was hard to believe that only a week ago he was chasing rebels in a completely different climate and scenery of La Paz, a province just three or four hundred miles northwest, where the Andes mountains were still capped in snow, and nights were windy and freezing. The days, however, were dry, pleasant, and comfortable. Rebels demonstrated great skills in camouflage, but once found they were easy to fight with. They did not have communication equipment and coordinating skills, so crucial during the combat. They had neither proper military training nor armaments. Brave, dedicated fighters, they were doomed in the very first encounter with a trained military unit.

Although they were enemies, Glenn understood what made them take to arms. The population was very poor; no wonder that some, disgusted by misery of their lives and hopeless, boring existence until the grave, decided to die as heroes, proud of themselves and respected by the living.

A cry of a parrot distracted him from reminiscing about the past. Glenn looked up at it; the bird's feathers were painted in red, green, and blue; its beauty and harmony were dazzling. There were as many of them around as sparrows in an American city suburb.

"Arára," said Maurizio, tracing Glenn's stare. That was what locals called this species of parrots.

Glenn smiled, trying to cope with the sudden pain in his stomach and a fit of nausea. Not good, he thought. Being sick during the battle is a sure way to the grave.

Lianas, exotic plants, and lush foliage interwove with each other, forming an impenetrable green roof. The sun could not break through its thick umbrella. Some of rays though managed to sneak through the small openings, brightening some leaves or small branches of the low growth.

Perhaps sometime in the future, he thought, it would be a wonderful country for adventure travel. In a comparatively small territory it had an amazing diversity of climate and scenery: snowcapped peaks of the Andes; alpine meadows; prairies, called pampas; floating islands; and, of course, the Amazon basin rain forest.

Glenn stood still, listening to the treacherous silence of the jungle and trying to discover a trace of human steps. Nothing suspicious so far. The rain had stopped, but all clothes remained wet. It would never dry out here, he knew that. It would be nice, he thought, to take a cool shower, and sit on a veranda with a glass of brandy and a cigar. But it was just a fleeting thought. Any blind bullet might make his wish obsolete.

The communication equipment, mounted on the

Maurizio's back, began speaking something hardly comprehensible with the background of static noise. A few birds, hidden in the crown of trees, responded from above to this mechanical sound with furious, protesting screams.

"They are over there," Maurizio explained, stretching his hand to the left. "Rene says that there is a swamp and a small lake at the back there, swarming with alligators." Maurizio grinned. "Let's give them some treats today."

The sharp, rattling drone of shots drowned out all other sounds of the wilderness. It was the time for Glenn to take total control of the battle. He had no doubt that guerillas had no way to escape; however, fighting them would not be easy. The dense vegetation gave them a good cover. Only the sound of a shot might give a trace of their whereabouts. Rebels, however, can easily notice the advancing soldiers and aim at the moving targets with deadly precision.

Glenn's unit was well trained. Soldiers advanced fast, now crawling in the undergrowths, and then hiding behind the trees, shooting, shouting commands and warnings to each other, reloading ammunition, and obeying Glenn's coordination. Glenn heard screams of pain from the edge of the swamp. These were wounded, perhaps dying guerillas. His soldiers were doing a good job.

He also began to shoot at where the plants moved. The roar of pain came from there, and the rebel jumped up to the open, holding his chest and shaking in convulsions. There was another shot from somewhere behind him. The bullet smashed the wounded guerilla, and he fell silent.

Glenn kept shooting blindly, in the direction of sounds. He knew that he was not doing a good job; his vision became blurred, hands and legs weak. For good measure, the piercing sting in his chest made his breathing harder. He knew for sure that this was not a wound, but what was it?

Fewer and fewer shots now came from the rebels' site. It seemed that the battle, as short as it was, was nearing the end. Shouts of his soldiers came from everywhere; a few guerillas already stood with hands up in surrender. The shooting stopped completely. In its stead, agitated voices of soldiers filled the forest.

To Glenn's ear, a shriek of horror from the left, behind his back, came as a contrasting dissonance to the military growling of the unit.

Summoning up all his willpower and remaining strength, Glenn rushed there. What he saw stunned him. His friend Maurizio stood on his knees, holding in his arms the upper torso of a man, stained in blood all over. With his blurry vision, Glen nonetheless made out the definite signs of death on the face of the still alive rebel. For sure, only a few minutes of life remained in this already unconscious body.

"Glenn!" Maurizio's yell vibrated with tears, horror, and pain. "Glenn! Please help. Oh, my God, why did it happen? Glenn, please do something. He is dying."

"Who is it?" Glenn asked. His legs no longer supported him. He sat on the ground with the wish to die.

"My nephew," Maurizio kept screaming. "God, why did he join them? Oh, my God!"

Somebody helped Glenn to stand up. He walked a few steps, then dropped on the ground, and drowned into the total darkness.

A few times, somewhere in the unknown space and time, he regained conscience, but did not see much. He felt like he was in flames, but his body was shaking, as if from a terrible cold. Then the darkness descended again.

After one of these breakouts, he woke up and opened his eyes. He was weak, hardly able to move a limb, but felt much better. Looking around he saw a clean, nice hospital room, and tubes attached to his body. A nurse from the locals came in and greeted him with a smile: "Buenos dias. Como esta?"

"I'm fine. Where am I?"

"In the hospital, of course."

"Where is it? What city?"

"Santa Cruz. I think I can free you soon from those tubes."

"Please do. What happened to me?"

"Malaria. The worst kind of it. We tried hard to pull you through. I am happy that you made it. You are a very strong man. And handsome at that." A smile of female appreciation brightened her face.

"Thank you. When you will let me go?"

"Soon. By the way, someone very important wanted to see you. He asked me to let him know when you were OK. Wait a few minutes. I'll fetch some food for you."

The next day, in the afternoon, he had a visitor. His boss Max Robertson, in charge of a few Latin America countries' intelligence, came in with a trace of smile on his inquisitive face. Bold, tall, in a formal civil gray suit, he would have passed for the president of large corporation.

"Glad to see you," he said, and sat on the bed. Glenn got up and sat beside him.

"How are you, Max?" he asked. "Something important?"

"You've done an outstanding job here in Bolivia."

"Thanks, Max. What is coming?"

"Bolivia has changed for the better lately." Max hugged him. "There are new hot places where we need you more."

"Such as…?"

"Argentina. Communists and leftist radicals have gotten more active there. The government is not stable, and neither is the economy. Many hotheads have been inspired by the Cuban revolution, or such heroes as Che Guevara. They also get some money for their activity, but we don't know the source yet. My guess is that the Russians are involved, perhaps not directly, but we don't know how. They also believe that the Cuban revolution could be exported."

"What kind of job is there for me?" asked Glenn.

"Mostly intelligence. That's what you wanted to do, right?"

"True."

"You will reside in Buenos Aires. Our particular interest, as I said, are radical-left movements."

"Would there be a similar job, like in Bolivia?"

"I'm sure that it will come to that. But for the time being just gather as much information as you can. Your Spanish is flawless, your skills are outstanding. See you next week. You will get all instructions then. Do you wish to have a short vacation and visit your home in the States?"

"No."

Max shrugged his shoulders. "Be well," he said and left.

Glenn leaned his back against the headboard and crossed his arms on his chest, reflecting. He loved America, but did not want to live there. Such a nice boring life! He could not live without the thrill of danger, the aroma of new places, the excitement of exotic women, the aura of different cultures, and the beauty of new scenery. He realized that one day he might pay a heavy price for it. Who lives by sword, dies by it. So, be it. He holds the sword not out of necessity, but by his choice. Argentina…Just south of the border, but a completely different country. Must be fun.

Chapter 2.

When Robert arrived at Buenos Aires airport, he already knew the city in minute details. Training with the KGB for his mission was brutal, relentless, and tiresome. Exams were not like those he had experienced in university – the passing mark must be 'excellent', as it was the only one on the scale of evaluation. He studied numerous maps of Argentina, its cities, customs, and, most importantly, maps of Buenos Aires. Not only that, but the instructors had given him stacks of photographs of this humongous city, and then, after browsing them, Robert had to tell whatever he knew about the building, street, or place shown on the one he picked up. His Spanish and German were flawless, and his story – his false biography – he remembered better that his real one. His forged Argentinean passport, issued in the name of Robert Chavez, did not arouse any suspicion. His outward appearance was as benign as his passport: a young, intelligent man in his late twenties, thoroughly groomed black hair neatly combed back, sensual lips and blue eyes. In a moderately expensive gray suit and unbuttoned shirt, he could pass for a not-so-long-ago university graduate on the way up in his career as a doctor, lawyer, engineer, or the likes. His appearance suggested a typical young man from a middle class family, who had been protected by loving parents from roughness of life, and whose major concerns were his education, career, money and girls.

Outside the airport doors, the air was hot, humid

and, it seemed, devoid of oxygen. In such weather, shorts and a T-shirt would be more appropriate, he thought, throwing quick glances around. To his surprise, he found that he was not the only one dressed in formal business attire.

"Amigo, amigo!" he heard a scream from the car stopped close by. In the frame of its opened passenger side window appeared the sunburned face of a taxi driver, serious and impatient. "Need a taxi, my friend?" he kept shouting in a hoarse voice. "Where do you wish to go?"

"Café Tortoni," Robert said.

"Sure, amigo."

Next moment, the driver was out of the car and approaching Robert with a few quick jumps. He was about to grab the suitcase, but Robert did not let him. He was warned that some taxi drivers were skilful thieves, able to quickly pick any lock and snatch a thing or two from the luggage while the client was in the car.

"Open the trunk, I'll put it there myself," Robert said in a commanding tone. The driver gave him a second, longer look, apparently realizing that his first assessment of this passenger was wrong. Robert closed the lid and returned the stare. The driver understood its meaning and took his place at the steering wheel.

Outside the airport the car turned to the main road, which was a mess of disorderly, maneuvering cars and cacophony of honking horns. The hot, humid, and densely polluted air was not suitable for breathing. For sure, the driver was not of weak heart. Miraculously escaping two sure-death collisions, he got into an argument with another taxi driver, shouting obscenities through the open window, and once, when the traffic stopped, wanted to jump out and teach him a hard lesson.

Dealing with police on the first day in Argentina was not in Robert's cards.

"Stop it," he demanded in a sharp voice. The taxi

driver nodded in consent, but under his breath kept mumbling obscenities, suggesting his disapproval of the other diver's sexual preferences. When out of words, he made an attempt to make a left turn to the road, which, Robert knew for sure, would make their trip longer and more expensive.

"Don't go there," Robert warned him just in time. "Keep going straight."

"I …" the driver stuttered, but Robert interrupted him.

"Take the shortest route. Bring me fast and safe to Café Tortoni, and I'll give you a good tip. Got it?"

"Sure, sure. Whatever señor wants." An appreciative smile of a small time crook, whose trick was not successful, manifested the change of his attitude.

"You know the city pretty good," he said with confidence.

"I lived here all my life," Robert said.

"I can see that, señor. Sure, I'll take you there in no time."

He did. Under Robert's watchful supervision, he removed the luggage, put it on the ground and accepted money with thanks, smiles, and best wishes. Robert walked through the door of Café Tortoni and gave it a quick look-around. All tables were taken except one, close to the entrance. Not the ideal observation point, as the end of the hall would have been, but at least he could sit there undisturbed and get on with whatever was supposed to be done. He took a chair and put his suitcase under the table.

"Coffee?" asked the waitress, slightly leaning forward to demonstrate her serviceability.

"Yes, please. Do you have a public phone here?"

"Certainly. Over there, near the entrance to the dancing hall."

He came to the open booth, dropped a coin inside the slot, and turned the slowly rotating wheel of the phone.

After only one beep, it clicked. The male voice at the other end said, “Hola”.

“Señor Fernandez? This is Robert.”

“Oh, yes,” was the calm reply. Robert told him the password and the voice gave him the right response.

“Do you mind coming to Café Tortoni for a cup of coffee?” Robert suggested.

“Sure, sure, amigo. I’ll be there in half an hour.”

When Robert returned, the coffee was already on the table, with a glass of water beside it. He didn’t order the water, but when he looked around he noticed similar glasses on other tables too.

“Clever,” he thought. ‘Coffee dehydrates, and water replenishes the lost liquid. Good service.” He leaned back and gave the place a thorough examination.

Everyone around was engaged in animated conversation. His impression was that something important had happened in the life of the country, and it had become a nagging issue of heated discussions. But through the drone of voices Robert caught patches of talk about fashion, for men and women, the latest news, or even personal matters of a very private nature. Nobody was concerned with being heard. Perhaps there was a grain of wisdom in such carelessness – only Robert was listening; everyone else was busy talking.

With a smile, Robert recalled the lessons of his team leader. ‘The mentality of a spy is opposite to the ordinary individual. Normally everyone wants to distinguish himself from the crowd, whether by dress, appearance, manners, or clever talk. A good spy must look so ordinary, boring, and unremarkable, that you would hardly notice him. It comes with practice.’

He leaned forward, reached for his coffee, and took a sip. Placing his left elbow on the table, he propped his head up with his open hand while studying the menu. He wore a ring with a flat, black onyx on his middle finger, which was meant to help the Resident to recognize him.

He slowly rolled his eyes, taking in faces, dresses, arrangements of tables, interior elements, and exits and entries. A few columns divided the space along the hall. Behind the closest of them, one table over, sat a woman, who drew his attention. Undoubtedly of North European descent, in her middle forties, she was very, very good looking. No doubt from a well-to-do household, she seemed a high maintenance lady: smooth white skin, blond, blue eyes, a string of large pearls tastefully crossing the space between her neck and ample cleavage. Her sleeveless dress exposed her nicely shaped arms, which she used now and then for reticent gesticulation.

Her female companion was hidden behind the column, but her also bare arms could be seen. They flew in sporadic flaps, then hovered slowly over the table, and withdrew out of sight behind the column when the woman with the pearl necklace spoke. The fingers of both women were heavily loaded with golden rings.

A funny thought came to his mind that a good artist could make a picture of them as, 'The Thrill of Gossip'.

It was a mistake to give this woman a second look. She caught it and stretched her sensual lips a bit in appreciative smile, apparently welcoming his attention.

'Try to avoid eye contact as much as possible in public places,' Tristan, the group leader, had instructed more than once. 'Without it, people won't remember you.'

Robert put his head down and, examining the remaining coffee in the cup, restored the woman's image in his inner vision. Her large eyes, the colour of a cloudless sky, were calm, fearless and conveyed a sense of the confidence of a lady with money and power. She could be Swedish, Norwegian, or even German. Well, if she is German, she might really be a catch. Who knows? As the Russian proverb says, the beast runs to the hunter.

He did not miss, however, a man who came in and stood at the entrance for a few moments. 'This is him,' Robert decided without any doubt, although he had never seen the Resident before and did not know how he might look. The new visitor, it seemed, did not pay any attention to Robert. Holding a leather briefcase in his hand, he lazily approached the table and said: "Do you mind if I sit here?"

"Sure. Please do."

Robert nodded, sizing him up and down. Below average height, in his late forties, brunette with silver glistening on his temples, dark eyes and a longish face, he gave an impression of a good-humoured Argentinean, dropping in for a coffee break. His formal gray, dark-striped suit suggested a man who had just left his office. He took a chair, sighed, and turning his head to the right, as if searching of the waitress, pronounced the password under his breath. Robert gave him the right answer. The man smiled.

"Jose Fernandez," he introduced himself. "You Robert Chavez?"

"Yes. For Argentina."

Jose laughed.

"Like it?"

"Don't know yet. Just arrived. Looks like a fun place. Much, much better than the place I was before."

"It is. But it is a crazy place too. With crazy people." While he spoke, Jose removed a large envelope from his suitcase and pushed it to Robert. "Take it. There is some money, the key for your apartment, your address, and your phone number. It was not easy to rent it for you, as landlords demand all sorts of references, documents, and assurance. You have enough money there to rent accommodations for the rest of the group. Now, I will give you my work number; remember it, but use it sparingly. You've been instructed how to communicate with me, so do it always this way, never in an open text. The telephone system in Buenos Aires is an annoying mess. Pick up a call, and there's a chance that you will hear conversations of other people, sometimes funny …"

"Coffee?" the waitress asked, leaning forward to Jose.

"Please, pretty," Jose agreed with as smile, and ran his hand over her bare arm. The young waitress did not mind. She responded with a permissive smile and moved away, wiggling her hips.

"Nice show," Robert remarked, tracing her retreat.

"Most women here are receptive to courtship from men of any age," Jose explained. "With your looks, you could have lots of fun here under other circumstances."

"I hope that I already have these circumstances," Robert said with a smile.

"Don't bet on it. If time permits. Now, in the envelope you'll find a few blank Argentinean passports. Later I'll give you some Bolivian and Chilean ones. If you need others, please tell me in advance. I was told that you know how to fix them."

"Yes, we have someone. Top notch specialist."

"My wife's name is Liz. You can speak to her the same way you speak to me. Whenever you obtain – he chuckled – account numbers and their associated names, give them to us over the phone, using our coding system, of course. Any question?"

Robert opened his suitcase and put the envelope inside.

"What's my address?" he asked. "I don't want to open the envelope now."

"In San Telmo." Josef told him the exact street number and name. "You can move to another place later, if you like. I think that it is the ideal one for you – not rich, but not a very poor neighbourhood; moderately priced, easy to make friends there or to abstain from any. I know that you'll need a house in the suburbs. I'll help you rent one, as this might be tricky."

"We need guns," Robert said.

"I know. You will get four Beretta's in two-three days. I have arranged that."

Coffee arrived, and Jose took a sip, sizing the waitress up and down. Robert looked at the woman with the pearl necklace. Damn it! Their eyes met again. This time he noticed a trace of a smile on her lips. Jose murmured, casting his glance down at coffee: "Noticed someone interesting?"

"She noticed me."

"That's okay. Any connection might be useful. You never know. One more thing. There is an antique dealer in Rosario, who is wealthy and has, as he boasts, Swiss accounts. His name is Gerwig Bosch. One of our agents is an antique dealer too, and, ostensibly, a friend of Gerwig. I will give you the address of his shop in Rosario. Worth trying. Now I have to go, though. Good luck."

Jose took the last sip of his coffee and left. Robert looked at the woman behind the column. She sat alone, holding a small mirror in one hand and lipstick in the other. No doubt she used this mirror to watch him.

He recalled his team leader saying that a good operative should catch whatever an ordinary eye would miss. This woman for sure is German, he thought. Worth a try.

Earlier he noticed that her companion had gone to the ladies' room. The moment was very convenient to test the waters. He stood up and approached the woman.

"I beg my pardon, señora, but it seems to me that we have met someplace before," he said. She put the mirror and lipstick in the bag.

"Maybe," she said, tilting back her head. Large eyes took up almost half of her face. Might very well be my mother, but still a beauty, Robert thought.

Spikes of a few wrinkles ran from the corners of her eyes when she gave him a gift of her nice smile.

"My name is Robert," he introduced himself.

"Bertha. I'm sorry for not being able to talk to you longer right now, Robert. Here it is..." She paused, fishing for something in her leather bag, and then gave him a visit card with her name and telephone number on it. "Please call me any weekday, but make sure that it is not later than five o'clock in the afternoon. Do you have a phone number?"

"Not at the moment. I just moved from my old place and the phone is not connected yet. I'll give it to you when I call you."

"Good."

Another gentle, promising smile. Amazing, how fast it goes, he thought, returning to his table. He paid his bill, went out, and called a taxi.

"San Telmo," he said curtly, and told the driver the exact address. "I'll tell you how to get to my place on the way there."

"I know where it is," the driver said and made a confident, albeit dangerous, maneuvre in front of the car to his left.

The scenery of the big city floated past Robert like an endless theatrical decoration. He was thrilled by this live stage, but at the same time, his mind was preoccupied with many tasks. He related real streets to the ones in the city map, so firmly imprinted in his memory from his training in the Moscow suburbs and in Cuba. He tried to memorize everything his eye caught. The excitement of adventure set his mind in the mist of happy intoxication, stronger than alcohol or any drug. He felt like a Spanish conquistador who put his foot down on a new, beautiful land, with determination to make it its own. All his life, as far back as he could remember, he was craving for risks and the shock of an adrenalin rush that comes with them. Danger was always a part of his life, be it a sport, like slalom, or encounters at night in the dark streets of suburbs, ruled by local riff-ruffs, and later, on the KGB missions.

He could not live long without heart-wrenching stress and intense action. They gave him a feeling of power over other people and circumstances, a joy of which was more intense than sex. Risky life was the goal and the best reward in itself.

In his university years in the Soviet Union, he read more than once in the newspapers that people in all countries around the globe want peace. Often he entertained himself with a question: what if, by some miracle, genuine peace could descend upon Earth? What would people like him do? Create danger for others for nothing, just to satisfy their craving for adventure? Sooner or later, adventurers would come to power and shatter the world into ruins. Perhaps now, we live in the most peaceful time in the history of humanity, because the wounds of the Second World War are still bleeding. They remind the world what risky business is all about.

"Here you are," the taxi driver said, pulling in at the side of the road. A horn screamed behind him. A woman driver did not like his sharp turn in front of her car. The driver spat out his unsolicited opinion about women in general and this one in particular.

Robert picked up his luggage and walked through the main entrance of the apartment building into a small lobby. It was empty: no concierge, no furniture, or decoration. There was a single elevator, with doors made of metal bars connected by hinges. There was no light inside it.

Robert pressed the button. This action produced no effect. The elevator remained quiet, as if it had nothing to do with what Robert did. He was about to press the damn button again, when the elevator got a second wind. Its metal doors produced a crunching sound and opened slowly, as if afraid of falling apart if it were to attempt a faster speed. Robert stepped in and selected the 5th floor. The door closed in the same manner as it had opened before.

The elevator moved up with nervous jerks, but stopped on the fifth floor as expected. After a moment of hesitation, it made another convulsive jump and fell calm, commemorating the trip with solemn silence. The door remained closed. Robert hit its metal grid with his fist, and it opened slowly with sounds of crushing bonds and the gnash of rubbing rusted steel.

Robert stepped into the short corridor and quickly found his apartment. When inside, he closed the door behind him and lingered at the threshold, observing his new dwelling. This was a spacious bachelor flat, with a small kitchen to the right, a large room with a sizable bed, dining table, a few chairs, and a love seat. Nothing suspicious so far. He crossed the floor, unlocked the patio door, and stepped out to the balcony. It was wide, running along the whole length of his apartment. Two plastic reclining chairs were set in the middle of it, and a bucket with a mop stood in the right corner. 'Nice view out there; looks like a beautiful European city. Hopefully we will enjoy the stay,' he thought, coming back inside.

He unpacked his luggage and took a shower. There was not much hot water, and it was not as hot as he liked, but it was still a pleasant one, refreshing and invigorating.

Naked, he went to the kitchen. There, he was greeted by a huge cockroach. The beast moved its antennas to assess the intentions of the large intruder. Apparently not expecting a happy outcome, it crawled into the crack between the sink and the wall. Robert opened the refrigerator. As expected, it was empty, save for a bottle of the local non-alcoholic drink in the door compartment. He brought it to bed, laid down, and lit a cigarette. It was a pleasure to have a rest after the hustle and bustle of the journey. After a few good swigs from the bottle, he took the visit card, which the woman with pearls had given him in Café Tortoni, and examined it diligently.

The name 'Bertha Jaeger' was adorned with strings of flowers and leaves. Beneath it was her telephone number.

Robert had twice been in love with a woman, and in both cases for a short time. He regarded love affairs as another sort of adventure, a challenge, for which the pleasure of sex was the reward. In Argentina, he had more important challenges. Bertha might not be such an easy prey, but she could be an exciting lay eventually in spite of her age. For sure, she was German, and might be of help for establishing useful connections or for providing information.

His memory brought him back to Cuba where he, together with other three team members, spent half a year in preparation, or, as it was dubbed, an 'adaptation' period. Besides continued intensive training, they had to mix with the local population, make friends, and even have love affairs, if that was someone's choice. The goal was the complete transformation of their personalities into the Latin American look and behaviour to such an extent that every local would take them for one of their own. It was fun; Cuban girls were lovely, hot, and entertaining. A little money at his disposal made him a king among the appalling poverty of the local majority.

Robert lit another cigarette and brought the bottle to his lips. The carbonated liquid tingled his taste buds agreeably. He glanced at the huge balcony window. It was already dark out there. The sounds of horns penetrated inside, together with strange voices from adjacent balconies and sporadic screams of kids from the corridor.

His memory drifted him farther back in time, to the very beginning of all this. Four KGB operatives were called to the meeting room, where the man in the general outfit told them about their new assignment to Argentina. The essence of it was not disclosed at that time.

"You certainly will know your real names from each other," he said, regarding each one with his heavy stare, "but you should never use them until you come back. Let me introduce you to one another by the names you should remember and always call each other." He stretched his hand in the direction of an unremarkable man sitting next to Robert on his right. Round face, thin lips, dark gray eyes and brown hair cropped short, and a blank expression conveyed the feeling of mediocrity – not worth noticing. Everything in him was average: size of shoulders, height and clothing. "This is Tristan," the general continued. "He is your leader. Obey his orders." Turning his face to Tristan, he asked: "39 years old, aren't you?"

Without a trace of smile, Tristan responded: "Will be in two months."

"Robert," the general stretched his hand in his direction, "is fairly new in the international division of KGB, however, he has been a few times on various errands in Spain and Italy. 27 years old, excellent analytical skills, fluent in Spanish, Italian, German and English without accent. Incredible capability in dealing with people. Photographic memory, sporty, and a sharp shooter."

"Not at a live target, though," Robert said with a chuckle. He understood the general's remark as a hint at the nature of the new assignment. Must be something dangerous, he though with a pleasant thrill.

"And this," the general moved on, nodding at the young woman sitting to the left of Robert, "is Lara. Only 28 years old, but has done a good job outside our borders. She is a registered nurse. Might be handy, if something happens to you, or your targets. She has many other important skills, though. Her Spanish is perfect. She has also a good knowledge of pharmaceuticals. Got it?"

Everyone nodded with an understanding smile.

Robert was well familiar with the department of poisons and drugs, which was established in this organization a long time ago, during Stalin's rule. It developed not only poisons of various effects, but also special drugs, capable of shattering the nervous system, destroying will power, and making anyone succumb to the demands of interrogators. It was clear what pharmaceutical knowledge of Lara the general alluded to.

"She is also a master of forging signatures, passports, and any other documents. At the start you will get Argentinean passports, but later we supply you with others, so that you can freely move from one country to another."

During his speech, Robert threw stealing glances at Lara. Blond, pretty, blue eyes and full lips, a bit snub-nosed, and with healthy, flawless skin. Good boobs, narrow waist, and nice legs. True bimbo, fun to play with, but she looked impregnable. Noticing Robert's interest, she stretched her lips into a smile. A small dent formed on her right cheek. She returned him a mischievous glance, in which he unmistakably read the question: "Got it?"

"And the last in the row is Sergio. He is 30 years old, an engineer."

"Former engineer," Sergio boldly cut into the introduction.

"Yah," agreed the general. "But still, a graduate of Moscow Energy Institute. Has strong arms; fluent in Spanish. German and English so-so. Can shadow anyone without being noticed, good with different sorts of machinery, also a good shooter and handles documents almost as good as Lara does."

Sergio responded to everyone's attention with a nod. Broad shouldered, with a thick neck, he looked very strong. However, his longish face with dark eyes and his brown, modern hairdo did not convey menace. Rather, on the contrary, the guy seemed gentle and intelligent.

"Details of your assignment, as well as specific training, you'll get in Cuba."

It was on the first day in Cuba when Tristan gathered the group and said, "After the adaptation period we will go to Argentina. The order is to find former SS members and prominent Nazis, who keep their money in Swiss banks, and obtain secret account numbers from them. We know from different sources of intelligence, including information from the former SS turned informers, that millions of dollars are there. Perhaps hundreds of millions, as our information is limited. Mind you, they robbed almost all of Europe. The money must be substantial. The risk for us is significant. Whatever remained of ODESSA got organized there and will be alerted as soon as one of them disappears."

"Disappears?" asked Robert.

"We cannot let them go after they give us their account numbers, can we, Robert? He would stir all the Germans, and the local police and secret service. We won't have a chance to escape, not to mention continue our mission."

"Do we have any information on them?" Sergio asked.

"Yes. We have a short list of those who might have Swiss accounts. We don't know how much money remains there, if any. They could've used all the money, or left it intact, we don't know. There is no way to know, other than through the confessions of the account holders, which I hope we will obtain eventually."

Everyone chuckled.

The memory of Cuba faded in Robert's mind. He took the last swig from the bottle, closed his eyes, and fell asleep.

***

He woke up in a merry mood, craving for breakfast and ready for work. In a small café down the street he had a hearty meal, coffee and cigarette, and then took a long walking journey to Avenida Corrientes, famous for its thriving day-and-night life. Missing nothing that came into view, he was nonetheless deep in thought. It became his second nature: think, analyze, and at the same time, imprint in his memory every image or event, which might be of interest in the future. Passing one of numerous cafés, he took a cursory note of an elderly man sitting at the table close to the pedestrian walk, reading a newspaper. Nothing of interest really, as all cafés look similar: the young and the old occupied tables inside and outside, talking, laughing, gesticulating, flirting and watching human traffic.

'Do all these people ever work?' he asked himself, and smiled at the thought. 'Kind of nice to waste time like that, sipping coffee and watching the elegant gait of girls on high heels, with mini skirts provoking the imagination.'

When the table with the elderly man was already behind him, Robert suddenly stopped. At first it was just an unconscious impulse, after which a logical explanation jumped into his mind in the shape of large letters, printed at the top of the newspaper, which the elderly man held open in full view: DAS ARGENTINISCHE TAGEBLATT. This was the biggest German newspaper in Argentina. In the past, there were many in its staff who ran from Germany in the thirties: some of them were Jews, some – Germans with strong anti-Hitler views, communists, homosexuals, and liberals of all sorts.

Robert turned around and came to the table. Now the newspaper totally hid the reader. Only his hands, densely covered with brown aging spots and wrinkles, dark-skinned from long exposure to the sun, could be seen, holding the newspaper at its edges. Light wind tossed its corners.

"May I sit here?" Robert asked, glancing at the

large print of the article titles. The newspaper folded at once, revealing the face of the reader. About 65 years old, almost bald, he combed back his remaining long hair. It only emphasized his baldness, covering nothing. Hard to guess what original colour his hair was, as even the eyebrows of this man were silvery gray. His eyes were sad, almost tragic, but a glimpse of hospitality flickered in them when he said, “Sure, please sit down.” No doubt, this man was glad to have any company.

“Hot day,” Robert said, grabbing an easy chair opposite the man. Making a facade of a friendly, lazy smile, Robert examined him. His long, suntanned face was carved with pronounced vertical wrinkles above the bridge of his nose, running up to the top of his forehead; from his nostrils down around his dense, silver moustache to his mouth; from corners of his mouth to his jawbone; and in the middle of his cheeks, along his whole face. All these made him look like a clown in grief, like something tragic happened to him, but the crowd couldn’t help but laugh, associating his look with something funny.

Below his chin, wrinkles ran in other directions: across the throat, in thick, fatty strips.

“Indeed,” agreed the man to the weather remark, making another messy fold of the newspaper. “What’s new in this country?”

“My name is Robert.”

“Claus,” the man reciprocated, and, bringing his cup to his lips, made the emptying gulp of his remaining coffee.

“Something interesting in the newspaper?” asked Robert.

“Not much,” Claus said with a tone of regret. “Not any more. It used to be a good paper when I came here in thirties. Many good journalists worked for it. I was among them, by the way. I am a writer and journalist, you know. I mean, I was.”

“Interesting,” Robert said. Indeed, it was.

The waiter appeared at his side.

"Some coffee?"

"Sure," Robert nodded, not taking his eyes off Claus. The waiter pronounced something incomprehensible and left. Robert took a moment to look around. People, people everywhere, lots of them, more than on Gorki Street in Moscow at that time of day. The smell of gasoline, mixed with the odour of melting asphalt, was nauseating. Traffic on the road was horrendous. One could watch it as a circus show where motorized acrobats manage to avoid fatal collisions for the amusement of the spectators.

"Some of us were anti-fascist, anti-Hitler, you know," continued Claus in brisk pace of speech, as if afraid that Robert would soon be bored of his old, trivial story. "There were many good articles in this newspaper at that time. Many German intellectuals found their home here, in Argentina. Who could guess at that time that the country would get into such a political and economic mess? Tell me, how could one guess?"

"Not me." Robert made a dismissive gesture. "I was born at that time."

"You surely were. What a time it was! I met with the finest intellectuals of our century here. By the way, I was a few times at small parties with Stephan Zweig. Have you read anything by him?"

"Of course I have." Robert's interest in this man doubled. "I have read everything he wrote. In German."

At this moment, the waiter was back with the coffee. He placed a steaming cup and saucer for Robert, and a glass of water.

"In German?" Claus cried. Switching to German, he asked: "You know German? Where from?"

"My mother was German. She died a few years ago. I love German."

"You have no trace of an accent, young man," Claus said, delight ringing in his voice. "Remarkable."

"Tell me some more about Zweig," asked Robert.

"Oh, Zweig. Of course. He was mentally unstable, you know. He thought that the Nazis wanted to kill him. He told me that he had seen men following him on the street, apparently in preparation for kidnapping him. He thought that Hitler wanted to bring him to Germany for an open trial, and torture him in a prison cell. It was not true, of course, but he indeed had some reason for being scared. In his Schachnovella, the protagonist, Chintovich, personified a brutal mental force, stripped of culture, humanity, and reason. Indeed, a fascist incarnate. No secret though that some in the local German community were sympathetic with Hitler. They could've helped, perhaps, to capture him, if Gestapo deemed it necessary."

"What happened since then with the newspaper?" Robert asked. "Sorry, I don't read it, I am more Spanish than German. Sorry, but…"

"Nothing to be sorry about," Claus interrupted him. "New generation has different interests. All changed at the time of Peron. Many Nazis were welcomed here, and the government put enormous pressure on the newspaper."

"Do you know any Nazis personally?" asked Robert.

"Yes!" Claus exclaimed triumphally. "I was an investigative journalist. I found some former SS, who immigrated to Argentina after the war. None of them was willing to talk. I was fired from the newspaper for my effort. At that time, I got a few threats. I knew they had a secret organization, which mission was to protect them if the government failed to do so. I think it is still strong, particularly after Eichman was kidnapped by Israelis."

"Very, very interesting," Robert encouraged the talkative mood of his new acquaintance. "Did the government have any incentive to offer them a refuge?"

"Many. The country's economics was in doldrums. Germans, whatever moral fabric they had, brought here money, education, professionals, and managers. They set up businesses, some very successful. They supported the government and the government supported them."

"Well, well. I think the German community must have accepted them. They probably know now all those former SS who came here. Why don't they report to international tribunals about Nazi criminals' whereabouts?"

"You are wrong, young man," Claus said, leaning forward with a quick jerk. "Many in the German community did not want to know them. The former SS though, preferred to integrate with the local population. It made sense for them to disappear under false identities, forget about the past and have a new life."

"If I were you," Robert said, "I would report to a German tribunal in Europe, or to Americans, about those SS men whom you found. Why are you silent about that?"

"I am too old for troubles," Claus said. "These people have lots of power. They have money. They can easily kill me, particularly at this time, when people disappear without a trace for no reason."

"I am not afraid of them," Robert said with a well-played emotional outburst. "I will do it, if you don't mind. Just give me the name and address of any one you know."

"Don't be crazy, young man," Claus said, smiling and leaning back again. "You are too young to risk your life."

"Listen, Claus," Robert said with a frown. "When you were young, you did crazy things, defying the danger. I am young. I want to take risks. I hate Nazis. These people have to be brought to justice. Would you give me their names?"

Claus nervously crunched the newspaper, and then gave Robert a long, thoughtful look. Robert tried his best to play naiveté, righteous outrage, and indignation towards Nazis.

"Well, I can give you some names," Claus

mumbled. “It was more than ten years ago, mind you. You may find none of them. I have something in my files at home. Give me some time to dig up my records. I will call you. Do you have a phone number?”

“Of course I do.” He scribbled his number on the napkin. “Do you?”

“Yes, I do.” Claus tore a corner of the newspaper and wrote his number on it. “Here it is. Let’s be in touch. I see that you have a good soul.”

Chapter 3

After passing the threshold of a small but exquisite restaurant on Avenida de Mayo, Glenn lingered a few moments in front of a mirror. With satisfaction, he noticed that he had lost the look of a typical American, which he had had at the start of his previous assignment. His face still held the saturated suntan of Bolivia. However, his blond, shortly cropped hair, blue eyes, and straight nose clearly identified his North European ancestry. In a tailored suit and with civilized, reticent manners, nobody would guess that he was a man on a special task force on dangerous assignments, living a rough, stressful life.

He dismissed a complaisant waitress welcoming new guests at the entrance and went straight to the table where his new recruit was waiting for him. This was one of the top-ranking policemen in Buenos Aires, and worth every penny on Glenn's payroll.

"Hi, Eduardo," he greeted him, taking the chair across.

"Nice to see you, Glenn." Eduardo responded with a welcome smile of a dog who was about to bite. "Unusually hot this time of year, don't you think? In your country it is spring; here is fall. Hard to adjust, I gather." Eduardo made a great effort to become amiable to the best of his ability. But nature gave him a face that was good only for conveying menace.

Eduardo did not know that Glenn had been in Bolivia, accustomed to the opposite seasons in the southern hemisphere. All he knew was that Glenn had a cover job in an American company in Buenos Aires, which was involved in the export of Argentinean agricultural products. He also knew that Glenn worked for the American secret service.

"First, my token of appreciation," Glenn said, and pushed across the table an envelope filled with money. Eduardo grasped it before it could finish sliding.

"Thanks," he said with the same weird smile. Glenn scanned the dining hall to make sure they did not arouse anyone's curiosity. Eduardo's look was not for public places. Although not a subject of newspaper articles and photographs, Eduardo attracted unwelcome attention. His large head was crowned with a messy hairdo, a few wisps of which hung over his forehead. Everything in his face was large: a bulbous, wide nose; Mediterranean, olive-shaped eyes; long, thin lips; and a protruding square chin, bony and strong, as if capable of withstanding any blow. Anyone would take this descendant of Italian immigrants for a mobster rather than a high-ranking policeman. A thought crossed Glenn's mind – he wouldn't like to be one of those whom this brute interrogated.

A tall waitress with shapely curves everywhere diverted his attention to her niceties.

"Anything to drink?" she asked.

"You first," Glenn suggested to Eduardo.

"Yes, a bottle of wine," was his guest's quick response, "and I am ready to order." He gave the waitress the specifics of his taste without looking in the menu. Obviously he had studied it many times before, as it had been his choice of a restaurant. Glenn asked for only a steak with the famous Argentinean sauce. When the waitress left, they resumed their dialogue on a more serious note.

"Both left and right radical groups intensified their activity," Eduardo began his reporting. "We have some informers in both. We know their leaders, their activists.

We don't know yet where the rebels in the provinces get their arms from."

"Do you know where they get money from?" Glenn asked.

"Not exactly. I know that Che Guevara has some connections here, as he, as an Argentinean, has plenty of friends, followers, and admirers."

"Is there any chance that we will see him here?"

"No." Eduardo decisively cut the air with the edge of his hand. "Not at this time. We will capture him as soon as he puts his foot on Argentinean soil."

"Sure?"

"Positive."

"Now. Back to money matters. I need to know where all radical groups get money from. I need to know who, if any, stands behind them."

The waitress came with wine and poured it into large goblets. Glenn looked out the wide window. The traffic on Avenida de Mayo was horrendous. A cacophony of horn screams, tire screeching, and the shouting of taxi drivers could be heard even inside the restaurant.

Such disorderly people, Glenn thought, waiting for the waitress to leave. I doubt that they will ever get organized. Hard to believe that most of them are of European origin. They all want to be heroes, cheaters, revolutionaries, and get social assistance for that. They want to distribute fame, money, and power equally among all. They hardly understand that if they did that, they would get not much more than they have.

"Some radical groups are supported by the government." Eduardo resumed his monologue, taking a large swig from the goblet. "There is pretty strong anti-Jewish propaganda, instigated by the German newspaper *Der Weg*. They support right radical groups as well."

"Interesting," Glenn commented. He tried the wine as well. "I guess *Der Weg* is supported by and large by the

German community."

"They became particularly visible after Israelis kidnapped Eichman," Eduardo continued. "So far, there has not been much violence, but their propaganda takes its toll. Perhaps it is just revenge directed against the Jewish community, or maybe there's some other reason as well."

"For instance?" Glenn asked.

"You see, it is nobody's secret that many recent German immigrants fear the same fate. They might be behind the scenes. This is just my guess, my hypothesis, so to speak. Nothing concrete."

"Can you try to find out?"

"M-m-m. I can try."

"Something bothers you?"

"Well, they have, through the German community, a strong influence on the government. I guess that they are well organized, as all Germans are, and very secretive, when they want to be. It would not be safe to cross their path."

"Who are they, that might be well organized?"

Eduardo took time for a few sips of wine, avoiding Glenn's eyes.

"Have you heard anything about the organization ODESSA, established by Otto Skorzeny?" he asked.

"I sure have," Glenn said. "There is a lot of hoopla about it, mostly highly entertaining and convincing fiction, but no one's found any material evidence of its existence."

"You never will. This organization is not like the SS or the Gestapo. It does not have a formal membership, listing of personnel, archives, or any paperwork for that matter. They do not pay wages to its executives, nor do they have membership fees. Actually, its members come and go, and even Skorzeny does not know everyone. I had a few encounters with SS people here and know a little bit about them. Trust me, they know how to keep secrets and how to be well-organized. Don't underestimate them.

Dangerous people."

Glenn did not respond, and Eduardo took it quite rightly as a sign of disapproval.

"It's not that I am afraid of something," he said, leaning forward and looking Glenn in the eye. "Just to let you know that it is not an easy task. But I'll work on it, if it is so important to you."

"Not much. Most important is information on communist and left radical groups. My bosses are concerned with the export of the Cuban revolution. With such economical disorder in all Latin American countries, anything can happen. We cannot allow Argentina to be a second Cuba. No way."

"Sure," Eduardo said. He watched the waitress approaching with their dishes in hand. He had a contented gleam in his eyes.

"Beautiful girl," Eduardo said when she left. His stare followed her until she disappeared into the kitchen. "You can have as many like her as you wish here."

"We'll see," was Glenn's uncommitted response. The business part of the meeting was over.

"Don't you like local girls?" Eduardo asked, while chewing a large bite of meat.

"I have more important tasks here."

"Come on." Eduardo clearly was skeptical about the importance of other tasks. "How old are you, may I ask?"

"Twenty nine."

"I thought you were older. Even more to the point. I am fifty. Believe me, a good lay is the best thing in life. When you are young, and a good-looker like yourself, you take them for granted and think that your attraction will last forever. Not so, my friend. Enjoy life. It won't last forever."

"We'll see," Glenn said in the same manner. "I want to do too many other things besides laying girls. I am always short of time. But you are right, I should enjoy life."

Chapter 4

Every day of the next week, Robert bustled about, arranging the settlements of arriving team members. Back in Cuba, they decided to rent a house for Lara; she needed seclusion, undisturbed privacy for dealing with drugs, poisons, and medical instruments, not to mention inks, papers, and other accessories for forging documents. Robert found the ideal place in the suburb called Villa Santa Rita. One of the three bedrooms inside the house was without windows; it looked like a solid cube, built of tiled floor, sturdy walls with electrical outlets for floor lamps, and a dull, brownish ceiling. The way in and out of it was guarded by a thick wooden door. Inside the room, the darkness was almost complete. It was good for psychological treatment of those who happened to be too stubborn during questioning.

Tristan and Sergio chose La Boca and Barracas districts, respectively. There, it was easy to vanish amidst the local poor population, los porteños, or people of the port, as they were called in Argentina.

Robert found the country annoyingly bureaucratic. Perhaps because of this, he learned a lot about payment procedures in banks, various duplicating paperwork for every administrative step, and myriad of other details of everyday life, which could not be taught in any educational establishment, even in KGB training facilities.

Tristan came next. Robert met him at Ezeiza International airport, where the group commander appeared impeccably dressed in a business suit, carrying a small piece of luggage. A careless smile brightened his face.

"How was the passport control?" Robert asked.

"Quick and easy. Anything interesting here?"

"I already have an apartment. You will stay with me until you sign all papers for your rent. It is in Boca, as you wished."

"Where have you settled?"

"San Telmo."

"Good place," Tristan nodded in approval. He knew the city well, as Robert did.

The taxi brought them to Robert's home in half an hour. When inside, Tristan took a moment to observe the place and to approve Robert's choice. He took off his jacket, rolled up the sleeves of his shirt, and opened his suitcase.

"Let's go out, Tristan," Robert suggested. "There is a good choice of restaurants on Defensa. San Telmo is the place with character. Hopefully we will have lots of fun in Argentina."

Tristan straightened up, holding a piece of cloth. He gave Robert the sharp look of a seasoned agent.

"Don't bet on it. It might turn out a busy place. Some of my previous assignments had something in common with this one. Sometimes we hardly had time to breathe."

"We'll see, Tristan. Now, do you wish to go out?"

"Not right now. Do you have something to drink?"

"Tequila."

"Poor me a glass."

Tristan sat at the breakfast table and watched Robert handling the bottle.

"Brief me about everything," he asked, slowly drinking from his glass. "Good stuff."

"I found a house for us. When Lara comes, she will have to sign leasing papers, as the house should be in her name. There is an apartment for Sergio as well. Mostly it's been kind of ordinary day-by-day life."

Robert refilled Tristan's glass and poured some tequila into his own.

"Cheers." He drank half of it and placed the glass on the table. "By the way, Jose gave me the address of a very interesting candidate. We shall place him on the top of our list."

"Tell me more." Tristan leaned back, crossed his legs, and locked his hands behind his neck, preparing for a long and lazy talk.

"He came to Rosario in the late forties, where he opened his antique shop. The city is about three hundred kilometers from here."

"I know that much," Tristan grumbled. Robert raised his glass. "The store front room, according to Jose, does not display the most expensive things, although some good stuff is there. The best is in the back rooms, where the owner meets with wealthy clients by appointments only."

Robert paused, swallowed a mouthful of tequila, and looked in Tristan's eyes for emphasis. "His goods are mostly from Europe. Bronze, ivory, or even gold statues, paintings and all kinds of other artifacts. He has a Swiss bank account."

Tristan's eyes glistened from the effects of the news and the alcohol. "Swiss bank account?" he questioned with delight. "How does Jose know about that? Did he hide as a priest at the time of confession?"

"One of our agents is an antique dealer in Rosario. He says that Gerwig – that's his name – makes no secret of his past. He brought truckloads of valuable things from Europe. A former SS man, all his life he was a big crook. During the war he plundered museums, private people, banks, whatever came handy. Drinks too much. When drunk, talks too much. Drunk most of the time."

Tristan tossed in the chair, hardly able to conceal

his excitement.

"Sounds like an ideal target. When can we go to Rosario?"

"Tomorrow we have to finish your apartment rent paperwork. All other days we will be busy with Lara and Sergio. The only window is the day after tomorrow, but—"

"Let's go the day after tomorrow," Tristan interrupted him. All his usual outward appearance of a calm, unhurried man now was gone. Impatience and an acute thirst for action took its place. Robert shrugged his shoulders.

"Whatever you wish."

"Do you have guns?"

"Berettas."

"We shall take them to Rosario."

"What for?"

"You never know."

***

They took a bus early in the morning, when the air still retained the fresh coolness of the night. The trip to Rosario took about six hours, so it was late afternoon when they arrived at the Mariano Moreno bus terminal.

"The shop is about a forty minutes brisk walk from here," Robert said. "I suggest we don't take any transportation to his place."

Tristan nodded in consent. "Let's go."

The city, it seemed, was bustling with joy under the end of the summer sun. Small cafés, antique shops, boutiques, and restaurants hummed with the drone of voices. It seemed that the only concern of people around was to kill time in the most pleasant way.

"Lazy folks," commented Tristan.

"It's a weekend," Robert said. "Hordes of tourists flood the city. On weekdays, it is not quite as busy as it is now."

"Have you been here before?"

"No. I read newspapers though."

"You stuff your head with tons of information, Robert. One day your brain will burst from the inner pressure, like an air balloon." A note of jealousy sounded in Tristan's remark. "How could you remember everything that you ever read or noticed?"

"It takes no effort on my side," Robert chuckled. "When I was younger, I thought that this was a stupid, useless talent, until the KGB noticed it."

"I wish I had that talent," Tristan said.

"You surely have some others."

"I don't know of any." Tristan turned his head around. "How far are we from the shop?"

"Must not be too far. Here, look across the street at the sign. Europeo Antiqueedad. This is him."

"I'll go first. Wait around somewhere until I get back."

"I'll sit over there." Robert nodded at the tables on the pedestrian walk. "Want something?"

"Not yet. See you soon."

Tristan crossed the street and went inside the antique shop. Robert walked to the end of the block and took a table beside the café's entrance door. It was nice to sit outside. The light breeze from the river was invigorating. The temperature was warm, but not hot. The day could have been a mix of lazy pleasure and information gathering, had it not been for Tristan's mysterious behaviour.

Robert ordered coffee. Observing the people sitting around and passing by, he recalled the details of the trip from Buenos Aires to Rosario. Tristan had not been in a talkative mood for most of it. Once, he even missed Robert's remark and his stare had dimmed with shadows of thoughts. When they got off the bus, Tristan became his usual self again. What was he contemplating?

Robert was half through his cup of coffee when Tristan came.

"I want to try Yerba tea," he said, throwing a sly glance at Robert. "In such a place, the local flavour is a must."

Robert stopped a passing waiter.

"Yerba for the señor," he ordered.

Tristan leaned back. He was all leisure and relaxation. It did not mislead Robert. He stiffened, as if preparing for a decisive leap.

"Tell me the story."

"I met Gerwig there and spoke with him briefly. He said that usually his salesman is in the store, and that he comes there for appointments with important clients. I told him that I have a partner with whom we have an antique store in Chicago. Asked him to accept us after he closes the store. He invited us to come at six."

"What do you wish to talk about with him?"

"Let's decide during the meeting. He has a drinking problem, this is evident. He also has a non-contagious disease, which is called verbal diarrhea. Can't stop talking. Which is fine, we will listen."

"What you are up to?"

"Nothing concrete so far."

"Not convincing."

"Look, Robert. Not everything could be planned and done as planned. Sometimes circumstances are in our favour, sometimes against us. In both cases, we often have to do something. As I said, now it's not clear to me where we stand."

Robert knew Tristan too well to believe him. The group commander had an incredible knack for assessing circumstances in a split second and making a decision.

"Actually —" Tristan continued, but suddenly stopped speaking, his stare fixed at some point in infinity. It seemed that a spontaneous idea had interrupted his monologue.

"What?" Robert prompted, sensing that there was something unusual on the commander's mind. His explanation did not follow though.

"Is there any other antique dealer close by?" Tristan asked instead.

"There are a few. Usually the same kinds of businesses cluster together. They compete with each other, but at the same time attract potential buyers with different tastes and budgets.

"Let's go and find some." Tristan's voice and manner suggested impatience for action.

"What's on your mind?" Robert was more than a bit puzzled.

"I'll let you know later. Let's go."

"We can ask the waiter which one is the closest," Robert suggested. "The locals should know better."

"No, no." Tristan's protest was too emphatic for such a trivial thing. Robert met his eyes; they were blank and unblinking. Robert shrugged his shoulders.

"Whatever," he said, rising. Asking further questions was useless at the moment. Everything will be clear soon, he concluded. An agent should be able either to guess his boss' intentions, or find out later the hard way.

Tristan took his last sip of Yerba tea, and stood up.

"Let's go."

They left the nice ambience of the street café and walked slowly past the Europeo Antiqueedad shop, basking in the last rays of sunset. All the ground floors of the buildings on the block were taken up by boutiques, small shops, cafes, and bookstores. Each of them had visitors looking for bargains or souvenirs. Between some buildings were small passages for cars; Robert and Tristan snuck through one of them to the back of Gerwig's antique shop, where they found a small parking lot, almost vacant save two cars — one of them a Mercedes.

"I bet it is his car," Tristan said. "Would be nice to take it for a test drive."

Robert watched him from the corner of his eye. When a sharp-thinking agent says such a thing, it's not just a nice dream. Tristan's face, though, remained impassive.

A few blocks down the road they found another antique shop. Tristan peered through the window at the display stand. After a minute of observation he turned to Robert. "Do you understand antiques?"

"A little bit. Not as a professional though."

"Still. Your head is stuffed with tons of information."

"What do you wish to know?"

"Look inside. Is there any really expensive stuff there?"

Robert leaned closer to the window. After a minute of observation he said, "Not here. A few items may be interesting, but more for tourists rather than antiques connoisseurs."

"Let's look around for another one."

A block down the street they found another store. It did not have showy displays or colourful posters. A modest sign displaying 'Berg Antiques' over the door was its only presentation to the world.

"This one is likely not for tourists," Robert said. "Want to try?"

Tristan nodded and opened the door. They went in, into the cool, air-conditioned show room. The walls were taken by exhibit shelves. Across the aisle was a long counter behind which a middle-aged woman sat reading a book. Her round face, brimmed with curly black hair, greeted them with a lukewarm welcome smile of marginal interest.

"Anything I can do for you?" she asked.

"We're just looking señora," Robert said. "You

have nice things here. Do you mind?" Under his breath he murmured to Tristan, "Here we are. I bet they have something more expensive over there behind the closed door."

"Do you have something for serious antique collectors?" Tristan asked.

"Yes, we do." The woman rose to her feet. Strangely, she was not much taller standing up. "It's in the back room. I can't let you in there, as it is by appointment only. You have to contact Señor Berg for that."

"Who is Señor Berg?" Tristan turned to shelves, as if he was not much interested in her answer.

"The owner," she said. "But he is not here. He will be back in about a week."

"Where is he?" Robert asked, then said, "Excuse me, it is not my business though."

"Never mind," The woman dismissed his excuse with a friendly gesture. "There is no secret. He is in America on a business trip. As I said, he will be back in a week or so."

"Do you have his business card?" Tristan asked.

"Not here. But we have a store business card, if you wish."

"Sure." Tristan approached the counter. "Would you kindly write on it the full name of Señor Berg? And his phone number?"

"Certainly." She scribbled something on a card and stretched it to Tristan. "Here you are."

"Thanks," Tristan said. "Hope to see you soon."

When they went out, Tristan brought the card closer to his eyes.

"Sebastian Berg," he read aloud. "Most likely he is German."

Robert's heart skipped a beat. Now he understood Tristan's scheme.

Five minutes before six, they passed over the Europeo Antiqueedad threshold. Only one man was inside. Robert had no doubt that it was the owner, Gerwig Bosch. Tall, in his late forties, his forehead seemed disproportionably large due to his receding hair. Beneath his watery blue eyes hung like a large, bulbous nose; purple, with a dense web of prominent blood vessels, it resembled an oversized plum. It served well as an alcoholic's identity card. At the sight of visitors, he left the counter and shook hands with them both.

"Wait a moment, amigos," he said, attending to the door. He locked it with a huge inside latch and then turned back, smiling. "It's over for today. Tell me some more about yourself and what you are looking for."

Tristan gestured at Robert. "This is Robert, my partner."

"Nice to meet you," Gerwig said, shaking hands with Robert once more.

Robert decided to speak with him in German. "You are German, of course," he said. Gerwig's face shone with a smile.

"And you, you are as well," he said with joy, as if meeting a soul mate. "No accent, although you don't look like a German."

"Who does?" Robert asked with a short laugh. "Even Hitler did not look like a typical German. My father said once that if he saw someone like Hitler walking on the street, he would arrest him as a Jew."

Gerwig burst into laughter. "Your father was an SS man?" he asked.

"Yes, he was. A very dedicated party member."

"I was in the SS, too," Gerwig admitted, taking his place behind the counter. "But I did not give a shit for Hitler's ideas. I went to the SS because that was the way to have a good life. I thought, if not me, somebody else would take this job. Nothing would change in the large scheme of things. Right?" He looked into Robert's eyes for moral support. "Why not take a chance? It was a step in the right direction. But I was sure then that Germany was heading towards disaster."

While he spoke, Robert looked around at the antique merchandise placed inside the locked glass doors of the display cabinets. There were nice bronze statues, pocket watches with golden or silver chains, silver cigarette cases and lighters, and some pictures. Gerwig noticed his interest.

"You like something here?" he asked Robert.

"Impressive," Robert said.

"Prices are a fraction of what it would cost in Europe or in Chicago," Tristan cut in. "We can do big business with you."

"Do you have business cards, amigos?" Gerwig asked. Robert threw up his hands in a gesture of disappointment.

"Unfortunately, we did not take them today. Stupid of us." Tristan spread his arms in surrender.

"Actually, we knew about you before we came here," Robert interfered. "Our friend Sebastian Berg advised us to visit you. He said, 'If you wish to get a really expensive stuff, go to Gerwig.'"

"Oh, Sebastian." Gerwig's smile got wider. "He is my friend, too. How long have you known him?"

"Quite a while," Robert said. "The last time we saw him was a week ago in America. He's coming back soon, in a week's time or so."

"Judging by the display, you really have many interesting things here," Tristan said, changing the course of the conversation.

"I have more than that," Gerwig said. "Much better stuff is in the storage rooms. Is there any particular theme you are interested in?"

"Do you have Art Deco?" Robert asked.

Gerwig's eyes sparkled.

"Yes, yes. I have Art Deco. Not a lot, but something worthy, that's for sure."

"Would be nice to see it," Tristan said.

"Hey, amigos," Gerwig exclaimed. "Why don't we go to the back room and have a drink there? I have a good German schnapps."

"Delightful offer!" Tristan was all excitement. "We have nothing to do tonight. Schnapps would be a nice finale to a pleasant day."

Gerwig led them through the door into a pitch-black space. He disappeared for a moment and then turned the electric switch on. Bright light, reflected in rainbow colours from numerous crystals of a huge chandelier, fell on the treasures of the spacious storage area. Robert was stunned. The value of all the things here was beyond estimation. Gerwig noticed the astonishment on faces of his guests.

"Where did you get all of these from?" asked Robert.

"This one," Gerwig pointed at one of the bronze statues, "is from Romania. This picture is from Poland. You like it, don't you? Please, sit down."

He cleared papers from two heavy armchairs and invited his guests to take a seat at the long wooden table, which, by its looks, could have once belonged to royalties.

While Gerwig was busy pouring schnapps into glasses, Robert observed the room. At the far end of it he saw two doors, one on the left and one on the right. In the middle of the back wall was another door, apparently the exit to the parking lot. The whole storage space was densely stuffed with all sorts of antiques. All the artifacts were selected by people who had a good knowledge of the trade.

"You have millions of dollars here," Robert said, taking his drink.

"Yes, yes." Gerwig raised his glass. "Cheers, Herr Robert. Cheers, Herr Tristan." His hand was shaking. After a sizable swig, the toxic tranquility smoothed the wrinkles on his forehead. He placed his glass on the table and watched Tristan and Robert drinking. “I was interested in antiquity from my young years,” he went on. “It served me well during the war. There was a group of us, all brave and reliable fellows. We gathered items from all over Europe. My school friend worked in Denmark. He was in charge of Jewish properties. I was mostly behind advanced armies in the east.” He chuckled. “When they advanced, of course. There were plenty of opportunities to collect valuable things. Who cared about antiquity in those days? Nobody was sure about the next hour, if not the next moment. When death was almost imminent, people had different values.”

“It must not have been simple to save all of these during the war,” Tristan remarked, filling up Gerwig’s glass to the brim.

“Oh, yah. And very dangerous. We had money, too, but we had to stash it somewhere as well. It was only after the war that I was able to deposit money in the bank. Under Hitler there was death punishment for holding money in foreign banks. You don’t drink much, Tristan. Do you like schnapps?”

“Of course I do,” Tristan said, raising his glass. “Not that fast though. Are you in a rush?”

“Not at all. I see, Robert, that you don’t take your eyes off that picture. Like it? I will sell it to you for a bargain price.”

“This is Art Deco.” Robert said, ignoring his offer of a bargain. “Likely, dates back to the very beginning of this century.”

“How do you know? Are you familiar with this artist?” Gerwig was impressed.

“First, it is not hard to notice that it is Art Deco. The building at the background has stylized geometrical shapes and lines, combining simplicity and utility. The result is a beauty of composition without details. All objects, including people, are flat, two-dimensional. Also the two women in the center are wearing clothes which were in fashion at that time."

"Amazing!" cried Gerwig. "You speak as if you lived at that time."

"This is Art Deco, too," Robert pointed at the tall bronze figurine of a dancing woman. She stood on one leg, her other one bent at the knee, arms up, small back arching.

"Yah, yah." Gerwig was all joy. "This is from Italy."

"It is beyond me how you managed to save all of these till the end of the war. Cheers." He clinked glasses with Gerwig, tentatively suggesting joining him in a drink. Gerwig frowned.

"We had a secret bunker near Stuttgart." A wry smile appeared on his face. "All the people of our group, except me and my school friend, were killed during the war. My whole family was killed when Dresden was bombed." He swallowed a mouthful of schnapps. "My wife and two sons." Gerwig was on the verge of tears. "Yes, the whole family. It would've been better if all this fortune was destroyed, but my family had survived."

Tristan came to Gerwig and sat at the table, facing him. Gerwig looked up and raised his eyebrows in a silent question.

"Look, Gerwig, enough sentiments for today," Tristan said, an austere frown darkening his face. "How much money do you have in your Swiss account?"

Gerwig opened his eyes wide and stared at Tristan with irritation and suspicion.

"Why do you care?" he asked.

"Because I want this money. Tell me your account number."

Gerwig gave Tristan another, more attentive look. He glanced at Robert in search of an explanation, bewildered by the sudden switch in tone from the established mood of the friendly business meeting. What he saw was obviously not to his liking. His face became gray and grim.

"You must be crazy," he half-whispered.

"Perhaps we are," Tristan agreed. "It makes dealing with us even more dangerous." He raised his voice to an animal growl. "What is your account number?"

"Why don't you fuck—" Gerwig did not have a chance to finish his curse. Tristan snatched the Beretta from his inner pocket and pressed its barrel into Gerwig's nose.

"Number!" he yelled. "Number, or I will shoot you right now."

Gerwig froze. "Here it is," he mumbled, and then pronounced the digits.

"What name is associated with it?" Tristan asked in a calmer voice, but still touching Gerwig's face with his gun.

"My name. Gerwig Bosch."

"Give me the keys for your Mercedes."

Gerwig fished them from his breeches and placed the bunch on the table.

"You prepared well for this robbery," he said in a low voice. "Know everything."

"Cheer up," Tristan chuckled. "We will take only the money from your Swiss account. You still have a fortune here, don't you? So far as robbery is concerned, you robbed all of Europe. We are just small crooks by your measures."

"That was a time of war." Gerwig protested, suddenly sounding dead tired.

Tristan jumped away from the table and got behind him.

"Now, Gerwig, this is one of the most important moments in your life. We will take you with us and keep you in a secluded place for a week or so, until we withdraw money from your account. Then we will set you free. If, however, you cheated us and such an account does not exist, you will be dead. Before your death, I will put you through hell. Understand?"

While speaking, Tristan was pulling black gloves onto his hands. Robert already knew what was going to happen.

"Yes. This is my account. I told the truth."

"Good." Tristan grasped the bronze figurine of the dancing woman. With a wide sweep, he landed it on Gerwig's head. The blow crushed his skull and split it open, sending red drops around. Gerwig died in an instant. His face became distorted, as one half of his head was deformed more than the other. Tristan dropped the statue on the floor, picked up his and Robert's glasses and threw them in the sink.

"Wash them and come to me," he commanded, and began walking to the front room. Robert quickly washed the glasses, placed them back in the cabinet, and went to the showroom where Tristan was.

The group commander, it seemed, was not in a hurry. He opened the drawer of the cashier's desk and murmured, "Look how much money is here. Nice to be an art dealer." He scooped up a heap of bills and shoved it by the fistful into his pockets. When the drawer was empty he said, "Now, Robert, open the latch of the front door."

When Robert did it, Tristan gave him a brief, sharp order. "Out. Rush."

They ran back to the storage room, then opened the latch of the back door and dashed out. Tristan unlocked the Mercedes door, took the driver's seat, and started the engine. When Robert had settled in the passenger seat and closed the door, Tristan drove off through the small driveway to the main street.

"Now, you are the navigator." He threw a sideways glance at Robert.

"Go left." Robert did not share Tristan's good

mood. “Over there turn right. We will soon hit the main highway.”

The distorted, solemn face of dead Gerwig floated in his inner vision with stubborn persistence. It seemed that he was silently talking to Robert. ‘Why did you do that to me, my friend? I liked you. You are a very cultured, educated young man. You are not a thug.’

“It will look like a simple robbery,” Tristan said. “I bet some people will come there through the open door and steal something. Police won’t have any clue.”

“It not only looks like a simple robbery,” Robert said. “It was.” His disgust was overwhelming. When Tristan smashed Gerwig’s head, Robert did not feel anything, because it was during the time of action. Now, he had a post-action syndrome. This was the first time in his life that he had taken part in robbery and murder. It was far from being an exciting adventure or a part of the interesting life he had dreamed about. A swarm of stinging thoughts and feelings attacked his soul with vicious vengeance. Tristan noticed his mood.

“Feel bad?” he asked.

“It was the first murder in my life.”

“I did it, not you.”

“True. It sucks.”

“C’mon. Don’t pretend that you didn’t know the score.”

Robert did not respond.

It was already dark outside. Although it was hard to read streets signs, Robert gave directions with confidence. When the car was on the highway, Robert opened the window and lit a cigarette.

“Now we have some solid cash to live on,” Tristan said, turning to Robert in an attempt to cheer his mood. “We can’t afford much on Jose’s meager budget.”

Robert said nothing, trying to cope with a shiver that originated somewhere in his guts. The image of the split skull refused to go away despite his best effort at concentrating on the road.

"I trust Gerwig," Tristan kept talking. "It did not make sense for him to lie. He is a rich man even without the Swiss account."

"He was," Robert corrected him. Tristan laughed.

"He was, he was. Smile, Robert."

"As I said, I have never taken part in murder or robbery before. Never wanted to."

"It is a useful experience. You still have never killed anybody yourself. You will have plenty of such opportunities with this assignment. We cannot let anyone live. The survivor would stir all German communities, former ODESSA members, and police. You knew it even in Cuba. We discussed it. Remember?"

"You said that you had no talent. You have one."

"Which is?" Tristan gave Robert a sideway glance.

"Criminal talent. You knew what was going to happen before we came to Rosario."

"Not exactly. But I was looking for such an opportunity. You are wrong though with your definitions. We are in a clandestine war, and we must do whatever clandestine soldiers are supposed to do. We should not be judged by the legal and moral standards of people out there. Our only criteria are the successes of our missions. Forget about your civil notions of legality and morality. You should've done it a long time ago."

"I was only on intelligence missions before."

"So be it. This was your Christening battle. You did an outstanding job. Now, let's go to any crowded plaza in Buenos Aires. We will drop the Mercedes there."

***

In a few days, Lara and Sergio arrived. Lara made drivers licenses for everyone. With Jose's help and Sergio's supervision they bought a used Ford with a huge trunk, capable of accommodating a bull. The car was in excellent condition. Sergio often touched its chrome and nickel sparkling parts as a man would touch a lovely woman. It was parked at Lara's house, registered in her name, and was available for anyone who really needed it. All were advised not to use it for trivial things. Driving in Buenos Aires was extremely dangerous. Accidents, often ending in fatalities, happened every day. The last thing the team needed was being investigated by the police or by some insurance company.

At last, when the dust of trivialities settled down, Robert called Claus.

"My friend, Robert!" Claus greeted him over the phone with sincere delight. "How are you, young man? I thought that your enthusiasm did not survive these couple of weeks."

"On the contrary," Robert assured him,"I was very busy with my business and personal matters. But now, I am comparatively free and eager to meet you whenever it is convenient for you."

Suddenly the line went berserk. A rattle, a hiss, and the barely distinguishable scream of a woman made Claus' response inaudible. Half a minute later the line became quiet, as if no interference had taken place.

"Do you hear me now?" Claus asked.

"Yes, I do. Can we meet?"

"Sure. When and where do you want?"

"How about today?"

"Super," agreed Claus. "I found something for you in my archives. What is your place of preference?"

"I know a nice café on Calle Defensa, close to Chile. How does that sound to you?"

"Good. I have no family or work. I have all time at my disposal. As a matter of fact, I like your company, you know. I found a few things that would be of interest to you…"

It seemed to Robert that Claus did not know how to stop speaking. Interrupting him would be impolite, but listening forever was not a good option either. Luckily, the communication quality of the telephone system came to Robert's rescue. The noise burst with a vengeance, this time mixing with the mewing of two young women.

"We'll have plenty of time when we meet," Robert shouted. "I will be there soon."

"Yes, yes," Claus agreed, and said something else, but his words drowned in the increasing noise. He recalled Jose's warning about the local telephone system. Indeed, if open text were used in conversation, you'd never know who would overhear it.

No sooner had he placed the receiver on the cradle, that it rang.

"Hola, Robert," Tristan greeted him cheerfully. "I will be nearby Florida-Corrientes this afternoon. Can we meet there?"

"Sure. Where exactly and when?"

"About four o'clock. Café Brazil."

"See you there."

Robert disconnected, picked up a jacket, and left his flat. After a short and silent negotiation with the lift, Robert descended to the ground floor and went out into the bright light of the day. After meeting Claus, he intended to walk on Defensa to Plaza de Mayo. From there, if time permitted, he would continue to the intersection of Corrientes and Florida.

Having lived for less than three weeks in Buenos Aires, he had already fallen in love with the city. It had a very European look, so far as the buildings and entertainment establishments were concerned, combined with the aura of a hot climate and a southern hemisphere temperament. Crazy, disorderly, but nonetheless beautiful and charming, Buenos Aires had all the contrasts and pains of capitalism, he thought.

He arrived just in time. Claus was already there.

"Sit down, sit down, my friend." He welcomed Robert with a smile. "I composed a short list for you, yah, as I promised. I was browsing my archives, yah, took a while though, but I don't mind, I have all time at my disposal as I live alone—"

"That was nice of you, Claus," Robert interrupted him. "May I have it?"

"Sure. Here it is."

Claus produced a piece of paper, which Robert snapped and unfolded at once.

"You see," Claus continued, "there are only four names there, with the addresses I knew for them at that time. I really don't know if these are their genuine names or not, but does it matter? Yah, I don't think so. If you wish to bring them to justice, I urge you to be very careful and observant. It is a dangerous and tiresome road, my friend. Yah. But I can read on your face that you don't care. I have seen many innocent and naïve souls like you who destroyed their lives in search of a good cause and an adventure. My advice to you is to get in touch with the Wisenthal Center in Austria. They may help you, as they…"

Robert let him speak without limit. Four former SS members were in his pocket. He smiled. Claus had no idea that the real danger was he, Robert Chavez, not the former SS. He was the hunter, and the most frightening type: invisible, daring, selected for the task by his quality, and trained specifically for this risky job. Behind him stood the KGB spy network and the humongous resources of his country.

"You are a good man, Claus," Robert said, while missing almost all the points of his speech. "I will do my best to reciprocate for your kindness and trust."

"Don't mention it," Claus said. Now his attention was distracted. Robert traced his stare. It followed a woman in high heels, her skirt slit to the belt, exposing a nice hip at every step. The entertainment did not last long; a few more short, lazy sways of her hips past their table, and she vanished among the passers-by. Returning his head back to face Robert, he said, "The older I get, the more pretty women I see. With the years, they multiply. Luckily, I am beyond any fling. Watching them and fantasizing about them is much more comfortable than chasing them. And safer, too."

"I'll spare this wisdom for a distant future," Robert promised. "But now, I shall excuse myself. I have to rush."

"Promising date?" Claus asked.

"Exactly. I will call you whenever I have any news."

Claus smiled and dismissed him with a nod. Robert stood up and left. Certainly, he would never see Claus again, he thought. The man had no use anymore.

His walk to Avenida Corrientes was long but interesting. He studied the signs above office entrances, took notice of bars, restaurants, and the locations of plazas and walkways through the courtyards and between the buildings.

Close to four o'clock, the sun was already rolling down in the late afternoon descent. This time, the narrow Calle Florida gets darker in the saturated shade of buildings, and it looked more like a canyon, squeezed by uninterrupted, tall stone walls. Robert observed it with the professional interest of a spy and the curiosity of a tourist. A cool breeze from the south was drying his sweat and filling his lungs with a welcome freshness. He was not in a hurry, rambling on towards the meeting place, looking around and at the same time brooding over his latest findings.

Large buildings, designed in the style of fine European architecture, stood like gigantic theatrical decorations on both sides of the pavement, which was artistically laid in different coloured stones or tiles. The people around were definitely of European descent. He felt like he was somewhere in Italy or Spain.

The street was closed to motorized traffic, but it overflowed with an influx of people. All of them were nicely dressed; many young women were in mini skirts, defying the common sense of older generations; others wore light, long gowns, emphasizing their femininity in a different way. Some men wore casual light outfits, while others stuck to formal suits and ties, ignoring the heat of the day. Like Arbat in Moscow, Robert thought, but the bright colours of a warm climate were predominant, and the faces were definitely not Russian.

He stepped into Café Brazil exactly on time. It hummed with a multitude of voices. Every table was a center of lively conversation, as it was anywhere else. Robert was already used to Argentineans' passion for talking.

There was only one quiet place, where Tristan sat. He was seemingly busy with examining a picture on the wall, but Robert had no doubt that his commander was watching the door out of the corner of his eye, and had noticed him right away.

"Interesting picture?" Robert asked, taking a chair across the table. Tristan nodded, turned his face to Robert, but said nothing.

"You are already loaded with coffee," Robert remarked, alluding to the empty cups and saucers scattered around.

"I got here an hour ago to make sure that we have a place." Tristan leaned forward and placed both elbows on the table. "I can see that you brought some news." Not moving his face, he rolled his eyes to observe the crowd, and then got back to Robert.

"Remember, I told you about Claus? The journalist?" Robert asked.

Tristan nodded. At that moment, a pretty waitress arrived with a smile and took to gathering the empty cups.

"Anything for the señors?" she asked, giving Robert extra attention. He looked her up and down. She was a really good-looking girl, with feminine undulations here and there, and nice lips, which made her smile seem very sweet.

"Four coffees," Tristan ordered, and winked to Robert. The rascal noticed Robert's interest.

"Four? For you two?" she asked flirtatiously.

"We are waiting for another two," Tristan explained.

"Good."

Robert watched her walk away. Her short stride and swaying hips made him feel an acute longing for sex.

"You began talking about Claus," Tristan reminded him with a chuckle.

"There are so many pretty broads here," Robert said with a sigh of mock frustration. "They are a tremendous force of distracting."

"Try to spare their images for a night of solitary enjoyment," Tristan advised. Robert laughed.

"For a serious job, I'd rather go to Antarctica. Penguins don't bother me."

"Right," nodded Tristan. "But penguins do not have Swiss bank accounts."

"Come on, Tristan. Don't you think it would be nice to fool around with the locals?"

"We certainly will. For that, we will use guns. Now, back to Claus."

"Yes. I talked to him this morning. He gave me the names and addresses of four former SS. Mind you, all of them had changed their names and came here with forged documents, which were almost genuine since they were issued by the Argentinean government at the time of Peron."

"Excellent," Tristan commented.

"In all likelihood, they have changed their addresses since then, maybe more than once. Without police help it will be hard to locate them."

"What is your game plan?"

"First, I will use the telephone book, although here it is not a reliable source," Robert said.

"Whatever. Deal with it."

When Tristan glanced at the door, his eyes lit from within. Robert traced his stare and saw Lara. She wore tight jeans and a loose, light, cream-coloured blouse, meant to hide her bulging breasts. It is unlikely, Robert thought, that she would escape men's attention, particularly those who like this kind of shape.

She took a chair, placed her new, fancy bag on the table, and gave both men a sly but sharp look.

"What's up?" Tristan asked. The light in his eyes did not fade. Robert had noticed his infatuation with Lara back in Cuba. It seemed then that she did not mind it, however, there was no obvious sign of them having an affair. If they were, it was with conspiratorial skills of top-notch spies.

Funny, Robert thought, that love seeps through even the impenetrable walls of intelligence operatives. No training or practice of self-control under extreme circumstances could stand up to its power over the human soul.

Robert felt a great temptation to make a teasing joke to Tristan, but he bit his tongue just in time. Let them, he thought. The life of people of their profession should not be without pleasures. Not only did they have the right to affairs, but also to love, although it was tentatively disapproved of by the KGB code of conduct.

The waitress came with four coffees at the same time that Sergio arrived. He measured the waitress with lust in his eyes as he took his cup from her hands.

"What is your name?" he asked, grasping her bare elbow and holding it until she responded.

"Rebecca." To Robert's surprise, she did not make any attempt to release herself from his grasp. A sting of jealousy poked his ribs. He knew for sure that he was much, much better looking than Sergio, and yet, this girl didn't favour him! Unbelievable. One never knows what attracts a woman or why.

"I am Sergio," he introduced himself. "May I talk to you later? Do you mind?"

"I finish at eight," she said.

Damn it, Robert thought. It happens that quickly! Is it because it is Argentina, or because she instantly liked Sergio? Robert had had occasional trysts many times before, and he attributed his success with the opposite sex to his singular male charms. And yet, he was fully aware that men, like women, who are possessed by an overpowering sex drive, tend to lose objectivity when thinking about themselves as sex objects.

"Before your date, tell me your story," Tristan asked Sergio.

"I started with Hans, the first one on our list. He still lives at the address that our bosses provided. I went to the superintendent of his condominium and took him to a restaurant. Told him that I am a merchant and need to know who lives in each apartment, in order to send everyone a personalized letter with my offers. Gave him some money to help him believe that it was true. You can bribe almost everyone in Buenos Aires."

"What else?" Tristan asked. Sergio sipped from the cup. "Come on, Serge," Tristan prompted him with impatience. "I know you too well. There is something else in your story."

"Right." Sergio lit a cigarette. "Hans lives in apartment 745. Nice, three-bedroom flat, with expensive furniture, original pictures, and decorative statues."

"Did he invite you for dinner?" Lara asked with a short laugh.

"Almost. I accepted his invitation before he knew about it. Superintendent keeps original keys in one place. I made a cast of the one from 745, snuck in there when nobody was in, and studied every paper I could place my hands on. Most importantly, I saw a large framed photograph of him hanging on the wall in the dining room. There he was in his SS uniform, young, smiling, and good-looking. No doubt that this Hans is the same one who is on our list. No doubt he has money. The only question is, if some of his money is still in Swiss banks. The only way to know it is to ask him."

"But we cannot take him before we know at least a few others," Lara said. "It would be better to process all of them in a short period of time and get out of this game. Otherwise all their community will be on high alert. If they really still have some remnants of ODESSA here, they would figure out what is happening and find us quickly. The local police would help them."

"I disagree," Tristan said gently. "People disappear these days and no one can find them. It is the police who do it. ODESSA, or whoever, would not be able to guess for a while what is happening. The first suspected culprit would be the police, the second, the Israelis. Let's start with Hans while we prepare other candidates. In any event, Sergio is right. The only way to know if their money is still in the Swiss banks is to ask them."

"I am with you," Sergio said.

"Me too," Robert joined.

"When will you be ready?" Tristan asked Lara.

"In a few days. It is not easy to find proper ingredients here for my medications. The names of the components are different, you know, and some are not available. Luckily, it is indeed easy to bribe everyone here. For money you can get everything, but we don't have much money either."

"We will soon," promised Tristan with a smile. He turned to Sergio. "Follow him. Find out everything about him and work on the plan of his capture."

"Will do," Sergio nodded.

Lara glanced at her watch.

"Who has the car today?" she asked.

"Me," said Sergio.

"In an hour, I have to meet a pharmacist at the other end of the city. Can you take me there?"

"Sure," Sergio said, rising. "Let's go."

Tristan watched Lara walk through the door, his lips parting in delight.

"I wonder why our brass sent us to Argentina, not Paraguay," Robert said. "To my knowledge, there are more Nazis there than here."

"Not exactly, but you are almost right."

"What do you mean by 'almost'?"

"Because ours is not the only group sent to Latin America. There was another one, seven people, trained for Paraguay and Chili. You know what, Robert? They were in Cuba at the same time as us."

"I certainly didn't know. I guess I understand why our bosses did not let us know each other."

Robert took a drag on his cigarette, looking at the passing waitress, and then, with a quick side-glance, he noticed something weird about the expression on Tristan's face.

"What?" he asked. "What's wrong?"

"They did introduce us." Tristan's face remained blank, but his eyes were sparkling.

"Come on, Tristan. What do you mean?"

"I was told about that before my departure from Cuba. Our brass made a funny test: if we met, would we, professional spies, distinguish each other from the locals? Neither did."

Robert kept looking at Tristan in disbelief.

"Are you … Gosh!" He laughed. "We met them? We talked to them? And everyone failed miserably! Ha ha."

"True," agreed Tristan with a grin, and took a sip from his cup. "And, at the same time, everyone passed the test with the highest mark exactly because of that."

"Anyway, time to go," Robert said, glancing at his watch. Through the glass wall of the café, the street looked pretty dark, but Robert knew it was because the sun had already set behind the buildings, and the shade from them was saturating into the evening twilight. When they left the café, Tristan led the way to Avenida Corrientas. Human traffic intensified towards the night with an influx of shoppers and nightlife enthusiasts, often blocking the way completely where street performers staged their shows. At one such place, Robert and Tristan joined the spectators. A man and a woman in their late twenties danced tango with professional deftness and elegance. The woman wore a light, colourful dress, short enough to reveal almost all of her perfect long legs. Her partner was in a formal black suit, quite appropriate for an important business meeting. When the man made her twist and turn, her gown flew up, exposing brims of her underwear, but this view, nice as it was, did not trigger any sexual fantasies in Robert. The dance was too professional, too showy for that, and it was a charming, impressive performance. The dancers' faces were serious, almost grim, as if some bad news had struck them a short time ago; sometimes their lips almost touched, and their eyes met in a disapproving deadlock, but the next moment the woman flew back, still holding the man's hand, and then made a quick, elegant twist with a speed and lightness that seemed to defying gravity. The wailing, romantic music of the accordion emphasized the tragedy of unrequited love, so vividly expressed by the dancers.

"Weird manner of dancing," Robert commented

after they left the show. "We dance tango differently. We hold the girls closer, sometimes dance cheek-to-cheek, and we smile when our eyes meet. After all, it is a great joy to dance with a girl and look into her eyes. Why do they have such grim, unhappy faces?"

"You are so romantic," Tristan teased. "Do you write poetry?"

Robert did not have a chance to answer. They reached Avenida Corrientas, on which a demonstration was moving towards the Obelisk. The small crowd carried huge signs written in large letters. Reading them, Robert couldn't believe his own eyes. "Jews, out!" screamed one of them, written in black on white. "Jews, go to Israel!" demanded the other in red. "Death to Jews," "Revenge for Eichman," called the others.

"What's going on?" Robert murmured and looked at Tristan. His boss' face was blank, but Robert noticed sparks of a gambler's excitement flickering in his eyes.

"I'll join them." Tristan said. "See you tomorrow."

He briskly walked to the demonstrators and disappeared among them.

Chapter 5

In April, the weather in Buenos Aires was still good, although the breath of approaching winter manifested itself in the chills of the mornings. Afternoons, nonetheless, were still nice, if rain and wind did not spoil the mood.

On one of such days, Glenn came into a café located in an old, low-rise building on Venezuela Street, where he had a date at three o'clock.

"Balcony, please," he asked the waitress. She led him upstairs to the second floor and offered the table at the corner of two railings. Glenn took a chair, ordered a beer, and leaned back, entertaining himself with the view of the bustling city. In his inner vision, though, he saw the girl whom he was waiting for. Twenty years old, a university student from a middle class family, she was pretty, but not a striking beauty. However, her large Spanish eyes, brown in colour and glowing from inside with the heat of the southern temperament, long eyelashes, black hair, and perfectly shaped eyebrows were a harmony of feminine features. With an ever-present sarcastic smile on her full lips and sparks of intellect in her eyes, she would pass for an actress or an artist.

He saw her for the first time two weeks ago among the demonstrators protesting against corruption of the government and excessive wealth of the ruling elite. She darted a cursory glance at him, passed by with the flow of her flock, and then turned back and smiled. Might be a useful acquaintance, Glenn thought then. With her help he could possibly meet left wing activists, if not communists, who were his primary interest.

He followed her all the way to Plaza the Mayo. There, after a few inflammatory speeches, the demonstration dispersed and everyone went their own way. He came up to her when she was talking to another young woman and introduced himself.

"Sorry for the intrusion. I am Glenn."

She looked him up and down and offered her hand for a handshake.

"Lollita."

A contemporary woman, confident enough to behave like an equal to a man, he thought. No stupid giggling, pretense of innocence, or false mannerisms of a well-bred girl. If you are Glenn, I am Lollita. I like you as well. That's it.

Her friend rushed to bid her farewell.

"I'll see you at the university," she said, and departed.

"You have some time today?" Glenn asked.

"Yes." She stretched her full lips in a friendly smile. Nice lips, but it would be impolite to stare at them for any longer. "What is your suggestion?"

"Café Tortoni, just four blocks away."

"Sure," she agreed. "Weather is nice, I don't mind walking there."

"I am an American, working for a company exporting Argentinean agricultural goods," he began his well-rehearsed lies. He knew by heart his part in the play.

"I am a student," she said. All the way to Café Tortoni she expressed her righteous communist views. Political convictions aside, she was smart, well-educated, artistic, and playful.

After their long rendezvous was over, he asked, "Where and when shall we meet again?"

"You still want to see me, after knowing my

political views?"

"I couldn't care less about your political views," he said. "You are fun to be with." Then he chuckled and said, "And not fun to part with. Such women usually leave a deep scar in men's hearts."

She laughed.

"Hopefully, I will have a chance to touch these scars with my own hand, just to count exactly how many of them are there."

They'd met twice since then. Each time he did not want her to go. He was sure, though, that this affair wouldn't last long.

His recollections were disrupted by a small, but noisy gathering of young men and women. Its procession stopped at the nearest corner of the street, and everyone flocked around the speaker. He climbed up on a small stool so that his head and shoulders towered above the crowd. Glenn had seen him once before at a similar meeting. This was Carlos, one of the local leftist leaders, a very active and daring revolutionary who combined Marxist slogans with emphatic gesticulation. Glenn was a witness to many such crowds. Radical ideas, left and right, stirred the minds of the younger generation, and influenced its way of life: jeans, miniskirts, unlimited freedom of sex and expression. No more respect for the hypocritical tradition of restrictions.

Glenn threw twice the amount of money of his expected bill on the table and went out. He did not see Lollita, but he knew for sure that she was there.

The gathering was already beginning to disperse. Lollita emerged from it, gently pushing her way towards Glenn.

"You came," she stated the obvious fact with a contented smile.

"Of course. I am glad that you made it, too."

"You have a very peculiar manner of conversing,"

she said, taking him by the arm and drawing forward.

"Really? Why is that?" he asked, looking at her face, which was now very close. Her dark, mysterious, and glowing eyes exuded consent for submission, shameless lust, and at the same time the superiority of a queen.

"You say pleasant things and give compliments without smiling," she said. "And sometimes you look aside, rather than in my eyes. As if something more interesting was happening elsewhere."

"It is hard to look into your eyes. It seems that you know not only my thoughts, but also my deeply hidden desires, which are not proper to reveal in the middle of the street."

"Good explanation," she agreed. "Where do you think is a better place to express your hidden desires?"

"I live a few blocks away from here. My coffee is as good as any on this street. But the ambience is more conducive to this type of conversation."

She gently squeezed his fingers and held them while walking along the street.

"I sense that you hide something from me. Before tasting your cup of coffee, I want to know what it is," she said, hitting him playfully with her hip.

"As you already know, I am an agronomist, graduated from a university in America, and now working for a company involved in the export of Argentinean agricultural products. Never been married. Unremarkable, boring life—"

"Spiced with numerous love affairs," interrupted Lollita.

"Not as many as you think."

"Liar. I hate liars. But I'm willing to make an exception for you."

"I believe that you will make my life more interesting," Glenn said.

"If you participate in our movement, you'd have

lots of excitement."

"And you will be a fringe benefit?"

"We'll see."

Entertaining themselves with small talk and flirtations, they arrived at Glenn's apartment. Its furniture and decorations amused Lollita.

"Nice," she said. "It's good to have money."

"Some coffee?" Glenn offered. Lollita stood in front of a tall mirror attached to the wall, examining all of herself and gathering her long hair at the back of her head. Glenn came up to her from behind and put his hands on her shoulders, looking at the reflection of her face. She kept playing with her hair and watching him in the mirror. Her consent was unmistakable. He embraced her from behind, breasts in his hands. She threw her head back, and gave in her lips for his hot, sensual kiss, then suddenly turned around, locked his neck in the ring of her arms and squeezed his hair in her small fists. After a few kisses, Glenn began working her skirt, but his fingers did a poor job. He began lifting it, watching with excitement as her bare legs appeared in the full-length mirror, and then her lacy underwear.

"It's not fair," Lollita whispered. "I also want to see you undress. Let's do it at some distance from each other."

She stepped backwards to the bed and quickly took all her clothes off. Stark naked, she was stunningly seductive. Glenn took her in his arms, and she pulled him to the bed, not hiding her impatience. All went like an agreeable fantasy. She was gentle and hot, submissive and egoistic, and in the flames of orgasmic fits. It seemed that she had been longing for this moment. She moaned, not too loud, but with no pause, in sync with his motions. In this toxic mist of joy, it came to his ever-alerted mind that his neighbours might hear them. From outside, the yelling of boys playing soccer, or football as they called it here, permeated through the open window along with a few rounds of car honking and the scream of a woman calling her son. To hell with the neighbours, Glenn decided.

With the last convulsion of ecstasy, Lollita covered his mouth with her swelling lips, and the next moment became soft, like a sleeping kitten. He felt her heart throbbing.

"Spanish woman," Glenn thought. "Lovely," he whispered in her ear.

"Don't go. Let's rest this way," she suggested. After a short pause she said, "Even better than revolution."

"Revolutions cost money," Glenn threw casually, rolling on his side.

"Lots of it," Lollita agreed. "This pleasure is free."

"Where do you get money from?" He asked, gently squeezing her breasts. "Where does Carlos get it from?"

"Carlos can only deliver speeches. He is not a man of action. Not many can do serious things, but everyone wants to be Che Guevara."

"Who of you can?"

"Does it matter to you?"

"Not at all. Just to support a conversation."

"Can you support it in a different way?"

"Sure. First, turn around and show me your sexy bum."

She gave him a kiss, rolled lazily, and put her forehead on her arms, crossed on the pillow.

"I love it," exhaled Glenn after a minute of silent observation.

"Could you direct your words to my face?" Lollita asked, a smile ringing in her voice. Glenn chuckled and ran his palm over the skin of her back, buttocks, and legs.

"This Carlos … is he your lover?"

Lollita delayed her answer.

"We did it a few times, but soon realized that we were not meant for each other. Now we are just friends, comrades in arms, so to speak."

"Don't you think that you and I are meant for each other?" he asked, caressing her legs.

"Looks like it, but you are too far from our movement. I mean, from Carlos, our ideas… You are the last who would be interested in all of these."

"You are wrong. I have a great deal of sympathy for your ideas. With your little effort I could become an ardent follower of them."

"We shall see."

She got up and began dressing under his admiring stare.

"I have to go. I'll call you soon."

No sooner was she out the door that Glenn grabbed the telephone.

"Eduardo? Can we have dinner tonight? Yes, today. At seven. See you soon."

He took a cigarette and lit it. Smoking always accompanied his analytical and philosophical reflections.

Interesting time I live in, he pondered. Women are changing the world, and with vengeance. They want the same rights and privileges as men had in all previous eras of humanity. The same sexual freedom, the same education, jobs, you name it. No more different moral standards for men and women. Mini skirts are a fashion hit even behind the iron curtain, in communist countries, as some observers say. Youth is obsessed with rebellion, revolution, and violence. They want fame, respect, money, but these commodities cannot be distributed equally. Were these trends the waves of the recent war, which stirred turmoil in human souls? Or, perhaps, it was a mysterious, cosmic power, which spread new ideas and thoughts over continents?

Chapter 6

Lara steered the Ford through the maze of suburban streets, deserted and sparingly lit by rare lampposts. Sergio was beside her, giving directions. He often turned back to the rear seat, where Tristan and Robert sat. He was in a talkative mood, perhaps from too much adrenaline pumping into his blood.

"Most lamps do not work here," he explained, with a grin. "The city government expropriates public money for private use, and whatever is left goes to road maintenance. As you can see, not much is left. In a sense, the local government helps us with our night job."

He chuckled at his own joke, but everyone remained silent. The tension was saturating in the car faster than the darkness of the night. Robert looked left and right; all the buildings stood in solemn, stony disapproval, their black windows watching the city.

Robert felt adrenalin rush into his veins as well. This job needs practice, he thought. He knew that its outcome was unpredictable at best, no matter how well one was prepared for it and how many people participated. Now, they were going to deal with a former SS, who had been likely well trained, albeit a long time ago, for all kinds of fights.

"This is it." Sergio pointed at the immaculately clean car parked ahead. Lara pulled in and moved back, close to its front bumper.

"You stay here," Tristan said to Robert. "When you

see me walking behind him, be ready. You'll have only two seconds at your disposal."

Sergio left, and soon vanished behind the corner. Tristan also went out, and followed Sergio at a distance.

Lara sat at the steering wheel, seemingly unperturbed. A devil of a woman, Robert thought. She turned back to him and smiled.

"Ready? Like it?"

"Sure."

Half an hour went by, boring and tense. They did not speak, fully concentrating on the street. Rare cars passed by, a few pedestrians strode along from time to time. Very hard to do this job super clean, Robert thought. Any witness could deal a fatal blow to the whole team.

Lara looked through the rear-view mirror and raised her right hand in a warning gesture.

"Sergio is coming."

Robert felt tension in all his limbs. Sergio appeared in front of their Ford, lifted the hood, and bent over the motor at the right side, as if busy with inspection. Robert did not look back, waiting for the signal.

"Hans is close to his car," Lara spoke in a monotonous drawl. "Tristan is closing the distance. I bet Hans does not suspect anything. There is someone walking two blocks behind, but he's moving away from us. Hans opens the door. Go!"

Robert was fast. He jumped out and was beside Hans in a split second. Deliberately holding the Berretta in his left hand, he pressed it against Hans' belly, holding his elbow with the right one.

"Do what I say. If not, I will shoot without warning."

"What is going on?" Hans stuttered.

Robert lifted the lock of the rear door from inside the car. Tristan opened it, yanked Hans back, and then pushed him inside at the rear seat. Robert took the driver's place and opened the passenger side door. Sergio quickly sneaked in. Tristan snatched the car key from Hans and handed it over to Robert. The engine started with the cranking sound and then settled in a smooth purr.

"Go, go," Tristan growled.

Lara's Ford still was in front of him, giving no space for a left turn.

"What happened to her?" Sergio asked, smirking.

"Something with the engine," Robert commented under his breath.

"I'll go and help her," Sergio said, grasping the door handle.

"Wait, wait. She's okay now," Robert said.

The next moment, Lara drove off, giving Robert space, and then stopped. Robert shifted the stick into first gear. The car jumped forward and turned the first corner in high gear. In the rear view mirror, Robert saw Lara following behind.

"What's the matter, señors?" Hans mumbled.

"Shut up." Tristan's voice was husky and menacing. "You'll know soon. Now, hands up. I'm going to frisk you." He was breathing heavily, as stress took its toll on him. "Clean," he declared.

For half an hour they drove in silence. Hans was sweating profusely, using his sleeve to wipe off his forehead. When Lara's home was in sight, Tristan said to Hans, "Listen carefully. Cooperate with us, and you'll survive. One wrong move, and you are dead. Got it?"

"Yes," Hans said, his voice trembling.

"When we get out, you walk in front of us. Don't look around, just keep going."

"Will do."

The car stopped. Robert went out, opened the rear door, and took Hans by the arm. Sergio remained close to the car, watching the street.

Hans was dead pale. He walked to the door

surrounded by his guards, making no attempt to resist. When they got inside, he asked, "Are you Jews?"

"You'll know everything in a few minutes," Tristan said, turning the light on. "Now, go this way." He pushed Hans to the room without windows. Robert went in after them.

"Move." Tristan gestured Hans to a single chair placed in the middle of the empty tiled floor.

"Take your clothes off," Tristan commanded. Robert was familiar with this technique. Naked, a man feels more vulnerable physically, humiliated emotionally, and helpless under pressure physiologically. Small trick, but it does wonders.

"What do you want from me?" Hans mumbled. He began mixing Spanish and German words. "Do you wish to kidnap me, like Eichman?"

"No. Do what I said."

Sergio came in.

"Everything okay?" Tristan asked him.

"Yes. She is already here. No tail."

"Where is she?"

"In the kitchen."

Tristan nodded. Vertical folds formed on his forehead when he turned his attention to Hans.

"I told you to take your clothes off," he reminded Hans with menace.

"But señors, all of this does not make sense." Hans was quivering all over. "Tell me what you want, perhaps we can settle everything between us in a mutually satisfactory manner. I have money, you know—"

"Clothes off," Tristan yelled suddenly. The sound of his voice made Hans shudder. Tristan removed a handle from his pocket and pressed the button. A glistening blade jumped out of it.

"Yavol, Yavol," blubbered Hans in a rush, taking off his clothes. "Whatever you want, señors. I just thought that we could come to mutual understanding."

"We will, we will," Robert promised. Hans' misery was not to his liking. It was one thing to fight a dangerous, armored foe, but quite another to humiliate someone who was helpless and craving for mercy. "Be patient, cooperate, and all will be cool."

When the last garment of Hans' clothes was removed, Sergio pushed him into the chair and tied his hands behind the back with a duct tape.

"You want to take me to Israel?" Hans asked. He was in despair. "If so, I'm not of much use for you. I have never worked in a concentration camp. I didn't do any work related to Jews. I was involved mostly in military operations, sometimes security, that kind of stuff."

He still had muscles of a sportsman, or a military man, but a protruding belly and sagging chest were clear indications of a sedentary way of life and lack of exercise. A swastika was tattooed on his right shoulder.

"Served in SS?" asked Tristan.

"No. Wehrmacht—"

"Listen, Hans." Tristan interrupted him in an unusually friendly voice. "This is the first, and the last time, that you lied to me. Once more, and I won't be able to save you from my brutal friends here. We know more than you might think. Don't risk your life for nothing."

"Yes, I served in SS," Hans admitted in a lifeless voice, hanging his head down. "But mostly I was involved in paperwork. Not often in actual operations." He raised his head and looked at each one in front of him. "I did not kill people, did not torture them, I assure you. Trust me. I swear."

"Open your mouth," Tristan commanded. Hans looked up at him, bewildered. "I said open," Tristan raised his voice again. "I am not joking."

"I beg your pardon." Hans frowned, apparently at a loss for what Tristan wanted from him.

“Open your mouth. Wider.”

Hans did. A yellow spark bounced from his golden prosthetic tooth.

“Good. You have golden teeth. I will remove them the way you did it in concentration camps. With this gold I can make a prosthesis for myself.”

“Please, make it clear what you want,” Hans pleaded. “If you are not Jews, we can make a deal.”

“We are not Jews,” Tristan said. “You are right, we can make a deal. We need your money. In the Swiss banks.” He paused, looking at Hans, whose cheeks jerked with a nervous tic.

“How do you know about it?” Hans asked.

“Funny, Hans, that you ask questions. When you were on the other side, you did not tolerate them, did you?”

Tristan spoke with a drawl, showing Hans that he had no need to rush.

“I don’t have much money left in my Swiss account,” he said. “A bit more than ten thousand dollars. I had withdrawn almost all of it at the time when I started the business here. I can give you the local money, if you wish.”

“We accept all currencies,” Tristan chuckled. “How could we withdraw it?”

“I can write you cheques. Let’s go to my office and I will sign them.”

“Give me the key to your office, and we will bring your cheques here. You sign them, we take money, and after that we will release you. Deal?”

“Yavol, yes, of course. The bunch of keys is in my pocket over there.” Hans nodded at where his clothes lay. “Bring it to me, and I will show you which one is from the building’s entrance door and which one is from the office.”

Robert removed the keys from the trousers and brought them before Hans.

“The big one is for the entrance. The one beside it is for the office. The address you know, I guess.”

Everyone laughed.

"You have a nice sense of humor," Sergio remarked.

"Let me do it," Robert volunteered.

"Sure," Tristan agreed. He turned to Sergio. "Give him his clothes back. He is a good chap."

Tristan cut the duct tape with his knife. Sergio threw Hans the pile of his clothes, most of which Hans captured on the fly.

"Where exactly are your cheques?" Robert asked.

"In my desk." Hans was busy putting on his clothes, apparently hopeful of a possible release. "My office is on the third floor, second door to the right from the elevator. The elevator does not work at this hour, so use the stairs. My cheque book is in the upper right drawer of my desk. It is locked, but you have the key."

"Is there any concierge, or security system there?"

"No. This is an office building, each office stuffed with papers, nothing worth the risk of robbing."

Tristan stretched a pack of cigarettes to Hans.

"Take it," he said. Hans put a cigarette in his mouth.

"I usually do not smoke," he said, drawing in a huge puff. "But in moments like this… Thank you, Señor."

Robert left the room. Tristan followed him and closed the door.

"Robert, take two rounds of ammunition, and be on high alert. If there is a trap, run away. If you are not back in two hours, we will finish him and be gone."

With traffic less intense at this late hour, Robert got to Hans' office in twenty minutes. He pulled in on one of the side streets, two blocks from the office building. No lights on in any window. Robert unlocked the front door and went in. The lobby was silent, not even a feeble rustle was heard. He took the stairs to the third floor. Also quiet, but at the end of the corridor he noticed a strip of light, seeping through the crack between the bottom edge of the door and the floor. Someone was there, of course, working late hours. Robert unlocked the second door to the right from the elevator and pulled it open. The door glided with no sound. German engineering, Robert thought with respect. Everything they use works. Without turning the lights on, he opened the top drawer and peered inside. After shuffling a few papers he saw the cheque book. When he took it, he heard a noise of approaching steps in the corridor. He squatted behind the desk and pulled out the gun. It was a false alarm though. The sounds of steps died at the staircase. The moonlighting workaholic was gone.

On the way back, Robert was thinking about what was going to happen, and he did not like it. He would rather not be there, and let Tristan and Sergio finish the job.

Lara opened the front door and let him in. It was impossible to guess what she felt or thought. Her eyes emitted the usual: politeness, formal friendliness, calmness, and indifference. Good nerves and good training, he thought. Remarkable woman.

"Got it?" she asked.

"Yes. How is everything here?"

"Not bad. He spilled out his two account numbers and names in the Swiss bank. Tristan has no doubt that he tells the truth. He told Hans that we would keep him here until the money is withdrawn, and set him free afterwards. Fritz believed."

Fritz was the generic nickname by which Russians called all male Germans. Lara attempted to be funny, perhaps to cheer Robert up, as she looked firmly into his eyes, no doubt understanding his mood.

"What they are doing now?"

"Sitting there. Friendly talk, you know. I even brought two stools for Tristan and Sergio."

Robert opened the door and entered the room. He found Tristan, Sergio, and Hans sitting face-to-face, talking and smiling. The small place was filled with cigarette smoke. A trace of worry was still flickering in Hans' eyes.

"Everything okay?" asked Tristan.

"Yes. And here?"

"Oh, we made friends with Hans here in your absence. Hans told us many interesting things from his biography. A remarkable person he is, this Hans."

Hans smiled, but suspicion blinked in his eye.

"Here." Robert produced the cheque book. "Everything is fine."

"I told you, amigos, that there will be no problem with money," Hans rushed to speak. "I—"

"Sign the cheques," Tristan interrupted him. "How much money is approximately there?"

"A-a-h. About thirty thousand. That's all I have now, señors. You see, I do not keep money in my business account because money should be for work, you know, it is just by coincidence that such amount is there—"

"Sign," Tristan interrupted him again, giving him a ballpoint pen.

"How many of them?" Hans asked.

"About ten. Whatever."

Indeed, Robert thought, even one was enough. Lara could forge any signature and even a top-notch expert could hardly distinguish it from the genuine.

Hans signed the first cheque and raised his head, holding the pen in the air.

"By the way, I forgot to mention that I worked a while in Russia," he said.

"Really?" Robert asked. Tristan and Sergio turned to Hans, waiting in silence for the story.

"Yah, I was there. It was in the thirties. Our group was sent to Siberia to study the Russian method of building concentrations camps and all associated administration and logistics."

"What's there to study?" Robert asked. "Build barbed wire fences, a few barracks, put guards on the towers, and that's all."

Hans shook his head.

"Not that simple, amigo. Russia had unique practices in extermination and in burying millions of people. That's what Hitler was looking for. When you deal with small numbers, it is simple. With large numbers, you have to know a lot: what equipment you have to use, how much of it has to be employed on each site, how much manual labour should be employed, the delivery of people, killing practice, record keeping, that kind of stuff. Time and money must be accounted for. The logistics are complicated with large numbers as well. But we developed a much more advanced technique later, with gas and other things, although our numbers even at the end of the war were still lesser than the Russians.

Hans took to signing again.

"Interesting," Robert said. "Really interesting."

"Yah." Hans stopped signing again, sensing a genuine interest in his listeners. "Russians helped us a lot before the war. Particularly with Jews. You wouldn't believe how many European Jews snuck to Russia for refuge. Russians turned them back to us. I was in the unit that received them at the border. We worked days and nights, there were loads of them, it was a hard job, you know. Some of them had a bit of jewelry, which was a sort of reward for us."

He chuckled at his small joke and took to signing again.

"Here," Hans said, returning cheques. "All good?"

Sergio took them from Hans and then took a few steps back. He threw Robert a fleeting glance, which Robert did not like. The next moment, he understood why. Tristan faced Robert and asked him in Russian, "Pri sebe pistolet?" (Do you have a gun on you?)

"Da." (Yes.) A nauseating lump stuck in his throat when he looked at Hans. Hans turned dead pale. His eyes, wide open, danced in fear, jumping from one of his captors to another. No doubt he recognized the Russian speech.

"Shoot him," Tristan ordered.

"Why me?" pleaded Robert. His anger and disgust for Tristan was overwhelming. "You do it, Tristan. I have done my work."

"What?" shouted Tristan. "Who gives commands here? You think you can tell me what to do, what not? Shoot him, I said. Hear me?"

"Señores, señores, please," Hans pleaded, pressing his hands against his chest. "You promised. I swear I told you the truth. I gave you all the money I have. Please, please."

"Why me?" roared Robert. "It takes nothing for you to kill a man."

"That's exactly the point," Tristan responded with matching anger. "You are the only one of us who has not killed before. Do it."

"I won't."

"You won't? Then look what I will do."

Tristan's voice sharpened in irritation. His usually blank, impassive features transformed into the frightening, aggressive demeanor of a vicious predator. He removed the knife from his pocket and pressed the button. The steel blade jumped out from its top end, reflecting the feeble light of the portable gas lamp in the corner. With a swift flap of his arm, he cut Hans' cheek. Hans screamed, grasped his face with both hands, and fell on the floor. His legs were shaking in spasms of unbearable pain. Robert glanced at Sergio. He remained impassive, as if nothing had happened. He wore the same expression as he would while asking for a cup of coffee, watching a show at the theater, or driving a car.

"You need more?" rasped Tristan, glaring at Robert with bloodshot eyes. "Look."

He poked Hans' leg with his knife. Hans yelled, and

then began talking fast, but incomprehensibly. Robert made no attempt to understand his words. He simply could not take it anymore. He took out his Beretta and pulled the trigger. The shot was accurate and deadly. Hans shook with a last convulsion, and then lay still, as if he was relaxing after a tiresome job. His eyes slowly opened and froze in an unblinking stare. The room filled with the tart smell of burned gunpowder.

"Not bad," Tristan said, returning to his usual cool composure. He folded his knife and threw it on the floor. "Let's rest a bit. We have to get rid of this corpse tonight."

He left the room and shouted, "Lara, make us some coffee, would you?"

"Sure," Lara raised her voice from the kitchen in response, cheer ringing in it. "Come here, boys. You deserve the best. I like sharp shooters."

Robert took a chair at the table in the breakfast area and looked aside, trying to avoid eye contact with his comrades.

"Cheer up," Tristan said to him. "If we manage to withdraw his money here, all of it will be ours. Got it? We cannot send it to the Center, nor do we have to report it. All is ours."

"This is fair," Lara said, busy at the stove. "I like it."

"Me too," Sergio agreed.

"My guess is that you have a woman," Tristan chuckled. "Is it the waitress who served us in Café Brazil?"

"You got it. She's a Jewish girl. Funny, she took me for a Jew, but when she found out that I wasn't, she settled with that."

"I guess I know how she found out that you are not Jewish," Lara said with a laugh.

"You are dead wrong, Lara," Sergio objected. "I told her that before going to bed with her."

"You are a knight of a man," she declared with

mocking respect. “I appreciate your honesty.”

“Now, you have to prove to us as well that you are not Jewish,” Tristan said. Everyone laughed, except Robert.

“Cheer up.” Sergio hugged Robert, showing his support. “First one is the most difficult one. We all have gone through it.”

“All of this is for the sake of our communist ideas,” Robert mumbled. “Rob and kill, like mobsters.”

“Yes, we rob them, we kill them in the name of humanity.” Tristan did not try to hide his irritation. “And our communist party clears us of all sins, as a priest in church. And you, Robert, are also a thug, a murderer, a member of a gang of professional killers. You knew it before coming here, didn’t you? You, like all of us, are almost a saint. Understand?”

“Stop your kindergarten talk. I am not a sadist. This goes beyond the crime.”

“Just imagine, Robert, that some of Hans’ victims could have suddenly emerged from the dead just now, and could have watched us dealing with him. Do you think they would disapprove of me? Do you think they would support you and interfere to stop me? Now, let’s finish with the coffee and go.”

“Regardless of how strong your arguments are, murder is murder,” Robert mumbled.

“You were so naïve that you didn’t know it?” Tristan said with a chuckle.

“Not so. But thinking about it is different from doing it. Our brass sent us to kill people for money. Nice.”

“We do not kill people,” Tristan said sternly. “We kill SS members. That’s the difference. There is no single family in our country that did not suffer loss during the war. Do you need any better moral ground for murder, Mr. Pacifist? With such attitude, people do not work for the KGB.”

He cursed, and then said, “Tomorrow, you, Robert,

give the resident these Swiss account numbers. Enough of this shit for today. Let's get rid of this corpse." He placed his cup on the table. "Lara, you stay here. Please clean the whole place." Turning to Sergio and Robert, he commanded, "Take him to the car. Serge, did you prepare the grave for him?"

"Of course."

They went back to the room where the dead body lay in the midst of a dark-red pool. Robert took a deep breath. He was disgusted with the dead body, with Tristan, and with the whole task. A rage against his bosses and the whole mission boiled in his mind and heart. For the first time in his life he felt a genuine contempt for the KGB system; good, righteous ideas could not be realized by establishing a foundation of crime.

Lara came back with a blanket. They wrapped the body in it and carried it out. The trunk of the car was already open; Lara had thoughtfully prepared everything without instructions. They threw Hans inside. Sergio took the driver's seat, Tristan the passenger, and Robert settled in the back.

"It's about a two hours drive from here," Sergio said. "The road in the country is pretty bumpy, but we have to hurry. We need to do this before the dawn."

For half an hour, nobody talked. Tristan opened the window and began smoking. Sergio also lit a cigarette.

"They have much better cigarettes here than in Cuba," Sergio commented. "But Cuban cigars are the best." He turned back to Robert. "They produce two good things, those Cubans: cigars and girls. Right, Robert?"

"Yes," Robert murmured. He understood that Sergio wanted to cheer him up.

Tristan joined the conversation with a much-improved mood.

"And both goods are cheap after the revolution. I think they'd be better off under capitalism. There is a great international demand for what they have."

Robert said nothing and took to smoking as well.

"What we do here is a nice promenade in comparison to the war," Tristan said. "I joined the army in 1943, when meat grinding was at its peak. I wonder how I managed to keep my sanity after that."

Robert chuckled. "Perhaps you didn't."

"War is always brutal," Sergio remarked, peering at the road in front in an attempt to avoid potholes. "Imagine the Roman wars, when soldiers fought with swords, standing against each other. Even scarier than the modern war."

"You are dead wrong, kids" Tristan objected, hurling his burning butt though the open window.

"You are just nine years older than me," Sergio cut in.

"All the same. One year in a war is an eternity. You've never been in a war. I was in hand-to-hand combat with the Germans. Got a wound and broken ribs. Good fighters they are, I should admit. Germans are always good at what they are doing. But you can't compare it to how it feels when you sit in the open trench, looking at the sky where hundreds of Messers are flying, dropping bombs on you. You know what? It seems that each bomb falls directly where you are. When it blows nearby, you think that it was just sheer chance that it missed you, but there is another one, already a few meters above, which for sure will finish your life. Do you know how artillery preparation for the battle feels? You don't, kids. I do. By the way, our artillery did even a better job than theirs because we had many more heavy guns. Sometimes the whole German defense was wiped out before our offense began. Often we broke into their bunkers and found soldiers there totally crazy. Laughing, chewing clothes, even jerking-off. Human psyche cannot sustain that load."

"What did you do with them?" Sergio asked. "Took

them as POW?"

"Nah." There was a lazy contempt in Tristan's voice. "We finished them. What could you do? They did not obey commands, did not understand a thing, they were not afraid of bullets. Crazy. What else could you do with them?"

He turned back to Robert. "If you were at war, you wouldn't feel any pity for Hans."

"But the war is over," Robert remarked. "We live in different times. Besides, it is hard to kill a human when he does not fight."

"You are dead wrong," Tristan burst in anger. "First, he is not a human. Second, the war is never over for humanity. We are living in a period of truce. If you feel any remorse about Hans, think what would have happened if the Germans had won the war, not us. Have your read Hitler's *Mein Kampf*?"

"No," Robert said. "But I read lots of comments about it, and even citations."

"I did," Sergio said. "I mean, I started to read it, but couldn't finish it. Such crap."

"Because you read it with the wrong mindset," Tristan said. "When I took it in my hands, published in German, by the way, I wanted to understand how this book inspired one of the most educated nations in the world. It could not be a complete crap, I thought, as many shallow thinkers believed. In it, Hitler laid the foundation for a new world. Now, after defeat, many Germans think that his theory was wrong and immoral. Bullshit! Just imagine what would have happened if they'd won. The whole German nation would be busy with establishing this new order. They would have killed many more people after the war than they did during it."

Sergio turned onto an unpaved side road, with many potholes and dents. The car jumped on them, tossing the body in the trunk and hitting it against the metal walls.

Outside the window was a pitch-black night, through which the car's lights managed to snatch a patch of the ground ahead. Robert felt as if he was in a surreal world; everything seemed unnatural, from the semi-philosophical conversation in the car, Tristan's sadistic calmness, Sergio's cool acceptance of everything, and the sounds of the jumping body in the rear of the car. It seemed to Robert that Hans was still alive, kicking and hitting at the truck lid in an attempt to break out from his captivity.

Sergio stopped the car where the last traces of the road disappeared.

"It's not far from here," he said, turning off the engine. "Let's take all his clothes off. It would be impossible to identify him even if he is found. In this soil, he will be completely eaten out by worms in a few days."

***

Robert reached his apartment well after midnight. It was dark inside, however he did not touch the switch, but went straight to the balcony, where he sat in the unstable reclining plastic chair and took to smoking. The street below lived its usual life. The laughter, the snatches of conversation, and the flow of human traffic set over the background of the dim street lamps were like a theatrical stage showing simple pleasure and joys, which were the things of the past. Real life now meant robbery, murder, interrogation, and mental and physical torture. A nasty sense of guilt stuck in his throat and refused to go away.

Although Robert was endlessly tired, he did not want to sleep. To be alone though was a welcome relief. The events and images of the day were utterly disturbing. Where did these nasty feelings and thoughts come from? Although Robert had never killed before, he considered himself to have a penchant for violence. A righteous cause could unleash his rage and make him blind to any reasons, feelings, or considerations of consequence. In his childhood and adolescent years he lived with his mother in a very rough quarter of the city. His father had gone off to war, and had never returned home from the front. He was not killed. He simply did not come back. In her grief, his mother did not adhere to strict morals. Who did at that time? But everyone, sinner or saint, was happy to condemn her or any other neighbour, whenever there was a chance.

In the overcrowded apartments of the post-war years, when a whole family seldom had more than one room to live in, people did not have privacy. Rumors and gossip traveled fast. Kids at school and in the neighbourhood, vicious with both their words and their fists, laughed while talking about his mother. He fought with them and was savagely beaten. When he came home with bruises, he never told his mother what happened. She never asked. She cried when she thought that he was asleep. Nothing but a miracle could have changed their life.

He loved his mother with all the passion of a neglected child, devoid of a father's love. He knew what was going on when his mother came home late, a bit tipsy, feeling guilty but somehow in a good mood. The stings of jealousy were painful and did not heal.

At the age of thirteen, he joined a boxing club. There he amazed everyone with his natural talent, including the trainer.

"You will be a champion," he praised Robert's performance. "You are adept at lightning speed, have perfect coordination, stay well on your feet, and master a hard punch. Also important is your resolve to win no matter what, and your rage, even hatred, against a tough opponent during a fight."

A few brawls with classmates in the schoolyard stunned the spectators. The poisonous tongues stopped their dirty insults. Many of his former foes wanted to become his friends.

When he was fifteen and already a regional champion in the youth category, his physical superiority was challenged by a really dangerous opponent. A new student, whose nickname was Ship, began his assault with insulting remarks. He was a well-known thug, protected by his older brother, a twenty-two-year-old mobster with a criminal record and a few years of prison in his biography. Robert made a great deal of effort to contain his rage and to avoid an open confrontation with Ship. It was too dangerous to stand up against his brother's gang.

He asked Ship to hold his tongue. Ship laughed and shouted obscenities against his mother, making sure that everyone around heard them. Robert lost self-control; with one expert punch he brought Ship down. With effort, Ship stood up, hatred blazing in his eyes.

"You will pay for this," he rasped.

This was in late spring, when most youngsters spent their evenings out. On that day, Robert played soccer in the forest clearing, not far from his apartment building. The game was half over when a few unwelcome spectators came, with Ship among them. Robert had seen some of them before; they were feared thugs — a terror to the whole neighbourhood.

They sat down on the grass and began drinking vodka from the bottle. Then, as Robert expected, they began shouting insults. Whenever Robert hit the ball, they laughed and swore at him at the top of their lungs. Everyone who played in the soccer field was scared. Everyone expected disaster.

Rage began boiling in Robert's chest. At some point, its heat blinded his mind. He hit the ball the last time, turned around, and walked toward the hoods. They smiled, watching his approach, a bit puzzled, not shouting anymore.

"Stop it," Robert said, standing a few steps from them.

"Ha. Stop it," repeated Ship, imitating Robert's tone.

"Stop it," his brother repeated the same way. They all laughed.

"Fuck off," one of the mobsters said.

"Listen up." Robert felt an urge to kick him with his foot. "Stop it. I don't give a fuck who you are. Just keep in mind, if you start beating me, make sure that I am dead. If I survive, I will kill you all. I will start with this little prick." He pointed at Ship, who did not smile anymore.

None of them expected such a warning from a fifteen-year-old boy. Robert's words were exactly to the point. While brawls and beating were a part of everyday life, murder was a serious crime, for which capital punishment was almost imminent. The best one could expect was twenty-five years in prison. Someone who was not afraid of it deserved respect.

Nevertheless, the brawl began. Robert was not a novice in street fighting. He knew that the best tactics were to press on, to assault, instead of defending himself. His first blow was directed at the nose of Ship's brother, who had already stood up and was the closest. He fell, likely with a broken nose bridge, screaming as blood poured down from his nostrils. Robert's next punch was not as accurate or strong, and neither were his following ones. When he felt that he was not able to take the mobsters punches and kicks anymore, he ran away. The gang was too tired to chase him for long. When they stopped, he also stopped, and shouted, "Remember, what I told you? I will kill you all. I don't care about jail. I will start with the little prick."

He walked home, blood stains all over his clothes. His neighbours and his mother were terrified.

"My God," she lamented. "Save my son. Please, have mercy. I am alone in his world."

The next day, Robert did not go to school. He was

trying to get himself into shape in preparation for the next, more brutal fight. His rage had no borders. He wanted to kill them, no matter how grim the consequences might be. His mother knew well the iron will of her son. She wept uncontrollably.

"What are you going to do?" she kept asking. "Please, tell me. What are you going to do? Please, don't do stupid things. Don't leave me alone."

He cut a stick from a tree branch. It was about ten centimeters thick and a meter long. On Sunday, armed with his new weapon, he took up a watching position not far from a kiosk that was selling beer.

As he expected, Ship's brother showed up late in the morning. One of the other mobsters was with him. They bought a jar of tap beer and headed to the park, which was a few blocks away. There they settled on the ground in a cozy clearing and began drinking. Robert did not give them a chance to enjoy their beer for long. He appeared in front of them with the stick in his right hand, ready for the final assault. Fear in their eyes elevated his joy to ecstasy.

"Remember, I said that I would kill you?" he asked. Determination in his voice and posture broke their insolence.

"C'mon," Ship's brother said. "Sit down, drink a beer with us."

"You apologize first," Robert said.

"Fuck off," the other mobster said, regaining his aggressive stance. Robert's stick cut the air with a hissing sound and landed on the mobster's back. His roar of pain was like music to Robert's ear. Ship's brother jumped to his feet. With the same speed and efficiency Robert hit his ankles. He fell, screaming and cursing. Whenever one of them made an attempt to rise, Robert sent him down with his stick. The execution did not last long though. The two, at last, came to terms with reality.

"Stop it!" Ship's brother yelled, no longer

attempting to stand up. "Enough. Let's talk."

"Will you apologize?" Robert asked.

"Forgive me," he said.

"What about this joker?" Robert asked, directing his stick at the other one. He was holding his chest with both hands, pain distorting his face. Robert raised his stick over his head.

"I apologize," the mobster said.

"Listen to me." Robert lowered his stick. "If you think of revenge, think twice. You won't have a second chance."

"Let's make friends," the Ship's brother said. "Sit down and drink beer with us."

"I will do it after I kill your brother," Robert said.

"Hey, don't do that. Let's forget about that. I will talk to him, don't worry, he will keep his mouth shut."

"Let me talk to him first," Robert said. "After that we will drink beer."

He walked away, not looking back.

Rumors flew fast in his district. Next day, during training in the sport club, fellow boxers surrounded him. Some of them were mobsters, too, and had good connections with the underworld.

"We want to help you," one of them said. "Tell us, what do you want to do?"

"Come to my school tomorrow after the last class. I want to impress the little prick."

During lessons, Ship was dead scared. He made an attempt to talk to Robert.

"After school," Robert said. "For now, fuck off."

The tension in class was thick. Ship remained pale and silent the whole day. There was not a trace of his contemptuous thug's composure. When he went out to go home, he was confronted by Robert and his mob. Large tears rolled down Ship's cheeks.

"I apologize," he said in a trembling voice.

"Remember, I told you that you will be the first whom I kill?" Robert asked. Ship crossed his arms and pressed them against his chest.

"Please, forgive me," he said, weeping.

"Punch him!" one of the Robert's friends shouted. "Snatch his balls!"

To his surprise, Robert realized that he could not do it. His rage, his hatred, had vanished. Without them, he was not able to do a thing.

A crowd of schoolboys gathered around them. Ship's total defeat, as well as his shame, was obvious to all.

"I will let you go this time," Robert said. "Remember though; if you think of revenge, think hard."

"Loser!" yelled one of his boxer friends. "Crush him! Tear his mouth!"

But he couldn't. Beating someone who was helpless and pleading for mercy turned out to be impossible for him.

His memory brought him back to the murder he had just committed. Whoever Hans was, he did not fight with Robert, did not insult him, and did not do him any harm, for that matter. Killing a defenseless person for money was nauseating. It was not in Robert's blood. No argument could clear his mind from the nasty feelings of guilt and disgust.

"Please, amigos …" he heard Hans' voice. Then Gerwig appeared in his inner vision. "You are an intelligent young man," he said. "How can you do that?"

Chapter 7

It was a late May morning when Glenn woke up and opened his eyes. About ten, he guessed, but could not check his watch, as Lollita slept with her head on his left arm, her leg resting on his body. Lovely girl, a pleasurable sight; like a cute kid when she was relaxed and in a deep sleep. Overwhelmed with affection, he could not restrain himself from kissing her warm, parted lips. Her eyelashes trembled and she opened her eyes. They were fogged with relaxed dreams. The next moment, she was alert; two vertical wrinkles of disapproval formed on her forehead.

"That wasn't fair, Glenn." Her voice was not clear yet, but gathering strength with every word. "You were watching me while I couldn't control myself."

"That's the best view." Glenn kissed her again. She returned the kiss. "I am fond of you more when you are a simple, beautiful girl, resting on my arm."

"I see. Not a rebel, as I am in life. That's what you mean?"

"Exactly. I believe that cruel things, such as war and revolution, should be the business of men, not women. The Lord created them for different missions."

"You are dead wrong." She withdrew her head from his arm. Her eyes hurled arrows of anger at him. "Women can do almost anything that men do. Millenniums of oppression took its toll, of course, but now it is time to change it. Yes, I am a revolutionary, that's right. I want to be like Trotsky, like Che Guevara."

"A female version of them," Glenn corrected. "Or, perhaps, like Jeanne d'Ark."

"Perhaps. I want to leave my signature on every year I live. As a typical American bourgeois, you cannot accept it. Your country gave women full voting rights less than fifty years ago. You Americans have the fossilized mentality of the Medieval Age."

"I am not a typical American," he objected.

She left the bed and bent over to reach her clothes. Astonishing view, he thought, observing her naked figure. This beautiful and fragile body is not for holding an automatic rifle.

"I am willing to do whatever I can to help you with this. I am your soldier, Lollita."

"How could you, a nice American gentleman who grew up with no hardships, be a part of a revolutionary movement?"

"Very simple. I feel compassion for the poor. With your influence, new ideas have come to my mind. I want to be part of your life. I don't know how to do it. Put me in touch with the proper people and I will prove my worth."

She regarded him with fresh interest.

"You sure? Your life will be tough and dangerous."

"I am ready. I am yours."

He felt obsessed with this girl. Poor thing! Would be nice to shield her from the dangers of revolutionary struggle. Little did she understand that neither America, nor Argentina would let radical leftists seize power. Nor did she suspect that Glenn was one of those who stood up against them.

Lollita lifted the phone receiver and dialed.

"Carlos? Hola. Remember, I told you about my new friend, the American?" She paused while listening, and then laughed. "Come on, Carlos. Don't be jealous. Actually, he is a nice guy. It seems that he sincerely wants to be with us. Yes, I am sure. Yes, it would be nice if Miguel was there. At one? What plaza? See you there."

After throwing the phone back on its cradle, she

said, "You heard everything. One o'clock."

***

Lollita led him to the outdoor court inside the rectangle of plaza buildings. A charming café was set up there on a tile-paved ground. Three men sat at a long table in the corner; one of them was Carlos; the two others were unfamiliar faces, distinctly Spaniards. When Glenn approached, Carlos stood up, stretched his hand for a handshake and said, "Hola."

"Nice to see you again," Glenn said.

"Again?" asked Carlos.

"Yes. I have seen you at a street demonstration."

"Oh, that explains it. Please sit down."

The two others did not move, watching Glenn with serious faces. The one who sat next to Carlos looked at Glenn with unblinking, disturbingly suspicious yes. His stare, it seemed, screamed at Glenn, "I don't trust you, bastard!"

Other than that, his round face, with bushy eyebrows, thin lips and puffy cheeks did not show any emotion. Around thirty-seven or thirty-eight, Glenn estimated, settling at the opposite side of the table.

"This is Miguel," Carlos introduced him to Glenn. Miguel nodded, but did not offer his hand, which was a bit weird for generally hospitable Spaniards. Glenn responded with the same indifferent nod.

"And this," Lollita pointed at the one next to Miguel, "is Flavio."

Flavio was a different type. He stood up, shook hands with Glenn, and smiled. Tall, about the same age as Miguel, slender and sporty, with a suntanned face and closely set eyes, he conveyed the impression of a healthy, well-fit, macho man. He looked like he could be on a poster depicting a strong, proud Spanish man riding a horse in pampas.

In his peripheral vision, Glenn noticed that Miguel kept watching him with the same steady, suspicious attention.

"How are you, Miguel?" Lollita asked, in an obvious attempt to break the icy atmosphere of the meeting.

"Good. Thanks." He still did not take his eyes off Glenn. Now it was time to respond, and Glenn did it with the same matching stare, conveying irritation at such inhospitable attention. It worked.

"We know from Lollita that you want to help us," Miguel said and darted a weird glance at her.

"Yes."

"It is a surprise to me that an American is sympathetic with communist ideas," Miguel continued. "Rich people usually do not care about the poor."

"Not all Americans are rich," Glenn argued. "We have millions living in appalling poverty, deprived of basic necessities, not to mention rudimentary dignity. However, there are many Americans, including well-off people, who do a lot for the poor. And not only in America, but throughout the world as well."

"Are you one of these?" It was Flavio who asked, eyes narrowed and with a sarcastic smile.

"No. But I'd love to do something."

The conversation stopped as the Spaniards took time to think. Glenn was the first to resume the talk.

"Do you have anything in mind as to how I can help you?"

"Not really," Flavio chuckled. "We need fighters, but you are not the one who would join us. I don't think it would be a good idea anyway. We need money, but it seems you do not have much to donate. And we need arms, which you do not have either."

"What kind of arms do you need?" Glenn asked. Like a seasoned chess player, he calculated in an instant all possible moves for all pieces on the board, and the likely outcome of the game.

"We need automatic rifles, grenades, ammunition, possibly some light, handheld grenade launchers, stuff like that. Why do you ask?"

The thrill of adventure made his blood pulsate in his temples. In such moments, an agent like him requires total self-control and the ability to remain calm.

"I may be able to help you with this." Glenn did not look at Miguel, but felt his frozen, suspicious stare. Clearly, he and Flavio were the real doers behind the scene, not Carlos.

"How?" Miguel asked. Glenn turned to him.

"It is much easier to buy arms in the States than in Argentina," he said. "I have connections there. It won't take me much to buy some stuff there."

"How about delivery?" Miguel asked.

"I work for an American company, whose business is the export of agricultural products from Argentina."

Miguel and Flavio nodded. Of course, they knew that from Lollita, Glenn figured.

"I deal with shipments a lot," he continued. "I know people who run the cargo boats. They must be greased, of course."

Everyone, including Lollita, nodded and smiled.

"But I will foot the bill, don't worry. I have money, not much, but likely more than you think. I can't promise a large delivery at first, you know, but let's start with something, and then we will see what to do next."

Miguel exchanged glances with his comrades.

"I like this," Carlos said. "It could be a good test for Glenn as well."

"Besides," Glenn kept talking, "when the doomsday comes, I may join you in the actual fighting. Don't write me off that fast. I am healthy, I keep myself fit, and do a lot of sports."

"We'll see," Carlos said.

"What's next then?" Miguel asked.

"I need some time to arrange everything. The first task is acquisition of arms in the States. Then, I will talk to the boat captain, and perhaps some others to take my cargo on board. If it can be done, I will let you know when it arrives here in Buenos Aires. Then, that would be the most risky part. We would have to take the load from the boat and smuggle it to the land. I will need some help with this."

"How many people would you need?" asked Flavio.

"I don't know yet. It depends on how big and heavy the stuff is. I'll let you know."

The ice of the meeting suddenly broke. Everyone began talking and laughing sporadically in the usual Argentinean manner. The Spaniards asked him many questions, mostly of a personal nature, and Glenn was happy to answer them. Almost all his answers were lies — facts of his false biography developed for him in detail by professionals. But the Argentinean love for talking was never to his liking. The flame of impatience for action was growing in his chest after his offer was accepted. He peeked at his watch and sighed. Everyone noticed his move.

"Are you going to leave?" Carlos asked with a note of disappointment. "So nice to chat with you. Next time we meet, I want to ask you more about America. Hopefully we will have time for a longer conversation."

"I am sure we will," Glenn agreed. "But now, I have to excuse myself. Mind you, I am a salaried employee and have to be in the office most of the day. I have flexible time, but to a certain extent—"

Lollita rose to her feet together with him.

"I will be right back," she said, and joined him on the way to the plaza exit. While talking, she looked at him with shining eyes.

"They liked you, Glenn. Will you really be able to

smuggle arms here?"

"I can't tell you for sure. I will try hard. It is important to me to show my worth to you and your comrades. I want to be one of you."

"How nice." She kissed him. "I have to go back. You know, they suspect me of being your lover."

"Shame on them! That is the greatest nonsense I have ever heard in my life!" Glenn exclaimed with theatrical indignation.

"Rascal!" she laughed, and pulled both his ears in reprimand. Then she abruptly turned around and went back with brisk, resolute steps.

While driving to the closest public phone booth, Glenn was composing a verbal portrait of Miguel and Flavio for Eduardo. It should have all the tiny details, be clear, precise, and easy to remember.

For sure these were not their real names. Such people usually hide underground, conspiracy being their second nature. They trust nobody, but would cooperate with anyone who supplied them firearms.

He pulled in, two blocks from the public phone booth, as all closer parking spaces along the road were already taken.

It was windy and chilly. Winter in the southern hemisphere was approaching. For Glenn, it was better than summer with its heat, humidity, and choking smog.

The telephone in the booth was in good working condition, which often was not the case. He lifted the receiver and dialed a number that only a few people knew. After a click, he was greeted with the usual "Hola."

"Eduardo, this is Glenn."

"My friend!" Eduardo's voice rang with joy. A call from Glenn meant that he would be getting some money. It was funny to hear Eduardo's arguments the other day that he needed money more than other people. Glenn smiled at the thought that Eduardo sincerely liked people who bribed him. With all fairness, Glenn had to admit that the service Eduardo provided was worth every centavo that greased his large palm.

"We need to talk. Have time now?"

"M-m-m." Eduardo paused. "Sure. Where?"

"Restaurant of your choice."

"The usual place will do?"

"Of course. I am not far from there."

Glenn hung up the receiver. On his way back to the car he was reflecting upon the meeting with the Spaniards, his promise of arms to them, and Lollita. His mind was preoccupied with organizing his thoughts and new information into mental boxes, some of which were marked 'Top Secret', some 'For Eduardo', and others 'For CIA Headquarters.' His love affair, however, although not a secret, was nobody's business. His involvement with arms would be known in the CIA, as they should help him with his plans. Eduardo should find out where Miguel and Flavio lived, as well as their connections. Particularly important was to find out where they got their money from. His best guess was that the Soviets here were involved, as they promoted all radical groups in Latin American countries, enthused by the Cuban example.

He was not far from his car when a powerful explosion shook him. The entrance door to the closest building was torn off its hinges and thrown onto the pavement. Shards of glass and splinters of wood darted in all directions. Glenn felt a sting in his temple, but not strong enough to be of concern. He jumped back out of sheer instinct, although it was useless after the blast. However, his constantly alert mind recorded that nobody on the street was hurt. For sure, whoever had set it off had chosen a moment when there were no pedestrians in range, and had used a remote control to activate the device.

A noisy crowd was quickly gathering around the debris, and the people were immediately engaging in loud discussions. Glenn looked up at the sign above the entrance: 'Zucker Joyas' was written on it.

"This is a Jewish business," he heard a male voice to his right. "As if our political problems are not enough for us."

"They deserve it," said the woman who stood nearby.

"Come on!" the man exclaimed with emphatic disapproval. "What wrong did they do to you?"

"Read *Der Weg* and you'd understand what wrong they did," she said with matching anger.

"That is Nazi propaganda!" the man shouted. "Crazy to blame someone for our stupidity. Look at the cars on the road. You think there are only Jews who drive them into so many accidents?"

A heated discussion sprang up around the rubbish on the pavement. Its drone paused only when three men appeared in the opening of the entrance. Two of them supported the third one on both sides. His face was bloodied. His large, black eyes were blurry. His skull-cap still clung to his hair, touching his right ear. A gust of wind yanked it off his head and flung it on the asphalt. Someone picked it up and handed it over to the injured man. He took it with a grateful nod, looking down at his feet.

He was about fifty, a bit overweight, dressed in a formal business suit. His injury was apparently not critical, Glenn concluded, as he still was able to walk.

The crowd parted, giving them a way to their car, and they drove away. Right decision, Glenn thought. It wouldn't be wise to wait for an ambulance or the police. With such crazy traffic in the city, they might take an hour, if not longer, to come.

Driving to meet Eduardo was a challenge, to say the least. Glenn could hardly contain his anger. A mess on the road could quickly convert a normal human being into a psychopath, he thought. When at last he walked into the restaurant, Eduardo greeted him by pointing his finger at his watch.

"You are more than half an hour late," he said. "Unusual for you." Suddenly his eyebrows shot up, forming into arches of surprise. "Oh, my friend, what's this? You have blood on your left temple. What happened?"

Glenn touched the sore spot with his fingers.

"There was a blast in the street," he said.

"A blast?" Eduardo repeated in surprise. "Serious?"

"Yes. In a Jewish jewelry store. The entrance door was crushed. One of the men inside was injured, not serious, I guess. Here," he pointed to his temple, "a small piece of something hit me." Glenn took a napkin and dabbed the small wound. "Nothing to worry about," he concluded, glancing at the small blood spot on it. Looking up at Eduardo he asked, "Who do you think did it?"

"Pretty sure Germans did it. *Der Weg* has gone crazy about Jews lately. They even bribe other newspapers to heat up the anti-Semitic propaganda."

"You said 'they'. Who are they? Not all Germans, I guess, and not *Der Weg* as such. Concrete people with a concrete purpose must be behind the scenes."

Eduardo took another draw on his cigarette. A long, crooked rod of ash on its tip was getting heavy enough to fall on the white tablecloth. When Eduardo exhaled, the ash fell, but the policeman did not notice it. Glenn understood that the rascal was deliberately delaying his answer to make Glenn understand how important, and hence expensive, this information was.

"I have a more or less educated guess," he said at last, but stopped talking when a young waitress approached him. He measured her up and down with his lustful eyes.

"A bottle of house wine," he ordered. "And steak. Lots of sauce, darling." He patted her bare arm and looked at her with a happy smile. It seemed that he was just about to fall down on his knees in front of her and say, 'Would you marry me?'

The waitress stepped back, giving Eduardo an embarrassing smile. After all, he was a valuable customer who always gave good tips. Well, not exactly. Usually it was his guests who paid, but still, money was money.

Glenn ordered the same, just to shorten the ritual of dish picking.

"I groped her ass once," Eduardo confessed, looking at her departing back, "but she wiggled it in protest. She said that she was married. Ha! As if the shape of her ass changed after the marriage ceremony."

"What is your educated guess?" Glenn asked, returning Eduardo to the rails of their previous conversation. "Who is behind the scenes?"

"I think Nazis of all sorts. Particularly former SS. There is a great deal of disturbance among them lately. Why are you interested in this?"

"I am pretty sure that our politicians do not like it. It might come to the point when America imposes sanctions on Argentina, or would not support the Argentinean economy in its predicament."

"With all due respect to your opinion, I disagree. Forgive me, but I think you are naïve. The American government would support any regime, if it were against communism. That's what our top brass thinks. Americans are practical people."

Eduardo was right, of course, but Glenn, as a man of an intelligence service, wanted to know more. One never knew where the dots of information were connected.

"Not so simple, my friend. What if Argentina was ruled by a radical right political group?"

"What about it? It would be our domestic problem. What if Argentina was ruled by radical left political group? It would become an international problem."

Glenn chuckled, but held a steady stare at Eduardo.

"Fine. Do you wish to know names?" Eduardo asked.

"Yes. Definitely so."

"I don't know them. It is hardly possible to know."

"Could it be whatever remained of ODESSA?"

"I am almost sure that this is the case. Perhaps not ODESSA as such, as there is no need for it anymore, but its former members; I am almost sure."

"Almost?" Glenn leaned forward, observing Eduardo's face with the utmost attention. "What makes you be almost sure?"

"Something very puzzling has happened in the last few weeks." Eduardo also leaned over the table, and looked left and right to make sure that nobody was eavesdropping. "It began with the disappearance of one of the former SS, a guy called Hans Pepke. He vanished, and so did money from his business account. Some stupid policemen even suggested that he took the money and left with a woman, but it was nonsense, you know, he was not that type of man. Then, another former SS disappeared, than another. Just like that, into the thin air. No witnesses, no clues, nothing."

Eduardo took another draw.

"So," prompted Glenn. He sensed something very exciting.

"So. They suspected the police, as they practice lately this sort of things. We assured them that we had nothing to do with it. We talked to their relatives, associates. They did not want media to make a great fuss of it. Don't ask me why — they have their own reasons. What I know for sure is that they all believe now that these deeds were done by Jewish hands, perhaps by the Israeli Secret Service, because the signature of professionals is certainly there. Local Jews might have helped them. Germans have suggested that the Israelis have decided not to provoke the angry Argentinean response anymore, like they did with

Eichmann. You remember that our government even demanded Israel to return Eichmann to Argentina for the local trial, instead of having it in Israel. I tend to think that the Germans are right. The Israelis probably decided to kill former SS without trials and media noise, because it is the best way they can get revenge."

Eduardo leaned back, as if tired after his speech. Glenn did the same, reflecting in a relaxed pose.

"Please, keep me posted, Eduardo. I would greatly appreciate it."

"Of course." Eduardo liked his appreciations and preferred to get them in hard currency.

"Now, some other things. I recently got acquainted with a local communist leader, whose name is Carlos."

"We know him," Eduardo nodded.

"With him were two buddies. One is Miguel, another is Flavio. For sure these are their nicknames. I will give you a detailed description of each one of them. I need you to follow Carlos and identify these two—"

Eduardo made a gesture of protest, but Glenn stopped him.

"I know that you have limited funds and a shortage of people. Do it. Send the best people you have."

"It is not completely under my control, you realize that," Eduardo warned. "But I will try."

"Please do. The ideal thing is to use a hidden camera to take a picture of each one. Just to make sure that there is no mistaken identity."

"What is on your mind, Glenn?"

"I think the Soviets are providing them with money. If so, there must be a Soviet resident here, if not a network. After Cuba, and particularly the Cuban crisis, they became very active here. Got it?"

Glenn saw that Eduardo indeed got it. Finding the Soviet spy network would take him to the highest level of his career. He would be at the pinnacle of power, beyond the limit of his fantasy, his wildest dreams. Eduardo lit another cigarette and began smoking with nervous puffs. When the pretty waitress came to their table with the meal he did not even give her a cursory glance.

"Tell me how they look," Eduardo said, when the waitress retreated. "I will do my best."

"Sure. And here," Glenn said, pushing the envelope with money across the table, "is the token of my appreciation."

Eduardo liked this 'token.' He smiled, grabbed it, and hid it in his inner pocket.

Chapter 8

It was already 10 o'clock in the morning when Robert woke up from gruesome nightmares, which always haunted him after an evening's indulgence in drinking until early morning. Even in a deep sleep he knew that it was not a reality. He only had to open his eyes and the terrible dreams would be gone, but somehow he could never do that until it was too late. Lying on the bed, he stared at the sky through the window, playing back the tape of the latest events recorded in his mind. He still believed that this kind of binge was justified by circumstances.

Jose, the resident, called to confirm that the two Swiss bank accounts extorted from Hans were genuine ones. Each one brought more than ten thousand dollars; not much, but good enough to start with. The local money from his account was not disclosed to the resident. It was their own loot, not taxable by anyone.

From the list provided by the KGB and then augmented with the names that Claus had provided, the group had selected three immediate candidates. Sergio did a good job in finding their addresses. Tristan and Robert followed them and gathered enough information for drawing the same conclusion: these people were very well off.

In two weeks, the group had captured the first three on the list. The job was exhausting and gruesome. Particularly revolting was Tristan; he gave complete freedom to his sadistic nature. The scenes of tortured, blood-covered human flesh disturbed Robert day and night. Tristan claimed that Robert was not made for the KGB job. Just because he could not do the same thing as Tristan did? Or, for that matter, because he could not stand someone's convulsions of pain? Sergio and Lara did not do it, and seemed to disapprove of it, but they said nothing.

In the past few days, Tristan had put another man at the top of the new list. His name was Rex Gruber. There was no doubt that he had been somebody in the time of the Third Reich. He came to Argentina with a great deal of money and was fairly rich now.

Tristan penetrated pretty deeply into the circle of people around *Der Weg*. Through them he found out that Rex was one of the most respected financial sponsors of the newspaper, as well as the anti-Semitic propaganda machine of the neo-Nazis.

There was also someone else. Tristan put him at the end of the list under the name of XYZ.

"I will explain to you later what that is about," he promised.

Today, though, was Robert's day off. He took a visit card from the night table with the name "Bertha" on it and dialed. After the third beep the phone clicked. A confident, calm female voice greeted him, "Hola."

"Bertha?" Robert asked.

"Oh." She paused for a second. "Robert. Nice of you."

"I am stunned." He was quite sincere. "How did you know it was me? It is hard to recognize a voice over the phone the first time."

"Yes, but you did it. Why can't I?"

"I knew that only you could pick up the phone."

Static somewhere inside the line made her response hardly audible. When the noise was gone, he heard a conversation between two young female voices, ringing with the joy of fresh life experiences.

"We were in my mom's bedroom," the younger voice said. "My mom and dad went to the theater. He grabbed me and kissed me."

"Can we meet today?" Robert asked. "Sorry for such short notice."

"No problem," Bertha said. "I have nothing special to do today."

"What was next?" asked the older female voice in the background.

"He put his hand on my hip," the younger one said.

"Your hip? Are you sure that you're telling me the right place?" her counterpart asked.

"Where is convenient for you to meet me?" Robert asked.

"I know a nice hotel. Write down the address and come there in an hour. There is a very nice café in the court inside."

The conversation in the background came back with a vengeance.

"What was after that?" the lower voice asked, vibrating with curiosity.

"He told me to stand with my ass up," the younger voice said, and giggled.

"Ass up?" repeated the contralto, trembling with joyful anticipation.

"I will be there soon," Robert assured Bertha and disconnected. A quarter of an hour later he went out with an elevated mood in anticipation of a new love affair. The fact that she was much older did not bother him a bit. Moreover, it turned him on. She was beautiful and seemed well-educated and smart. In his first university years, Robert felt intimidated by women with intellect. But with some experience, he concluded that many of them are much easier to socialize with, and more pleasant to deal with than just a dumb beauty who considers herself to be a queen.

With Bertha, he expected at least a witty, entertaining conversation, and, with a bit of luck, a refreshing romp. Intellectual women were sometimes surprisingly receptive to bypassing a courtship and foreplay. Some of his older friends confessed that with age, a woman's passion for sex and her appreciation for men grow in her heart and body, if time and health permit. Actually, this woman could be useful. For sure she knew who was who in the German community of the rich.

With a little effort, Robert found the hotel, went in, and crossed its opulent lobby, decorated in a modern Renaissance style. At the far end, the head waitress blocked his way with a smile.

"May I help you?"

Robert returned the smile.

"Someone is waiting for me over there," he said.

"And who is that?"

"Her name is Bertha."

"Oh, yes." The waitress sounded apologetic. "Please, follow me."

She led the way through the rear entrance to the large court. It was a secluded place, hidden from the curious eyes of the street passersby behind the walls of the surrounding buildings. The café was in the far corner, two sides of which were a wrought iron fence with fancy ornamentation and hanging baskets of bright, colourful flowers. The floor was paved with large marble tiles. When Robert passed the iron door he saw a dozen tables, all of them vacant, save the last one in the first row. There, facing the entrance, sat Bertha, a bottle of champagne and a goblet, filled almost to the brim, in front of her.

"Hola," he greeted her.

"Please, sit down," she invited. Her blue eyes sparkled. "Some champagne?"

"Sure." He nodded and took the bottle, while observing her. She wore a green, sleeveless gown, generously open, showing her shoulders and a lot of her sizable breasts. Her skin was white and smooth, with no signs of aging. He met her eyes, and in them he read her understanding of his desire.

"You may find it unusual that a woman comes to a date earlier than a man," she said, taking a sip.

"I do not—"

"Stop it." She indulged in another sip. "You do. I like this place. Sometimes I sit here alone, drinking and talking to myself."

"I hope to be no less interesting in conversation as your second self," Robert said.

"For that, you will have to dilute your blood with wine as much as my first self." She brought the goblet to her lips. "I like good wine. It carries me to the world of fantasy, which is way better than the real one."

"In vino veritas," Robert quoted the Latin phrase and drank half of his glass in two swigs. "With its help, the world of fantasy becomes a new reality."

She laughed.

"And we do stupid things, which we don't regret."

Her sweet smile and warm blue eyes, understanding and playful, made his mouth dry. He finished the glass. The tart, tingling liquid carried him into a relaxed mood.

"Frankly, I am surprised that you called me," she said.

"Because I am much younger than you?"

"Yes."

"Do you wish to know the true reason, why I called you?"

"Certainly." A trace of anxiety stiffened her mouth.

"Because I like you."

"Liar." She leaned back, stretched her legs and brought the glass to her lips. "I like liars. They make life pleasant, at least for a short while."

"You are a gorgeous woman," he said, and took a

sip.

“Thanks. Do you like this champagne?”

“Yes.”

She watched him closely. The expression of her eyes could not be misinterpreted. In them, he saw a raw, hot longing for rough sex. Could she really be that quick and easy?

Robert finished the second glass. She smiled while watching him.

“I’d love to know more about you,” Robert said. “You probably have had an interesting past behind you, as any beautiful woman does.”

“Oh. You mean, a lot of secret love affairs?” She laughed, throwing her head back. “Not quite. I am forty-five years old.” She sipped from her glass, giving him a sly glance. “As a woman, I take the liberty to shave a couple years off my biological age. Do you mind?”

Robert chuckled. “You are beautiful. That’s what counts.”

“Thank you. Do you wish to know anything else about me?”

“Yes.”

“Why?”

“Because I hope for many pleasant dates with you. Are you married?”

“Yes.” She smiled. “Do you mind dating a married woman?”

“Not at all. You have a strong German accent.”

“I am German. My husband and I came to Argentina in 1950.”

“Oh. Have kids?”

“One. A bit younger than you. He is twenty-four.”

“Drop it. No need to comment on your age anymore. Why did your husband decided to immigrate to Argentina?”

“Can we skip this question?”

"Sure. If you wish."

She stretched her arm and touched his hand.

"Don't be offended," she said. "Perhaps I will tell you more some day, if our relations last."

"They will. That's why I want to know more about you."

"Enough for now."

"Why?"

"Because I don't want to tell you the truth. However, I never lie, or prefer not to. That's why I'd rather say nothing. Tell me about yourself. Now it is your turn."

"I also always tell the truth," he lied. "This is my main principal in life."

His words were a great surprise, even for himself. Everything about him was a lie, a very thoroughly invented and thought over 'legend' in KGB parlance. His identity, name, nationality, and the names of his parents were lent to him for this particular task, and would be changed for the next. His way of life was a lie, and his profession was crime. And here, a woman, perhaps the wife of a Nazi, preferred the truth, while he, a macho man sent out on a noble mission, was a liar. Paradox.

"You are too young to have any secrets to hide," she commented. "When your sins pile up, you will feel the necessity to lie. That's when it becomes more difficult to tell the truth. Anyway, enough philosophy. Tell me about yourself."

"I am an engineer. Work for a small engineering firm." He told her the company name, which was prepared well in advance for similar occasions.

The first bottle of champagne was soon empty. Without a reminder, the waitress came up with another one. Robert stopped talking and raised his glass to cheer Bertha up for more drinking. He did not like talking about himself, as he knew that regardless of how well the legend was imprinted in one's memory, sooner or later some mismatches might creep up in the mind of an attentive listener.

"So, you are an engineer." Bertha stared at him with her large, beautiful, and serious eyes. "What else?"

"What particularly do you wish to know?"

"You look so calm, cool, and confident, as if you did not have, or do not have, any troubles in your life. As if you don't care a bit about your future. Am I right?"

"You are absolutely right. I was born into a well-to-do family. I never struggled with poverty or had to solve any puzzles of survival. My parents paid for my education, all necessities, and more. The only big stress I had was when both of them died in a car accident. Since then I have been on my own, but some money still remains from my parents' fortunes. No wonder that I am a careless, spoiled brat who thinks that he is the king of the world."

"That explains it. I envy you." She half-closed her eyes, enjoying the taste of the champagne. "My life was full of troubles. War, deaths, losses. You name it."

The pace of drinking accelerated, and soon Bertha became tipsy. Her full lips moved in tune with her slow drawl. By this time, a few people had come in and taken tables nearby. It became uncomfortable to speak in a flirting manner.

"I suspect that some of our neighbours are curious to hear us speaking." Moving his eyes, Robert showed Bertha the couple at the table to their left. "I think these two damn Jews are too nosey."

"You hate Jews?" Bertha asked.

"Well … You could say so. Let me put it this way. I don't like them. Not that I want to kill them all, but I'm happier when none of them are close to me."

"Hah. You are my soul mate. I don't like them either. Let's get out of here and go to my room."

She rose to her feet and went to the hotel's rear door, not looking back. Robert followed her, watching the deliberate swaying of her hips with acute desire. Her gown, made of light fabric, boosted his imagination. She definitely knew well what she was doing. In the elevator, they stood near each other, keeping some distance, not touching, just exchanging stares, and emitting frank, shameless lust. Robert looked down at her cleavage, and then up at her sensual lips. They smiled in understanding and approval. When the doors opened, she stepped out, walked quickly to the door of her room, unlocked it, and let him in.

Chapter 9

Closer to winter, the days were getting shorter. Rain and gusty winds often made walking on the streets a nuisance. At such times, it was nice to stay in bed at least a few minutes longer, stare at the creeping dawn, and analyze whatever important things had happened recently, and whatever might happen in the near future, in relation to the task at hand. Today though, Lollita did not give him this chance. She woke up early, before dawn. As if struck by unexpected, troublesome news, she suddenly jumped up, brought her watch to her eyes and rasped, "Oh! I have to rush."

"You didn't tell me anything yesterday," Glenn complained, watching her dress. She was indeed in a hurry.

"I didn't want to. Glenn, darling—"

"What are you going to do?"

"Please, Glenn. Later. Do you love me?"

His heart skipped two beats. This was as unexpected as a shower from a clear sky. He gasped.

"Yes, I do."

They had never exchanged those simple, magical words. A thought crossed his mind that only those possessed by love know their sacred power and charm.

She was already at the door when he pleaded, "Please, don't go. Stay a bit longer."

She came back and kissed him.

"I will call you. Love you."

"Love you, too."

He had told her the truth. His mental state of

deception and cool calculations vanished for a brief moment. When she left, he began his mental preparation for the day.

His colleagues often praised his ability for making fast and good decisions in tough circumstances. He knew too well that quick wits were never enough. The key was to develop the likely scenarios to the tiniest details, predict what might go right or wrong, and make the best of it. This was a sort of mental game, which he always played before the real one began. It was practically impossible to take everything into account, but when the time of action came, he was well-prepared because most of his responses had already been thought over.

Many people try to do this, but not in the right way. The trick was to not let emotion drift you away from cool calculation. Like everything else, it took time, effort, discipline, and practice.

With all his smarts and experience, he was at loss with Lollita. Her behavior was often unpredictable, even defying common sense. When such things happened, Glenn did not rush to conclusions. He realized that he simply did not understand her reasons, and she did not care to explain.

The quiet of the morning did not last long. The ringing telephone, loud and irritating at this early hour, yanked him back to the world of action.

"Glenn, this is Jeff. Come to Puerto Madero at five p.m. By the bridge, you know where."

"Will do."

A week ago, two secret agents had arrived to Buenos Aires. They were older than he, but junior in rank, and supposed to be his subordinates. He had not seen them yet.

Their choice of meeting place was probably for a reason, he guessed. Before coming to Argentina he had read a lot about the city, and particularly about Puerto Madero, the old port at the very end of the Boca district where the people working in the port, los porteños, lived.

At the beginning of the 19th century it was a modern, busy port, accommodating a large number of oceanic ships. Jobs were in abundance for porteños, not only inside the port, but also in the neighbourhoods. Sailors, mostly young, strong, and healthy men, flooded the sleazy joints of Barrio, Boca, Montserrat, San Telmo, and Micro Centro. Drinking binges, fighting, often with knives, and all kinds of wild parties ravaged at nights all over the districts. Tango, the dance of local prostitutes, whiplashed sailor's longing for sex and violence.

In a few decades, though, Buenos Aires had grown rapidly and became one of the largest cities in the world. The technology of marine transportation grew by leaps and bounds as well, meeting the demand for goods in different parts of the globe. Huge marine vessels began crossing the oceans; they were too large for docking at Puerto Madero. Its location left no room for expansion, which was why the new port was built not far from it. Puerto Madero, with its channels, buildings, and dock facilities, deteriorated rapidly. By the sixties, it became an enclave of dilapidated, abandoned buildings, cracked asphalt, unusable roads, and scattered rubbish. Criminals, drug addicts, the homeless, and all kinds of outlaws swarmed the old port. This was the place where, at five o'clock, Glenn pulled in beside a long, low-rise building, close to the rear bumper of the only car parked there.

It was not completely dark yet, but the sun had already set and a few surviving street lamps were on. Their reflection in the black water under the cloudy sky painted a scene in surrealistic colours.

Two men stood across the street, leaning on the channel railing. One of them was more than six feet tall, dressed in a long and light spring raincoat. His longish face, with a proportionally long nose, tall forehead with a few wisps of blond hair hung over it, and large blue eyes, was serious, but friendly.

"Jeff," he said curtly, offering his hand for a handshake.

The other man was short, also lean, and apparently quite fit. His face was round, with puffy cheeks and shifty dark eyes. He did not smile either.

"Brad," he introduced himself. Glenn knew their names, but now he could attach faces to them.

Both of them were in their early forties, likely at the peak of their careers. They were known as good professionals at their level.

"Let's go closer to the Laguna," Jeff suggested. "We will show you where the boat with your guns will drop her anchors."

"When will she come?" Glenn asked.

"Next Monday."

Jeff began walking across the bridge toward the ocean.

"The ship will not dock at the main port until you get your load." Jeff slowed his pace to let Glenn and Brad catch up with him. "Will you be able to get there on a small boat? Do you have a small boat?"

"I'll take care of everything."

When they reached the other end of the bridge, Brad began talking.

"At night, there is almost nobody here. Perhaps some local thugs, but no police, that's why this place is the best for you. Don't worry, I will be around, just in case."

"I don't need anyone," Glenn objected. "Who will meet me at the boat?"

Jeff turned to him. "I will. Everything is arranged with the captain. I urge you, though, reconsider your decision regarding Brad. It is good that police avoid this place, but instead of it, the mob rules here. There could be a problem."

"That's fine. I'll deal with it."

They came to the shore and stood there, observing Laguna, the endless space of the ocean and the streets of Puerto Madero.

"The waters could be rough," Brad remarked. "There is no other way, though, to get your goods."

"Whatever." Glenn turned around. "Look, next Monday I'll come here in the afternoon, just to make sure that the ship has already anchored. If the weather is really that rough, we should find some other ways."

"They are even riskier," Jeff said.

"I know. I know. Okay, let's solve problems as they come."

Dusk settled, painting the run-down streets in shades of gray. Glenn glanced at his watch and began walking back toward the cars. Jeff and Brad followed him on both sides. At the end of the bridge Glenn saw two men, watching their approach. When Glenn got closer, he made out their faces. There were puffy, blue sacks under their eyes, indicating heavy alcohol abuse.

"Could you spare some change?" one of them asked.

"You see," Brad said pointedly, not giving a glance to the beggar, "you never know what might happen here. I can hide someplace here; nobody would notice me."

"No," Glenn objected with resolution. "I will be with people who can handle that."

"There," Jeff said, pointing in the direction where their cars were parked. "We already have company."

Indeed, a few people were standing there, smoking. One of them was sitting on the hood of Glenn's car. They were obviously waiting for the car owners in order to negotiate a deal with them.

Not uttering a sound, Brad grasped the man sitting on the hood and yanked him off, like a light doll. The man landed in the surrounding rubbish like a sack of potatoes. His head hit a boulder with a cracking sound. He groaned, made a few attempts to get up, but then gave up and lay still, holding the injured spot.

Brad and Jeff were about to deal with the others, but they had already run off.

"Do you still reject my help?" Brad asked.

"Yes." Glenn was sure about that. "I'll manage. Thank you. See you on the boat, Jeff."

Back at home, with a glass of brandy on his night table, Glenn kept dialing Lollita's number. Cold, indifferent mechanical beeps were the only response. He called Carlos a few times, with the same result. Glenn cursed.

"What kind of revolution could these people stage?" he pondered with contempt. "They can't organize even the simplest thing. They are busy with slogans and speeches, but not real actions."

Close to midnight, Carlos picked up the phone.

"Hi, Carlos. This is Glenn. I was trying all evening to contact you."

"Any good news?" Carlos asked.

"Yes. The ship with the goods will arrive on Monday. We need a small boat, preferably a kayak, not a canoe, as the water could be rough and either fill it up, or turn it over. The kayak usually has a protective canvas cover, water proof, you know—"

"Look, I don't know much about that. I will let Miguel call you soon. He will organize everything."

"Where is Lollita?" Glenn asked. Carlos paused before answering:

"I don't know."

Glenn was tempted to scream, 'Tell me the truth, shit head,' but he held back. These days, the police had adopted very nasty and scary tactics. They picked up those whom they did not like for their political activity or public protests, either on the streets or in their own homes, with no formal charges or legal procedures. This was not occurring on a large scale yet, but it was suffice to scare many.

People just disappeared without a trace. If this ever happened to Lollita, he would never be able to save her. Even Eduardo would be helpless, as all who disappeared were quickly in graves without any identifying tombstones.

Half an hour later, Miguel called. With him, the discussion was short and to the point.

"After the ship drops her anchors, I will inspect the place and find the spot from where to launch the kayak. The small boat should have enough space for two, and for the goods."

"Sure," Miguel agreed. "We will bring a German portable kayak, which could be assembled on the shore. We have someone who has good experience with this."

"Who is going to be there?" asked Glenn.

"Me, Flavio, and another guy. His name is Bajardo. Nice chap. Do you need someone else?"

"No. Your car must have a big trunk. Mind you, Puerto Madero is not a safe place to stay for long. Local trash could be a nuisance."

"You tell me. But we know how to handle that. The worse thing that might happen there is police, but it is very unlikely, if not impossible. They do not dare to go there at night even when shooting and killing takes place."

"Let's go in my car. Okay? The fewer cars the better. Agree?" Glenn asked. "I can come to your place, or you come to mine. Your choice."

"Don't worry. I will be in Puerto Madero."

"By the way, do you know where Lollita is these days?"

"No idea."

"Could it be that the police have picked her up?"

"Unlikely. We would have known."

"Okay. At nine on Monday, then."

***

It was about ten o'clock when Glenn arrived at Puerto Madero. Flavio and Miguel were already there, standing with someone else near a large American car. Flavio greeted him with a smile and a handshake.

"Glenn, this is Bajardo," he introduced his companion. "You will like him."

The feeble light of a distant street lamp behind Bajardo's back did not help much to see his face. Glenn strained his eyes while shaking his hand, and managed to make out Bajardo's smile, which was far from being a sign of welcome. It would be better for him not to smile, Glenn thought. The very rough face of the about forty-year-old man transformed into a mask of thick wrinkles when he smiled. His large eyes, large teeth, and thick hair, conveyed a sense of his aggression and brutality. His big, round shoulders and iron grip confirmed this impression.

"He's going with you," Miguel said, giving each of them an encouraging hug. "Flavio and I will stay here. Give me the key to your car, Glenn, just in case. You never know when the port police might appear."

Flavio opened the trunk of his car and gestured for Glenn to come closer. Bajardo removed a large rucksack, which seemed heavy, and put it behind his shoulders with ease, as if it was a weightless feather. Glenn took out two oars.

"Follow me," Bajardo commanded and headed towards the waterfront, not looking back. Glenn did not like accepting orders from anyone, and more so from a stranger. It was just a fleeting thought though. Soon they reached the shore, where Bajardo stopped, dropped the rucksack on the ground, and quickly removed its contents; wooden parts, joints, and a long canvas.

"You know what this is?" he asked, squatting down, and picking up a piece.

"Yes," Glenn said. "This is a Klipper, a German portable kayak."

Bajardo looked up at him. His face was hardly visible, but his voice expressed his feelings good enough.

"How do you know?" he asked with a great deal of respect.

"I'll tell you later. Let's assemble it together. I can do this job with my eyes closed."

As he bent over to pick up some parts, he noticed that Bajardo had spared a moment to glance at him again.

In less than ten minutes, the frame was put together, and the canvas hull was stretched over it. They fastened the cover with two openings in it and then hauled the kayak to the water. Glenn crawled into the first opening. Bajardo pushed the kayak farther into the water, and deftly slid into the second opening, behind Glenn. Glenn tightened the rope around his waist. This way the kayak would not sink even if waves covered them or the kayak flipped upside-down.

The wind was light. Nonetheless, the ocean was rough. Its choppy waves, although not high, required a lot of strain and power to advance through. Glenn felt that the man behind him was a mighty paddling machine. Obeying their synchronized strokes, the kayak glided like an arrow, slightly touching the water's surface, towards the humongous, barely distinguishable rock of the black ship with a few lights on its deck.

"Where did you get such training?" Bajardo asked, his breath becoming a bit heavier.

"In a hiking club," Glenn lied. "Traveled a lot in the American wilderness. Canoeing, kayaking, hiking, those sorts of things."

"Americans," Bajardo grumbled with notes of contempt and puzzlement. "Rich people are always looking for ways to kill their time."

Glenn did not respond. The ship was approaching fast. When it was less than a hundred meters away, he said, "Never have had such a buddy."

A flashlight blinked from above, and Glenn responded with his. When they approached the hull, Glenn tied the kayak with a rope to the ladder and began climbing up. When he reached the top, a dark figure greeted him, "Hi, Glenn."

"Hi, Jeff."

"Take it fast," Jeff commanded. He stood a few meters away by a pile of large bags. Glenn took one of them, with shoulder straps on it. It was heavy even for a strong man like himself, and, to his dislike, seemed fairly large for the kayak. He passed it back to Bajardo, who already stood behind him. The Spaniard took it and hurried down. Glenn grabbed another one and followed Bajardo. He was sweating profusely under its weight. When he reached the bottom, he noticed that Bajardo had already managed to unclip the top canvas and stash it somewhere at the bottom. Then he put it inside his bag and took one from Glenn.

"We can't cover them," he explained. "No way."

He stabilized the boat to let Glenn take his place. They started their way back to the shore.

Luckily, the wind subsided, although the water still was not calm. The scanty lights on the shore were their guides. A few times, their kayak was close to flipping upside down. Less experienced people would certainly have found themselves on the bottom, Glenn thought.

His eyes, adapted to the darkness, distinguished the line of the waterfront in close proximity, and soon the kayak pulled onto the shallow place with a scratching sound. Glenn jumped out, pulled the boat further onto dry land, and grasped the closest bag. It produced a crunching metal sound. Ammunition, Glenn thought. Bajardo was already behind him with the other bag behind his shoulders.

Miguel and Flavio appeared from the darkness.

"Is there anything else?" Flavio asked.

"Yes. There are another few bags on the ship. We

have to go there again."

"Great. Great. Leave it here, leave it here." Miguel was talking fast, excited by the thrill of success. "I'll handle it with Flavio. He'll be putting it in his car anyway. He will go right away, doesn't make sense to wait. Go, go guys. Go."

Glenn pushed the boat back to the water, Bajardo took his place, and off they went. Glenn's trousers were wet, his boots full of water, but he did not feel cold. Again, he saw the familiar flashlight, climbed the ladder, and gave Bajardo a bag, lesser in weight than before, but bigger. His was approximately the same. After the quick descent, they were again in the kayak.

"You were in a hiking club?" Bajardo asked, when the shore was very close.

"Yes."

"It seems to me that you have military training."

"Bullshit," Glenn said. "All my life I was in sports. Basketball, weight lifting and, of course, wilderness travel. I was involved in hunting, too, you know."

When the kayak touched the bottom, Bajardo stepped into the water with a splash and said, " You are a good comrade. I like you, you know. With people like you, we can do a lot."

Miguel approached them with quick steps.

"Hurry, hurry," he said in a husky voice, taking one of the bags. "I saw someone, although far away. If it is a port police, we're in trouble."

"You go with Miguel," Bajardo said to Glenn, again in a commanding tone. "I'll handle the Klipper, don't worry."

When on the street, Glenn and Miguel had to put the bags down and sit on them, hiding from two drunken couples passing by. When the street became deserted again, they quickly crossed the road and squeezed their luggage into Glenn's trunk. Glenn crawled into the driver's seat;

Miguel took the passenger's. Glenn inserted the ignition key in its slot and turned the starter on. The well-oiled engine purred smoothly, almost noiselessly, on the parking gear.

"Where is bloody Bajardo?" Miguel asked, and turned around. "Ah!" he exclaimed, and leaned to Glenn. His eyes were all fear.

"What's up?" Glenn sensed trouble.

"We are in deep shit," Miguel said. "Policeman. Asshole."

Glenn looked back to his right. Indeed, a policeman was approaching the passenger side of his car with confident, unhurried strides. Alone, with no reinforcement in sight! Unbelievable! Was he a total idiot? Anyway, this was one of those unpredictable cases, for which Glenn was not prepared.

The policeman stopped by, looked inside the car, and then walked around to Glenn's side.

"What are you doing here?" the policeman asked. He blinded Glenn's eyes with the strong beam of his flashlight. Glenn squinted and moved away from it.

"Waiting for two girls. They will be here soon. What's the problem, Señor?"

"Two girls, indeed," the policeman repeated. "How nice. Give me your driver's license."

This one was tough, but there was no choice. Glenn gave him his license, which the policeman snapped up and brought to his eyes, directing his flashlight at it. A few seconds later, he turned the light off, put the license into his pocket, and commanded, "Get out." Glenn obeyed.

"You stay in the car," the policeman said to Miguel.

"Sure, Señor," Miguel said.

"What's the problem, officer?" Glenn asked, and took out his wallet. "Please accept our appreciation of your—"

"Hold on," the policeman said. "Later. Now, open

the trunk."

Unbelievable! A police officer not taking a bribe? Were they in Argentina, or what? Perhaps he wants to negotiate a higher price?

In his peripheral vision, Glenn caught a glimpse of Bajardo, his figure moving soundlessly like a cat on grass.

"Come on, officer." Glenn went behind the car and inserted the key into the trunk lock. "Would five hundred pesos do?"

"Open the trunk," the officer repeated, this time in a more abrupt manner.

"Okay, okay, no problem," Glenn said, feverishly thinking what to do with the policeman if he discovered the arms. "We have some booze in here. Do you want some? One thousand pesos will do?"

The policeman said nothing. Glenn opened the trunk. To his horror, the policeman turned his flashlight on again and directed its beam inside, at the bags.

"What's in them?" he asked.

"Some belongings, and booze. Come on, Señor, here is two thousand—"

The policeman bent over and touched a bag. At that moment, Bajardo was already behind him. Glenn saw a swift, fast sway of his fist in the air. It landed on the policeman's neck with the crunching sound of a breaking bone. The policeman fell on the ground without uttering a sound.

"There was no other way out," Bajardo said in an apologetic manner. Miguel left the car, came around, and turned the policeman on his back. The eyes of the body were half open and not blinking. Glenn had seen death too often before to err. However, just to rule out the slightest chance, he touched the corpse's artery on the throat.

"Dead?" asked Miguel.

"Yes. What did you hit him with, Bajardo?"

"Knuckleduster."

"Let's get him seated in the back," Glenn said. Now it was he who was in command. "Bajardo, place your Klipper bag on his knees. Sit next to him. Go, go. Let's get out of here."

Glenn removed his driver's license from the pocket of the dead policeman and hauled the body inside. It was not an easy job, but together with Bajardo they did it with the utmost speed and efficiency. With the kayak's huge bag on his knees, he looked almost like a live passenger, if not for a strange tilt of his head.

Everyone took their places. Glenn turned on the engine, and let the tires of his car hit the road.

"Listen, this is what we're gonna do," Miguel said. "We'll go to Flavio's place, unload the bags there, and then run out of town. We'll move the corpse out of your car and off you go. We will take care of him outside the city. This way you will be out of danger."

"It is too late to care about danger," Glenn said firmly. "Mind you, we have to deliver the arms to people anyway. Why don't we go to them right now? No need to stop. This way we will avoid any unexpected troubles and we won't waste time."

"Good, Glenn, good," Bajardo raised his voice from the back seat. "He's right, Miguel. Let's move on."

"Well… actually, it's a good idea. Turn to De Mayo, Glenn."

"Okay," Glenn agreed. In his mind, he brooded over the killed policeman. Not good at all. If the police captured Miguel or Bajardo and find out the truth, Glenn would have to run out of the country. The question was if he would have time for it. The punishment might be swift and brutal. However, now he would be delivering arms directly to rebels, and he would have the chance to find out exactly where they were.

Chapter 10

At the end of May, days in Buenos Aires became noticeably shorter, as it was already late fall in the southern hemisphere. As darkness saturated, the streets of Palermo Viejo became deserted, as life moved to various entertainment establishments. On one of these evenings, the hunt for Rex Gruber began. Tristan dropped Robert and Sergio near the entrance of the Barcelona Bar.

"I will park the car and come back. I'll be around, outside," he said. Tough, reliable Tristan. Although disgusted by his sadistic nature, Robert respected him and even liked him at all other times.

According to Sergio, Rex was a man in his early fifties, slender, tall, sporty-looking, likely kept himself in good shape with some sports or fitness activities. His head was balding from the forehead up and back; his hair was cropped short. His blue eyes, as Sergio put it, were 'icy cold, like polished steel'. He lived in Barrio Norte, the district of Buenos Aires populated mostly by the middle class and some wealthy families. He often entertained himself in the barrio Palermo Veije, where bars and restaurants were in abundance. His preferred place was the Barcelona Bar, where on Fridays he usually picked up a girl for a short rendezvous, and then went home. A respectable German 'bürger', a good family man, and a valuable community member.

At eight o'clock, the bar was half empty, as it was too early for the hustle and bustle of the nightlife. Sergio chose one of the vacant tables close to the bar stand.

"Two draft beers," he asked the passing waiter.

"I do not expect Rex to come before ten," he said to Robert, "but we need to have a strategic place. Look around in the meantime. Nice joint, isn't it? This is the priciest one in this barrio, and not for nothing: it attracts people with money, and, as it usually goes, good-looking women."

Robert rolled his eyes. Massive wall candelabras shed dim, relaxing light, evenly spread all over the place. Sufficient enough to see your neighbours, but not enough to notice any flaws or marks of age on their faces. The counter, though, was brightly lit by lamps, shaded by ornamental glass or crystal, that hung from the ceiling.

Robert sipped his beer while looking into Sergio's eyes. This waiting time was good enough for a frank conversation, which Robert had contemplated before.

"It seems that you have good luck with Rebecca, don't you?" he said, and threw a pack of cigarettes on the table.

Sergio diverted his stare to the entrance.

"What makes you think so?"

"Intuition. She is much younger than you. Nice girl."

"She is. A week ago was her twenty-third birthday."

Robert lit a cigarette, and took a draw. He said nothing, whereby giving Sergio a clear sign to continue.

"She is very useful. Her older brother works in the driver's license bureau. Case in point, it was him who helped me to find out Rex's address."

This was true. When the address of Rex was known, all other intelligence was just a matter of technicalities. Sergio had followed him and found out his place of work and where he spent his free time. His occasional romps certainly did not escape their attention.

Tristan got credit for this case as well. He had made good connections with the *Der Weg* people, as well as with some radical anti-Semitic groups, through which he found out that Rex was one of those who supported *Der Weg* financially.

"It seems to me that Rebecca is not just an occasional tryst of yours," Robert said.

"What makes you think so?"

"Because you try to explain your affair with practical considerations. It does not work with me, buddy. It is none of my business, though."

"I don't mind telling you everything about my affair with Rebecca. Before I do that though, I want to ask you a question. You have an affair, don't you? Who is she?"

"Does it really matter? Buenos Aires is a city of hot broads. It is hard not to get one. I like this city."

"I like this city, too." Sergio frowned. "You heard my question?"

Robert turned his attention to the entrance, watching two couples coming in.

"Could it happen that Rex won't come today?" Robert asked.

"Look at me," Sergio grumbled. "I asked you a question. Answer it."

"Well … There is one broad that I spend some time with. Not worth mentioning though."

"Why?"

"Because … she is much older than me. But really a good-looker. And fucks like crazy."

"How much older?"

"She is about forty-five, or older, but you would never tell that. She looks like thirty, or thirty-two."

"Is she Spanish? Italian?"

"No. German. That's the whole point. I think I can use her somehow."

"Do you know what I think?" Sergio asked.

"No. What?"

"You explain your affairs with practical considerations, to use your own words. I think that you like her. If not more."

"Does it matter?"

"It does."

Robert chuckled. "Since when is it of interest to you whom I …?"

"Not that. Liking her, that's what is of interest to me."

"And why, may I ask?"

Sergio placed both elbows on the table and put his chin on his fists. A weird, unfamiliar glow of intense emotion lit his eyes from inside.

"Let's be frank with each other, okay, Robert? What we do here is a crime. I don't like it, and you don't like it, either. All that rhetoric that we do it for the righteous course of Communism is just bullshit. You want to know the truth, Robert? Here it is. Your guess is correct. I love Rebecca. I want to marry her." Sergio paused, regarding Robert steady with unblinking eyes. As if satisfied with the effect of his words, he continued:

"Yes, marry her. I don't want to go back to our shitty fatherland, the Soviet Union. Enough of that for me. I have no qualms about allegiance to the pack of stupid, vicious dogs, which we call our government. I like the free world. It is huge, diverse, and beautiful. I believe that you feel the same."

Robert lost his ability to speak for a few moments. He simply nodded, at the same time trying to cope with a chaos of thoughts and emotions.

"It is not the right time and place for such conversation," Sergio continued, "but it never is. You know what I suggest? I suggest robbing another two or three Fritzes, taking the money, and ducking out. We have a good supply of passports and all the expertise to vanish without a trace. Now, speak."

"How would you tell this to Tristan?" Robert asked.

"I will answer your question in a moment. But first,

I want to hear your answer. Are you with me?"

"I confess that I did not know you well, Sergio. I am with you. As a matter of fact, I was planning something like that, and was about to discuss it with you. I thought of running away without money and settling somehow in any English-speaking country, like Australia or America."

"Now, about Tristan," Sergio said, and squinted at his watch. Robert did the same. It was a quarter to ten. The time was approaching at which the Argentinean bars began bubbling with laughter, flirting, and dancing, and picking up ladies of the night.

"I will take care of him, Robert. I am almost certain that he, as well as Lara, are on the same footing. You know as well as I do that they are in love with each other. They will never return, never. Trust me. Let's talk about it later. I think Rex will come soon."

They took to smoking, drinking beer, and observing the coming visitors with the seemingly lazy disinterest of locals who came here to kill time. Tension was growing though, as it always did when the risky, violent action was in the making.

"Lara is a typical blonde," Sergio said. "White skin, blue eyes. I wonder if it would get Rex alert, or even suspicious, when she starts talking to him."

"Not in this place." Robert dismissed this suggestion with a wave of his arm. "Many East Europeans live in this barrio: Lithuanians, Ukrainians, even Russians."

"How do you know?" Sergio was surprised.

"I studied every barrio in my spare time." Robert chuckled. "I remember tons of information, which I for sure do not need. But sometimes it comes in handy. Tell me, Sergio, do you know what exactly Lara prepared for Rex? She was not sure at the time of our discussion, as she did not have all ingredients for each remedy."

"It's 'dura'."

'Dura' was the general term for a stupid female in

Russian. The drug earned this nickname because of its affects. When taken, particularly with alcohol, it works differently at certain intervals of time, about twenty minutes or half an hour each. At first, it elevates the spirit of a man, or a woman for that matter, and at the same time clouds the brain in narcotic happiness. This is the time when those affected by this drug behave like stupid drunks. The next stage makes them physically weak, incapable of putting up any resistance. After that they become fully incapacitated. These effects usually last from two to three hours, with no noticeable side affects thereafter.

"She found all the components for it," Sergio said. "Luckily, she knows their Latin names, so she could speak with pharmacists intelligently. She is a clever girl."

His stare suddenly hardened and he cast his eyes to his mug.

"He's here," Sergio spoke in almost whisper. "Don't look at him. I will go out and let Lara know. He is at the bar stand. Avoid his eyes."

"Don't teach me," Robert murmured. "I know my part."

Sergio left the bar. The waiter came up right away.

"Anything for the señors?"

"Another draft. My friend will come back in a minute."

"Certainly, señor."

Robert rolled his eyes, observing the bar. He recognized Rex without a trace of doubt; Sergio's description was precise and easy to match. His posture and gestures suggested a man of power, confidence, and dominance. Well, we'll see, Robert thought.

Sergio came back a few minutes later and sat with his back to the bar. His attention, it seemed, was drawn to the distant table, where a few young women sat.

"Nice broads over there," he commented aloud, with the intention of being overheard by their neighbours.

"Don't you think, buddy?"

"Would you pick someone up?" Robert asked, playing the game.

"Something happened?" Sergio said in a low voice.

"A nice girl came in," Robert commented, watching Lara walking from the entrance to the bar counter. A few heads turned after her. With a sophisticated hairstyle, a low neckline, and large blue eyes, she was quite a view. Her narrow waist and sizable breasts, emphasized by her tight gown, enhanced the harmony of her looks. She had painted her lips scarlet, as hookers do to distinguish themselves from the rest of the women's lot.

"Where is she?" Sergio asked.

"One couple is between her and him. Here, he noticed her. Now he's taking his glass and coming over to her. Hey, it seems that he's hooked."

Robert took a swig from his mug to wet his dry mouth. Rex began speaking with Lara, but she did not give him even a casual glance. When the barman poured her a drink, Rex was quick to pay. This time she gave him the gift of her smiling eyes. Gosh, she could be a movie star with her deliberate makeup. Her eyes sparkled in happiness, as if she had found the prince of her dreams at last, and had fallen in love with him at first sight.

"What?" Sergio asked with impatience.

"He paid for the drink."

"What else is new," Sergio commented. "That's how all men fall into the trap."

"Here," Robert kept murmuring, "our friend just got a gift from Lara, something really nice and sweet in his drink. He didn't notice anything. In a few minutes, his mood will improve even more. I suggest, Sergio, that you go out first. I will pay the bill and be ready to follow this nice couple."

When Sergio left, Robert began watching the bar with no precautions. Rex was standing with his back to the hall, leaning to Lara and very busy talking to her. Lara was all smiles. She raised her eyes up, gazing at Rex with coquettish admiration. Their conversation became visibly animated.

Rex moved his lips to her ear and said something. Lara's face grew serious; she nodded in agreement, placed her glass on the counter, and walked toward the exit. Rex followed her a few steps behind. Half a minute later, Robert went out, keeping some distance from them. Once outside, he glanced to the left; the silhouettes of Sergio and Tristan lingered there in the darkness. To the right, he saw Lara and Rex walking away. Rex was wobbling a bit; 'dura' had begun working, Robert concluded.

Rex opened the passenger door of his car and let Lara in, as a gallant and courteous cavalier. After she settled, he went around the car, noticeably limping, and crawled inside to the driver's seat. The lights of his car went on and moved ahead.

At that moment, Tristan pulled up in his Ford and Robert jumped in. They followed Rex in silence, peering into the dark, poorly lit streets.

"Where are they going?" Tristan grumbled. "Look, this jerk cannot handle the steering wheel. He is already done. If Lara does not take care of him right now, who knows what will happen."

Indeed, Rex's car began zigzagging as if some struggle was going on inside.

"I trust though that Lara will handle him," Tristan kept talking, apparently to himself. "Clever girl she is, isn't she?"

"Indeed. Where are they going?" Robert exclaimed, noticing the name of a street as it flashed in the beam light. "We are now in barrio Villa Ortuzar."

"How do you know that?" Tristan even turned back to look at Robert. "I also studied the city, but I am not able to recall in an instant where the street on the map is and in what direction to go from there. Such a memory."

There was no time for Robert to comment on it. The car in front of them suddenly stopped, forcing Tristan to hit the brakes close to its rear bumper. A few moments later, Lara appeared in the Ford's front lights holding the bunch of keys. She made a gesture, which was the signal to them to jump out.

"He's ready." Lara pointed at the driver seat. "Cannot move a finger. Take him out."

Tristan pulled open the driver's door and yanked Rex to the pavement. Sergio and Robert picked him up and threw him in the back seat. Rex was heavy; as immobile as if he were dead, with his head dangling about as if his neck could not support it.

"Lara, you drive the car." As usual, in tough circumstances, Tristan was in command. "I will be in the back with him, just in case. You, Robert, drive the Ford, as you are the best at navigation. Lara and I will follow you. Go, guys, go."

In less than an hour, both cars pulled in by Lara's house. They took Rex, who was already in a deep sleep, to the room, and laid him on a mattress, which Lara had prepared for this purpose. They took all his clothes off, except his underwear, tied his hands behind his back with the duct tape, and left the room. Tristan locked the door and led all his team to the kitchen, where they settled around the breakfast table. Lara was busying herself with making coffee.

"You need a boost, boys," she said. "This is going to be a sleepless night. He will wake up in two to three hours. It will be fun."

Tristan turned to Sergio and Robert.

"Put our canvas cover on his car," he said. "Early morning, we will have to take it somewhere and hide it. He will be done with by then."

Lara was right. At about two o'clock in the

morning, a powerful kick at the door shook the house. Tristan unlocked the door. Rex stood there, furious and defiant, his hands behind his back.

"What is this—" he yelled, but did not finish. With an expert blow of a well-trained boxer, Tristan sent him down. Rex tried to balance while falling back, but failed. For sure, he was well-trained for a close fight. He touched the floor with his right leg, then squatted, and rolled on his hip, side, and shoulder. It was a rather automatic response, which usually develops over prolonged and extensive martial arts training and practice. If not for that, he might have smashed his head.

"Let me help you out," Tristan said in a pacifying tone. Robert helped him pull Rex up. "Sit down here, on the stool. Yes, here. Sorry, we are very poor people and this stool is the only furniture we have."

Sergio brought a portable gas lamp and lit it.

Rex sat, rolling his eyes from Tristan to Sergio to Robert. He did not show any fear; only hatred, mixed with regret was on his face.

"Are you Jews?" he asked.

"Shame on you," Tristan reproached him. "You, a brave and experienced SS officer, cannot make out a Jew from a non-Jew? I consider it an insult to be called a Jew."

Tristan lit a cigarette and took a draw.

"Who are you then?" asked Rex. "What do you want?"

"We want your money."

"How much?"

"I cannot give you a specific number." Tristan exhaled rings of smoke and watched them melt in the air. "We want to know your Swiss bank account numbers and associated names. That's all. As soon as we get them, you are free."

Rex went pale. His face suddenly aged a good ten years. His show of self-confidence and commanding posture was gone. He put his head down and stared at his feet.

"I don't hear any response," Tristan resumed his talk. "You ignore me, as if I am not here. Do you wish to cooperate with me, or not?"

Rex raised his head.

"A few of our people have disappeared. It was you, who kidnapped them?"

"We know nothing about this. Who disappeared?"

"My former colleagues."

"You mean, former SS officers?"

"You can put it that way."

"No, we have nothing to do with that. Interesting. Most likely it was Jews who did it. They hunt after you guys, you know, and even Germans themselves are after you. But what does that have to do with my offer to exchange your money for your life?"

"How would I be sure that you won't kill me after you get what you want?"

Tristan chuckled.

"There is no paperwork involved," he said. "You have no choice, though, but to trust me. It would take approximately a week, or a bit longer, to take your money from your Swiss account. You will stay here until the money is in our hands. After that, we have no interest in you. We will let you go."

Rex put his head down again. It was clear that he had no illusions about his destiny.

"I will help you," Tristan said, and went behind him. "Let's start."

A cracking, dry sound was followed by a piercing scream. Robert knew that Tristan had begun breaking Rex's fingers.

"Stop it!" Rex yelled. "Stop it! Let's talk!"

Tristan did not stop. With a sadistic, insane smile on his face, he kept breaking his victim's fingers, screwing up his face after each crack. Disgusted and furious, Robert threw him back with a powerful push of his hands.

"Stop it," he said. "It won't do any good."

To his surprise, Tristan did not insist. He went around and faced Rex again. Rex was dead pale; his face was a picture of total exhaustion and grief.

"You see," Tristan said, "my friends are against violence. Will you tell us your account numbers? Will you?"

Rex did not respond. His eyes hardened again, as if he had just got a second wind in his guts.

"Asshole," he rasped.

Tristan was about to move behind Rex's back again, but Sergio grasped him by the shoulder and took him to the distant corner. Robert joined them, as he wanted to say something as well.

"He is a hard nut, Tristan," Sergio said. "What if he dies on you? Let's give him a dose of 'rastormozka'. I think there is a lot of money at stake here."

"Yes, Tristan, I agree," Robert joined. "This is the only way."

"The only way," Tristan repeated. "Rastormozka sometimes does more harm than good. However … Let me discuss it with Lara. Luckily, she managed to bring it from Cuba. Watch him. I will be back in five minutes."

He left and closed the door behind him. Rex remained sitting with his head down, not looking at his captors. Robert was pondering about the drug, which Tristan called 'rastormozka'. He knew too well what this Russian nickname for the drug was about. It was developed in the KGB medical laboratories for use on those who stubbornly refused to spill the beans. Mostly these were dissidents, deeply devoted religious people, or dedicated enemies of the communist regime. Some of them showed astonishing capabilities of resistance even under torture. Torture, though, was not an ideal means, as some died under it.

The ability of humans to resist pain, exhausting interrogation tactics or psychological pressure was called a brake, or 'tormoz' in Russian, which strong-willed people applied against the natural urge to ease the pressure of interrogation or avoid pain. 'Rastormozka' meant 'releasing brakes.' When administered, it reduced or completely paralyzed the human capability to resist any stress, be it physical, mental, or psychological. The trick was to apply it with the right dosage, but the dosage was not firmly established yet. It varied from one individual to another. Taken in an amount above one's biological endurance, it made him or her mentally ill with no chance for recovery, and useless for interrogation. Although extensively tested in special psychological prisons on those whose lives were doomed for the sake of medical or political 'progress,' it still produced unpredictable results. Tristan was therefore rightly concerned. It was possible that Rex might die under torture.

The door opened. Lara came in, holding a syringe full of liquid in her right hand. Tristan entred after her. When Rex saw Lara, he stared at her with inhuman rage, following each of her steps.

"Here you are, shit of a woman," he said. "I would love to see you in my hands, if it was twenty something years back."

"Time's changed, darling," Lara responded, giving him a shot in the neck. "Now, we will let you feel what it is to be in someone's hands like yours. Got the idea?"

"Shit of a woman," growled Rex. He began talking in German, but Lara was already on her way out.

"You thought that she was German, ah?" Tristan asked him. "As a matter of fact, she is. How else would she speak German without an accent? Your donation therefore would be for the good of Germans anyway."

Rex remained defiant, staring into Tristan's eyes

with the same hard hatred.

"You still think, son of a bitch, that you belong to the superior race," Tristan kept talking. "Don't you? In a few minutes, you will realize who belongs to it. I can tell you my definition of a superior race. It's the one that holds the power. Here I have it, therefore I belong to that race, and you, subhuman asshole, belong to the shit race. Understand?" Tristan suddenly screamed. "Understand?"

Rex shuddered. 'Rastormozka' had begun its work, crushing his nervous system.

"How much money do you have in your Swiss account?" Tristan kept yelling. He knew well that shouting at 'rastormozka' victims doubled the effect of the drug. None of them can tolerate loud sounds.

"About three million dollars," Rex rasped. His eyes were red. A dense nest of wrinkles appeared on his face. His head and shoulders began shaking, as if he was under a high fever.

"Numbers. Numbers and names," Tristan kept yelling. "Spill the beans, shithead, and I will let you go now. If not, I will tear your guts out with these hands." He moved closer to Rex, looked in his eyes, and raised his hands for emphasis.

"Numbers and names. You hear? Another few seconds of delay, and I will do what I promised. One, two—"

"Fine, fine." Rex began to cry. "Here are the numbers. Please, let me go."

"Write it down, Robert," Tristan commanded, not looking back. "Done?"

"Yes."

Robert handed him over a piece of paper. Tristan brought it to Rex's eyes.

"Is this right?"

"Yes," Rex nodded. "Please, let me go."

"Wait a moment. It won't take long."

Tristan left the room. Rex looked at Robert and Sergio, his eyes overflowing with tears and fear. Robert turned his face away. He knew too well what was going to happen.

Tristan returned in a minute, went behind Rex, and captured his neck in a garrote. When Rex began shaking with mortal convulsions, Robert went out and settled in the kitchen. Sergio followed him and closed the door behind. The rasping, choking sounds of breathing became muffled, and then stopped.

Chapter 11

Beyond the boundaries of Buenos Aires, the roads became a challenge for any driver, however, Glenn proved to be efficient in maneuvering between their undulations of decay. In an hour or so, he caught up with Flavio. They stopped for a brief talk, and to relieve themselves, as the urge was always greater with stress.

The further north they drove, the warmer the temperature became. Vegetation changed to more tropical species, with rainforest trees, dense undergrowth, and lianas. The paved roads soon ended, merging into gravel ones. Eventually, even the gravel roads, bad as they were, ended as well. In their stead, dirt roads appeared, often hardly distinguishable in the night. They often became a long succession of potholes, dents, and deep trenches, made by heavy trucks in rainy weather.

Miguel asked to stop by a lake populated by caiman crocodiles. They pulled the dead policeman from the car and threw him into the water.

"A special treat," Flavio commented.

Glenn strained his mind to memorize every fork and crossing in the roads, as well as natural landmarks, which later might help him repeat the voyage.

They reached the camp late at night. In the bags, they found grenades, light grenade launchers, M-14 rifles, and plenty of cartridges for them. Glenn got a few appreciative hugs from those who came to take the delivery.

They slept in a shack, which, it seemed, would collapse under the weight of a few raindrops. Miguel woke him up at dawn.

"Sorry, I can't show you all our facilities here this time," he apologized. "Flavio and I have to rush back. Let's get going."

Driving back to Buenos Aires, Glenn tested his memory. It did not fail him. Almost everything worth remembering was imprinted in his mind.

After the days of gut-shattering driving on Argentinean unpaved roads, it was nice to return to his apartment, take a shower, and have a long, peaceful sleep.

In the morning, after a hearty breakfast, Glenn took to arranging a meeting with Eduardo. A hotel, with private enclosures for selected guests in an exquisite restaurant would serve the purpose. When all was settled, he called Eduardo.

"This time we will meet at a place of my choice," he said.

"Why is that?" Eduardo asked in a merry tone. He knew that Glenn had good taste.

"It's a nice, secluded place. Conducive to serious conversation."

"Where is it?"

"In a hotel. I will give you the address."

"When?"

"Tonight. Between six and seven. Will do?"

The restaurant of Glenn's choice was spacious, sparkling with crystal and cutlery. At the end of it were private sections.

"Nice place," Eduardo commented after taking his place at the table across from Glenn. "Appreciate that. What is the special occasion, may I ask?" He opened the menu. "Oh, French cognac. Prices are crazy these days, aren't they?"

"Whatever," Glenn said.

"Shall we take a bottle?"

"Why not. Choose the steak. It's the best in town."

"I trust your judgment. Look, Cuban cigars! You like them?"

"Whatever. Enjoy life, Eduardo." He was tempted to add, "at the expense of other's," but he only smiled instead. Valuable information and police help were worth good money. The American government would foot the bill.

"What's on your mind?" Eduardo asked.

"I want to exchange news."

"You have news for me?" Eduardo took his eyes off the menu and stared at Glenn with arched eyebrows.

"Yes, but first, tell me yours. It seems you have some."

They stopped talking as the waiter came to take orders. When he left, Eduardo was the first to resume the conversation.

"We have had considerable success. Your description of Miguel was very good, I should say. We managed to identify him, as he was often with Carlos, the leader of this group, or small party, if you will. Miguel is not his real name, as you guessed, and not the only one. Quite elusive, I shall admit. Following him was not a trivial task."

"What do you mean?" Glenn did not like this sort of remark.

Eduardo took a sip from his water glass. Ignoring the question, he continued.

"Our people found out where he lives. Not only that, but a week ago, he met someone at one of the cafes on Avenida Corrientas. It seemed to our agent that Miguel received a parcel under the table from him. Our agent suspected something interesting, and followed the man, instead of Miguel. We have smart people in our police, don't we?"

"No doubt," Glenn agreed. He took the liberty to withhold his true opinion.

When the appetizers arrived, Eduardo diverted his attention to eating, thus adding a flavour of suspense to his narration. He took a few sips of cognac, defying the ritual of having it with a cigar after dinner. Through all this maneuvering, Glenn made out that Eduardo was not comfortable with the story.

"Nice," Eduardo continued, and placed his cognac glass on the table. When he took up his fork and knife, Glenn gave him a mild mental push.

"Well. What else did your agent say?"

"You see, something interesting happened. The man, whom he followed, suddenly disappeared. Vanished, seemingly into thin air."

"What?" Glenn stiffened. "Vanished? Is this a fairy tale?"

"Hold on, hold on," mumbled Eduardo raising his palm, as if to defend himself from an assault. "Please, listen. Our agent was good at shadowing, I assure you. His target was a professional in spy work. In all likelihood, he had prepared his escape well in advance."

"What do you mean?" Glenn asked in a calmer tone. He sensed the reason in Eduardo's explanation.

"I mean, the target was on alert the whole time. For sure he noticed the tail, but behaved as someone who suspected nothing. When he ducked into the closest plaza, our agent followed him fairly closely, but was not able to assess on the spot all the small passages between the buildings and the entrances into them, through which the target could disappear. I shall admit that I did not expect the discovery of a professional, but on the other hand, look … now we know that there is one, and, for sure, others — perhaps an organization. You know as well as I do that dealing with professionals requires a different level of skills, and adequately trained, sufficient forces. I think that we deserve credit for what we have discovered."

Glenn sipped his cognac as well. His appetite was gone. He lit a cigar and took a draw.

"That makes sense," he agreed.

Eduardo, encouraged by this remark, resumed chewing with fresh vigor.

"I did not want to make a decision without your consent," he was saying through a full mouth. "I suggest arresting Miguel and making him speak. He would have no choice but to cooperate with us. What do you think?"

"Don't do that," Glenn said emphatically. "If it was indeed money that he received, he will get it again. Their shitty revolution devours money like a hungry monster. I am pretty sure that the Russians are involved here, either directly, or with the help of their Cuban servants.

Eduardo finished with the steak, pushed the dish off, and took up the glass of cognac.

"Now, it's your turn," he said, fumbling with the cigar. "What's new?"

"I know exactly where the military training camp of this group is," Glenn said. The effect of his words was stronger than he expected. Eduardo coughed and choked on his cigar smoke.

"Sorry. How come?" Eduardo raised his left eyebrow up. His left eye, wide open, conveyed an air of surprise, while the right one, half-closed, remained stern and keenly investigative.

"I was there."

Eduardo took another draw on his cigar.

"How?" This time both his eyebrows were arched.

Glenn let this question pass.

"I shall confess to you about my past. I spent two years in Bolivia fighting against communist guerillas there. I am an expert in jungle fighting. If your government decides to send troops there, I would like to offer my help. I could be either an instructor, or I could actually help the commander during the battle. In any event, I know how to get there. I remember the roads well. I can't show them on the map, as most of them are dirt roads, zigzagging in tricky ways.

"Interesting," Eduardo remarked, observing Glenn with fresh interest. He quickly returned to his usual jovial mood. "Our special police forces are in infancy now. They lack professional training, not to mention experience. I will talk to my bosses about you. But you have to prepare a good explanation on how you got there."

"Very simple. I'm having a love affair with a girl who is very active in this group. She introduced me to Miguel. I offered them my help with my car. We brought some supplies, such as clothes, food, and some other stuff, I don't really know for sure what was inside some of the bags. They believe that I am a strong sympathizer, if not one of them in spirit."

"Well … Not very convincing, but plausible. Likely our brass will contact your bosses in the CIA to confirm your credentials."

"Please do. Next time, however, if you discover something suspicious or interesting, please contact me immediately. Now, just to change the subject, you obviously know about the abduction of a Jewish girl. As the newspapers put it, she was tortured, dismembered, and her body parts were scattered about the streets. Have you found who did it?"

"No, we haven't. We never will."

"Who do you think did it?"

"There are a few groups of young people, mostly descendants of German immigrants. They made it clear that this was the act of revenge, but did not say what for. We know though that one of their most respected sponsors of *Der Weg*, Rex Gruber, disappeared not long ago. Everyone, including the police, believes that there is no chance to find him or his remains. For sure he is dead, as are a few others who disappeared before him. Many in the German community believe that this was the deed of either the local Jews, or the Israelis."

"Still, crime is crime. I would agree with them if they did so to those who killed their people. But to tear apart an innocent girl? What kind of macho fighters are these shitheads? Worse than their fathers."

"You know better than I do," Eduardo said slowly, as if tired of explaining trivial things, "that we won't arrest them. They belong to the right radical movements, which are counterbalances to the left ones. Left movements are our main concern. When we finish with the communist threat, we will start dealing with the right radicals. I am sure that our government will even go as far as to reprimand them for their wrongdoings in the past. But now … you know the rest."

"Do they get professional training in fighting?" Glenn asked.

"Yes. Former SS officers are their instructors. I think they must be good at that."

"Okay, Eduardo. Thank you. Here is my appreciation. Keep me posted."

Chapter 12

Before coming to Buenos Aires, Robert fancied this assignment as a mix of business and pleasure. There would be exciting romps with local girls, spicy food, entertainment, and an aura of a remote, exotic country, he thought. Both sides of the coin, called reality of life, showed him their ugly faces.

The job of hunting former Nazis took long, often boring hours and at times was intense, exhausting, and nerve-racking. The pressure was constantly on the rise, as the time and opportunities were running out. Their targets became scared, cautious, and alert. *Der Weg* supporters, whom Tristan befriended, told him that the Israeli intelligence service was doing a job of revenge with the help of local Jewish community. That was how it had been with Eichman. There was no doubt in their minds that without powerful local support these actions would be impossible.

Each time it was harder to trace, capture, and extort information from their prisoners. They spilled the beans only under Tristan's sadistic tortures and use of Lara's magical 'medications.'

There were plenty of indicators that former SS got organized quickly, with German efficiency and discipline, sharpened with war expertise. Robert, as well as other team members, had no doubt that the remnants of ODESSA, in cooperation with local police, were already after them.

After Rex, the team 'processed' two others. The unanimous decision was not to give the resident their Swiss account numbers, but rather take the money and defect, each going his or her way. The only issue was when to stop their operation. However, they were in the dark regarding the validity of obtained account numbers.

One Wednesday, when the last corpse was buried, they returned to Lara's house in early morning. Lara served brandy and coffee, as no one wanted to eat. This time it was Sergio who took the initiative regarding crucial discussion.

"We can't stay longer here, Tristan," he began, looking firmly at the group commander. "They are all on high alert. We hardly have time to beat it out of here. Mind you, we already have the Swiss accounts from the last three. We have substantial money to share. Good enough to start a new life with."

Tristan swigged from the glass before answering. This gave Lara an opportunity to speak.

"Indeed, Tristan, let's get out of this mess. Right now. We will have a wonderful life. I will take care of all passports. I suggest going first to Uruguay, or Paraguay and from there the whole world is ours." She took a sip from the coffee mug and said with a dreamy smile, "I prefer Australia. What do you think about Australia, Tristan?"

"We do not know for sure if we indeed have this money, or not," Tristan argued. "When Robert passed account numbers to the resident, we had his feedback. Now we don't."

"So far, all the accounts were in good shape," Robert cut in. "In all likelihood these accounts are good as well."

"In all likelihood," Tristan repeated. "But not for sure."

"Money, no money, I want to withdraw from the fray," Robert said firmly.

"Hold on, hold on," Tristan responded. Now he

talked not like a commander, but rather as a friend, sharing Robert's concerns. "I agree that time is running out. But listen, we are very close to the biggest loot. I found the end of the rope, which leads to the major sponsor of *Der Weg*. He had been a big shot in Germany, and he is now. He has millions in different Swiss banks, I am almost a hundred percent sure."

"Who is it?" Sergio asked. His firm stand, Robert noticed, was shattered.

"I haven't seen him yet," Tristan replied, "but soon I will. All *Der Weg* Germans trust me. They take me for a psychopathic Jew-hater."

"What else do you know about him?" Sergio asked. Robert looked at Lara. Her eyes sparkled with excitement.

"His name is Kurt, that's what I know so far. Listen, guys, it is not only money that I am after. I really want to talk to this big shot. Face to face." He finished the brandy in one gulp and banged it on the table. "For all he did to us during the war, I want to remove his soul from his guts. Listen, guys, this is the last one, I promise."

"It might be the fatal one," Robert cautioned.

"I know your reasons, Robert." Tristan's reconciliatory tone made its way, Robert noticed. "We shall see. If it becomes too risky, we will call it off and go. Millions of dollars, guys. Millions. Agree?"

"Yes," Lara said.

"I agree," Sergio joined.

Reluctantly, Robert said, "Okay. The last one."

"Today is already Wednesday." Tristan glanced at his watch. "Take a rest till the end of this week. Relax. Let's meet here on Saturday night. I will update you on everything. If I have not found Kurt by then, off we go. Lara will have all documents finished for you by then."

***

On Thursday morning, in anticipation of a nice, relaxing day, Robert lingered in bed thinking about Bertha. He was infatuated with this woman. Was it perhaps because she treated him sometimes like a kid? He had little of his mother's love in his childhood. Well, forgive her God for all sins, but she neglected him. He did not blame her. She lived in the time of war, poverty, and misery of life. His father never came back to see her or him. He envied other kids who had both parents. In Bertha, with her motherly tenderness and understanding, he found more than just a beautiful body of a Nordic woman, mixed with the hot passion of the south. Her political and racial views often disgusted him, but hey, she was not a soul mate. After all, she was sincere, whereas he was a liar and even worse, a professional killer and robber.

His unleashed craving for sex with different women did not haunt him anymore. To some extent it was due to prolonged fits of nausea after each murder. The feeling was getting less severe, but did not vanish altogether, as Tristan and Sergio claimed it should.

Robert glanced at his watch. Nine o'clock, too early to call her. Lovely woman. If she were here, he fancied, he would take her pink buds, which were on the top of her boobs, in his mouth, and caress them with his tongue until she moaned. He would touch the triangle of her small blonde hair, pat her smooth tummy and hips, and play with her legs. She would kiss him all over, heating herself up for a stretch of their sexual marathon. Oh, how she loved it! She never got tired of it, or bored with it. While resting between these intense bouts she caressed him, and kissed him, now like a lover, and then like a mother.

Robert stretched his arm to the telephone to call her, but it rang when the receiver was in his hand. He brought it to his ear.

"Hola."

"Hola, Robert." It was Jose. In his coded language,

he said, "I need to see you today. Important. Urgent."

"Where?"

"Plaza Lavalle. At noon."

"For how long?"

"Fifteen minutes, or less."

"Okay."

"Bring with you a paper bag with a sandwich. We will exchange the bags."

"Will do." Robert placed the receiver back on the cradle with a click. What the hell is it, he thought. Something went wrong. When it happens with a resident, everyone is in trouble. He dialed Lara. She picked up the phone after the first beep.

"Hola, Lara. Is Tristan there?"

She did not answer. Instead, Tristan took the phone.

"What's up, Robert?"

With the same code, Robert said, "Resident called. Urgent meeting. Shall I go there?"

"Yes. Mind you, he has to give us money. He missed already two pays."

Indeed, the resident knew nothing about the money they got from Gerwig and Hans. He was supposed to provide enough of it for the on-going activity.

"I think it is not our money that he is concerned with."

"Find out what it is. Where is the meeting?"

"Plaza Lavalle."

"Do you think you need support?'

"I don't think so. He would have said that."

"I will be here. Call me right after the meeting."

Close to noon, a taxi brought Robert to Plaza Lavalle. He walked around it, studying human traffic, buildings, and location of benches. Nothing suspicious so far, although a shallow observation is never conclusive. Sometimes even good professional spies could not detect the tail at the first glance.

He reached Viamonte street and then strode to the Fountain of Dancers. Figures of the dancing man and woman were cast in expressive poses, as if a magician caught them in the highest spirit of performance and converted them to stones to save the beauty of the moment for eternity. Streams of water around them enhanced the charm of the composition.

The resident sat not far from the fountain on a bench, with a paper bag beside him. As soon as he noticed Robert, he took to chewing a sandwich. Robert settled on the same bench and placed his bag close to Jose.

"Good," Jose said under his breath, staring in front of him. "Notice anything?"

"No."

"Take my bag. There is another sandwich and some money. Sorry for being late with it."

"Thanks." Robert removed the sandwich and began eating. Then he placed the bag between his legs. "Something happened?"

"Yes. A week ago, I had a meeting with one of the local communist leaders. I had known him for quite a while. Everything had been okay. The last time, though, I detected a tail after me. I am sure that it was the first time. I managed to shake it off, but can't take a second chance to meet him again."

"For sure."

"Yes, for sure. But at this moment I can't send anyone to meet him. All local residents are very busy. Under no circumstance should they take this risk. This was the order from the Center. However, the communist movement here is on the rise. With our help it might become the most powerful political force here. Unless, though, the army takes the power, which is very likely. Then, there would be a real mess here."

"Perhaps," Robert said. "Why do you tell me about this?"

"In the bag, only one third of the money is yours. The rest must go to the local communists. You shall meet my contact and give it to him."

"Me?" Robert was furious. "You risk us, instead of—"

"Don't rush with conclusions," Jose interrupted him. "I have told the Center that you are in a tough corner here. They called off your mission and ordered you back to Cuba. From there you will go home. Got it?"

"Yes, but what—"

"Hold on. Listen. There is some risk, but not much. They won't arrest everyone whom my communist contact meets. There is a small chance that they may follow you. Be prepared to shake the tail off. You can leave Argentina right after that."

"Who is going to help you after we leave?"

"Our agents are on their way to Argentina. Thanks to your job, there is some foreign currency in the Center to support local communists."

"I see. Goodbye then, Jose."

"Wait a second. You haven't brought me new Swiss accounts lately. What is going on?"

"As I told you over the phone, the whole nest of SS wasps is in turmoil. They are on high alert. Now they have their own security people who safeguard them."

"They can't safeguard them all," remarked Jose.

"True. But those who have money can afford it. Those who can't, don't have Swiss accounts."

"I will tell you over the phone when and where you should meet my contact and give him money. His name is Miguel. You will easily recognize him. Here is how he looks."

Robert listened, missing no detail. I won't be here by then, he thought.

"Now, you go first. Good luck," Jose said.

Robert walked from Plaza Lavalle at a leisurely

pace, trying to notice a tail. There was none. When the last trace of doubt was gone, he took a taxi and went to Lara's house. As he expected, she and Tristan were there. Lara asked him to sit at the breakfast table and took to brewing coffee. None of them asked questions. Robert placed the bag with money on the table.

"What is it?" Tristan asked.

"Money. One third of it is ours, the rest must go to the local communists."

"Local communists?" Tristan repeated.

Robert gave him a detailed account of the meeting. Corners of Tristan's mouth went down in display of contempt and irritation. Lara left the stove, came to them, and put her both hands on the table.

"None of our business," she said, and supplemented her opinion with a few dirty words. Robert had never heard her speak that way. Tristan remained silent, squinting his eyes in deep thought.

"Let's take all the money and forget about it," Lara suggested. "After all, we are out of this game anyway. In two to three weeks we will be far away from Argentina."

"And take the money, which belongs to local communists?" asked Tristan.

"You know whose money it is." Lara began showing her temper. "Why do you care?" She began raising her voice. "Are you still a communist? Aren't you?"

She was talking to him as if he was her husband, with whom she had equal rights. This had never happened before, so far as Robert could remember.

"There is nothing wrong in being a communist," Tristan said, surprisingly in a reconciliatory tone. "It is people that made it as it was. The ideas themselves are good."

"Good?" yelled Lara. "Perhaps you wish to go back to our shitty fatherland? Where was it good? Cuba? You wish to go to Cuba and live there to the rest of your life?"

"Cut it out." Tristan remained unperturbed. "What do you think, Robert?"

"Well… I do not have a firm opinion. I do have greater sympathy to local communists, than the former SS."

"No doubt," commented Tristan. "But the question is do you mind taking a risk, albeit minimal as it is?"

"I think so. If you back me up."

"Don't worry about that. I will arrange everything."

"You are crazy," Lara interfered, beyond herself with irritation. "We, Russians, are the nation of masochists. Our barons can rely forever on our patience and obedience. Stupid. I wonder what Sergio would say about that."

"We can't get him till tomorrow," Tristan said. "He is with his Jewess. Funny, ah? It seems that he is in love."

"I am sure that he would be against it," Lara said.

"Don't bet on it," Tristan said. "I know him. He does not like our rulers, but he is pretty strong in his communist convictions." He turned to Robert. "Let's do it this way. If we get our last target by the balls before the resident calls you, we will be out with all the money. If not, let's give the money to the communists and then decide what to do next."

"What if Robert notices a tail?" Lara asked.

"I don't believe that the local police is able to trace us," Tristan said with confidence. "However, if there is a tail, we will shake it off and run away the same day. So, what is the consensus? Agree?"

"Yes," Robert said.

"Assholes," Lara grumbled, pouring coffee in the cups.

"If you need me, call late at night," Robert said.

***

He called Bertha from a public phone. When she heard his voice, her tone became mellow.

"Sweet boy. You haven't forgotten me. How nice." Bells of joy reached his ears.

"Can we meet, Bertha?"

"Of course. But it is too late for today."

"I miss you."

"I miss you, too, my dear boy. How about tomorrow, the same hotel? At eleven o'clock. It is nice there, isn't it?"

"It is."

"Wait for me in the court.

"Good. At eleven."

The next day, as Robert expected, Bertha was right on time. She never tried to test his feelings by being late, never played stupid girlish games, as some women do till old age. And she was always sincere. Robert liked it.

"Let's not waste time here," she said, taking him by the arm. "I am hungry for you. I am always afraid that I meet you for the last time. Where do these feelings comes from?"

He stood up from the bench and put his hand around her waist.

"I have no intention to part with you. If there was a chance, I would commit myself to living with you for years."

She laughed. Holding his arm, she led him inside the hotel.

"What happened with my intuition?" she asked, entering the lift. "It never failed me. With you, it is on a swampy ground."

When they entered the room, she locked him in her embrace.

"My boy," he heard her hot whisper. "My dear boy. It is terrible."

"What is it?" he responded, also in whisper.

"In my age, to fall in love… with a young man. It is a disaster. I am helpless."

"What if—"

She covered his mouth with her lips.

"Not a word," she said, catching her breath. "Take your clothes off."

As he expected, their lovemaking was long, strenuous, and acutely enjoyable. She pulled his hair, scratched his back with her long nails, caressed him, and sang a sweet song of blissful moaning. Then, after the climax, the silence of their happiness conquered the room.

Head on a pillow, she fixed her large, unmoving eyes on Robert and stroked his hair and cheek with her soft palm. She seemed to be deep in thought.

"What are you thinking about?" he asked. She did not answer, lovingly patting his head. Her swollen, pink lips formed a lazy smile, showing a teasing white strip of her teeth.

"You are beautiful," Robert said. Her lips mesmerized him. They were wonderful when she was serious, and even more so when she smiled.

"Men say this compliment before, not after," she chuckled, pulling his ear as a gesture of motherly reprimand.

"Your lips are—"

She silenced him with a tight, wet kiss.

"Main kinder," she said in German with a sigh. "If you only knew, how I love you. If you only new. In evenings, when I am alone in my drawing room, I think about you and I want to cry."

"Cry?"

"Yes. From being heavenly happy with love. From fear of losing you soon."

"But you won't," he objected.

"You are a sweet, innocent boy with no experience in life. We have about twenty years of difference in age. Soon, I will be an old and ugly woman, but you—"

"I don't want to hear that," Robert protested. "I love

you." This was the first time he did not lie to her. "I want to have you in my exclusive possession." She was about to say something, but Robert interrupted her.

"Let's change the topic of our conversation," he suggested.

"What do you wish to talk about?" Her lips returned to a teasing smile.

"Something of no importance. Have you read in the newspapers about a Jewish girl, found murdered on the street?"

"Yes. What about her?" She raised her eyebrows, still smiling.

"Well… I think it is a bit too much. Anti-Jewish slogans is one thing, but quite another is the actual killing for nothing. Don't you think so?"

"I don't." She got serious. "It is not for nothing."

Robert was perplexed.

"It sounds like you have a personal vendetta against Jews," he said. "Do you believe, like Hitler did, that all of them must be exterminated?"

"You can say so. They are the cause of trouble to the whole world."

"But Hitler wanted to exterminate other nations as well. He wanted to kill the Russians in even greater numbers, as far as I know."

"There is a great deal of difference in his approach to other nations," she said. "He wanted to exterminate Jews entirely, whereas the other nations he wanted to reduce to manageable population. After all, we Germans, needed space. Mind you, there was no plan to reduce population in Northern Europe. So far as Hitler was concerned, most of us Germans loved him."

"What for?"

"In just a few years, he brought Germany from moral and economic abyss to the pinnacle of might and prosperity. We all felt respect and fear from all nations."

"You all paid a heavy price for your love for Hitler, didn't you? He brought on you the greatest disaster in German history."

"You are right. But it is only a temporary defeat. The game is not over yet. By the way, the girl was killed not for nothing. You don't know many things, which go on behind the scene."

"Perhaps not. Do you?"

"Yes."

"What is it?"

"Don't tell anybody. Okay?"

"Sure. I am too far from these things."

"Jews became more active lately. A few former SS members disappeared without a trace. This is for sure the deed of Jewish hands. Some of them are high in the government and apparently snatched the names and addresses of our people from secret archives. Most likely they killed them. They kill us, we kill them. They cannot commit this kind of crime and get away unpunished. After all, we are still well organized and have means to defend ourselves."

"I am puzzled," Robert said. "Do you have a secret organization?"

"Sort of. It is my husband's domain though; he deals with it, not me. We have gone too far in our chat, Robert. Let's not talk about that. We break the main rule of social pleasantries, never talk about politics."

She snuggled her head and arm on his chest, submissive and soft like a young girl.

"Sure. No politics." He yanked the blanket off the bed, exposing her naked body to the broad daylight.

"Shame on you!" she shouted joyfully, making no attempt to cover herself. Such a lovely woman, kind and gentle, with so devilish ideas, he thought.

"You have a body of a twenty-five-year-old woman," he said, observing her with acute lust, and put his hand on the blonde hair between her hips. “Maybe you know where the fountain of youth is?” He squeezed her gently.

“Yes. Your hand is on it.”

Robert burst out in laughter.

“Come on. Don’t be so cynical.”

“I have to. In my age, being romantic is stupid, if not ridiculous. Being a laughing stock is the worst of what may happen to a woman heading for menopause. A coquetry of the eighteen years old would seem nothing but affectation. But the insatiable craving of this thing, where your magnetic hand is now, for men, mobilizes me to be in shape and stick to a strict diet. I have money and time at my disposal.”

“You said that you always tell the truth.” Robert looked into her glowing, blue eyes. She did not blink.

“Yes. Did you catch me lying?”

“You cheat on your husband, don’t you?”

She rose on her elbow.

“Yes and no. I know that he has a lover in Tigre. When he tells me that he goes away for a business trip, I know where he goes. I have never made a scene about it. We have not slept together for about two years. So, I feel free in that sense. I know for sure that he does not care.”

“Weird, isn’t it?” Robert said. “Not to sleep with such a beauty?”

“Beauty, or no beauty, love has its beginning and end, like everything else. Sometimes it lasts a few days, months, or years, but very seldom to the grave. Its time span depends on personality. But he is a wonderful man. I still respect him.”

She pushed Robert on his back and put her hand on his chest.

“You say that you always tell the truth.” She was looking at him with loving, but investigating eyes. His heart skipped a beat.

"Yes. You don't believe me?"

"I feel tremendous strength of your character. It is just female intuition, nothing more. But it does not fit into idiosyncrasy of a spoiled brat, as you put it about yourself."

Robert ran his palm over her shoulders and back.

"Don't forget that I am Spanish. Every Spanish is a macho man."

Bertha kissed him and then pulled his hair.

"It is much more than Spanish machismo, that I sense in you. Mind you, I had encounters with men possessing enormous guts. My husband, for instance, is like that."

"Who is he? You always avoided a conversation about him."

"Now he is just an engineer. He owns a construction company. But he was—"

"He was…" Robert repeated, prompting her to continue.

"He was an SS high-ranking officer," she confessed, smug for her husband's honorable stature.

"All SS people were strong?" Robert asked.

"Not all. But those who were in elite military units undoubtedly were. Kurt was once in the team of Otto Scortzeny. Anyway, that's not the point. I sense, right or wrong, a devilish strength of your heart and mind. That's what I like in men. Inner strength."

She gently grasped his crotch and laughed.

"This is the only weak place in a macho man, and women use it to the fullest. You have a strong body, too. Lots of exercise?"

"I was in sports from childhood."

"It shows." She sighed. "Time flies. I have to go home. I want to take a shower. Do you wish to bath with me?"

"Sure. Go there. I will smoke a bit and join you in a minute."

When the stream of water was loud enough, he picked up the phone and dialed.

"Tristan? I am in a hotel now. With a woman, yes, smartass. You or Sergio must come here. I will come out with her, and then one of you should follow her. Find out her address. She is Kurt's wife. Details later. Here is the hotel address…"

Chapter 13

Sunday morning greeted Glenn with rainy dark clouds. Lollita slept on her side, back to him, stark naked, her hair spread on the pillow. He did not see her face, but he knew well how it looked; her long lashes, parted lips, and all other features made up the soft and peaceful harmony of a young woman. Himself being an early bird, he was careful not to wake her up. His habit was to get up early, exercise, and then work all day long to the point of exhaustion.

Breakfast, lunch, and dinner had never been a part of his schedule; eating was just an event that happened amidst his hectic activity: meeting someone, waiting for someone, or preparing for a deadline. Lollita made exceptions to the rule. Instead of exercising, he cooked breakfast for her and enjoyed doing nothing. Throughout all of this, his thinking, calculating, and investigating went on as an automatic process. It did not take any effort on his part. It was his second nature, something he did unconsciously.

Glenn loved his way of life. He knew more than most, took notice of things that ordinary people missed, understood more than most, and had the power of the exceptional few.

Slowly, he rolled onto his back, put his hands behind his head, and gazed at the window, reflecting upon his life during the past month. For sure he was doing a good job — he was praised by his brass — but nonetheless it did not give him a good feeling, as it had before. He knew what had gone wrong. Lollita was the name of the culprit. Her image disturbed him too often during his stressful days; he longed for her on the nights when she was not with him. She had become his addiction, both in flesh and spirit. This was certainly not good. An intelligence agent may fool around with women, may be a womanizer even, but still be good at his work as long as there was no real attachment.

In his thoughts, Glenn tried not to use the word 'love', but it came into his mind with stubborn persistence. He was afraid of it, and to a certain extent, ashamed of it. A soldier, a spy, a macho adventurer — in love? Who in his profession could afford such a weakness?

As if overhearing his intensive thinking, Lollita sighed, turned toward him, and put her right leg and arm on his body.

"How long have you been awake?" she asked in a sleepy voice. Her eyes were still blurry with the remnants of her dreams.

"About half an hour."

"What have you been doing all this time?"

"Looking at the sky through the window."

"Something new over there? Any greetings or promises from above?"

When he didn't answer, she pulled a few hairs on his chest to draw his attention.

"Someone in your bed is speaking to you, buddy. Please be courteous and engage in conversation."

"Just a weather forecast. It will likely rain soon."

"Any conclusions from this?"

"Two."

She rose on her elbow and leaned over him, blocking his view of the window. He embraced her waist.

"What are they?" she asked. "I am curious to know what kind of thinking is inspired by staring at the window."

“My first thought was that it was going to be a nice, lazy day for us. I will cook breakfast, after which we will spend time here till noon.”

“In bed?”

“Yes. It is cozy enough for pillow talk, isn’t it?”

“It is.” She whispered in his ear, “What is the second one?” Her words sounded intimate and sexy. She knew how to make simple things seem interesting and exciting.

“We will go to Teatro Colon in the evening. A famous ballet star will perform tonight.”

“Lovely, but all wrong.” She dropped on her back. “I can stay with you just another two hours. That’s all.” She tossed the blanket off and stretched, groaning in pleasure.

“Why is that?” Glenn could not hide his disappointment. Busy as he was, he had put aside all urgent matters for this day because he wanted to be with her. He felt betrayed.

“I have a meeting with Miguel at half past two this afternoon. Before that I have to do some important errands. Smooth your forehead, darling, don’t look so grim.”

“Where are you meeting him?”

“In Seagull restaurant, on Defensa. He wanted to see me sooner, but he got a call for an urgent meeting there at two o’clock. He was sure that it wouldn’t last longer than half an hour. All his important meetings with someone who we don’t know are short. Isn’t that how big deals are made?”

“Perhaps.”

He kissed her lips, but his lust had dissipated. His usual habit of thinking, making decisions, and rushing headlong into action replaced all his emotions and sentiments. Work, as it had always been, came first, leaving no room for such trivialities as love, friendship, or even personal necessities. A plan of action was assembled in his mind in an instant.

"Let's have breakfast someplace out," he suggested casually. "From there we can go our separate ways. I have to do a few important things as well."

"Good," she agreed, crawling off the bed. "I'll take a quick shower."

When the hissing of running water behind the closed bathroom door was loud enough, Glenn picked up the phone and dialed. The receiver on the other end clicked after the first beep.

"Hola."

"Hi, Brad. Be in café Seagull at half past one. Tell Jeff to be outside. At two, Miguel will be there. Don't follow him. Follow the person he meets with. I will be on the other side of the street, so watch my signals."

"Understood."

"Tell Jeff to drop inside and have a quick look at the target. He should be able to give me a verbal description. All clear?"

"Yes."

Glenn hung up the phone. A needle of a nasty thought pricked his heart. What would Lollita say if she knew who he was? There was no other way, though. People of his profession have a dual personality by definition. One part has to be loyal and honest, but only to his organization. The other has the freedom to break any moral or criminal code, or to neglect even rudimentary decencies, as long as it helps to achieve the goal. But still …

She came out of the bathroom with pink cheeks and shining eyes, wrapped in a cream-coloured towel from the waist down.

"You're already dressed!" she exclaimed with disappointment. "What's the rush?"

"Just a change of mood from leisure to business." It was a delight to watch her deliberately and slowly pick out her underwear; she did it with a sly, naughty smile and a challenging, shameless stare. Well, we will have plenty of time, he thought. She is lovely. An adorable girl. He said aloud, "Well, I hope we will have plenty of good time in the near future. What do you think?"

"Who knows," she said, pulling up jeans. "The future is not cast in stone."

The usual coquetry of a woman who wants to keep her man's interest, he decided. That's good. He will make her happy.

Their breakfast in the nearest café was short and not spiced by their usual exchange of jokes and funny observations about the people and things around them. It was obvious that she was preoccupied with something that Glenn was not supposed to know. Glenn was equally preoccupied; as much as he enjoyed her company, he now wanted to part with her as soon as possible. When they had finished their breakfast, she said, "Darling, I can't tell you everything, but I won't be able to meet with you for a little while."

"Come on, Lollita. What's the matter?"

"Please, do not hold a grudge against me. I love you. It's true. But I have more important things in my life than love. I will call you as soon as I can. Bye for now."

Close to two o'clock, he was on Calle Defensa, across the street from café Seagull. It was not raining yet, not windy, and rather pleasant. The usual Sunday flood of pedestrians helped his aim of not being conspicuous. He saw Miguel go into the café. There were a few others who came in after him, but none of them seemed suspicious.

Ten minutes later, Jeff showed up. He went inside where Brad, no doubt, was already on his duty. Soon, Jeff came out and began walking slowly toward the port. Glenn crossed the street and joined him.

"He's talking to a funny guy," Jeff reported, not turning his head. "Looks like intelligent man, college-boy type, about twenty-seven or twenty-eight years old. Black hair combed back, well groomed. Blue eyes, low forehead;

seems like a typical Spaniard. Dressed in a gray jacket and blue shirt."

"Good. Now, let's go back. You pass Seagull and stay there at some distance. Brad will follow him anyway, so we will not lose him. If you see me walking toward the port, go the same way. If I see you walking in the opposite direction, I will follow you. But I have the gut feeling that he will go toward the port."

They crossed the street and walked back. When café Seagull was one block away, Glenn stopped.

At about two-twenty, the so-called 'college boy' went out. If not for his self-confident manner of walking, he would really have passed for one. However, he did not look around, or so it seemed. He did not show any sign of being alert or concerned about being followed. He was indeed walking toward the port. Brad followed him at a safe distance.

When the 'college boy' was approaching Plaza Dorrego, a thought struck Glenn that he might lose him there. He quickened his pace, crossed the street, and walked ahead of him. Not looking back, he went into the plaza, and at the same quick pace he moved across it to the opposite exit. He didn't know whether it was telepathy, or just his oversensitive intuition, but he felt in his guts that he had made the right decision.

The place was humming with sounds of the day-to-day small pleasures of life. People were sitting at tables under sun-shielding umbrellas, eating, drinking, and laughing. Most of them were engaged in animated conversations and were gesticulating emphatically.

At the edge of the broad, paved path, he passed a middle-aged couple. A tall man stretched and squeezed a huge accordion, whose bellows were breathing out a charming Italian tune. The woman beside him sang a heartbreaking love song; her sorcery would have stopped Glenn at any other time. Likely, she was a professional singer without a job. There were many like her around in these difficult times.

At the corner of a dilapidated house, built with the impressive architecture of a distant past, three musicians played tango for a young couple of dancers. The woman wore a short, provocative dress and tight net panties, hiding nothing, revealing everything. The man was in tight breeches, a business style jacket, and a black brimmed hat. They moved fast, looking sternly into each others' eyes, like strangers who did not like each other. A few people stood around, watching the performance.

Here and there some older folks played chess, silently concentrating on the pieces on the boards; others, the lonely ones, drinking coffee or beer, followed passersby with their dreamy, slightly sad eyes.

An uneventful, peaceful, and seemingly happy life ruled this place, as if there was nothing troublesome beyond its bounds: no guerrilla groups gathering strength all over the country; no communists dreaming of seizing power; no former SS and Nazis involved in their sneaking way in the Argentinean politics.

None of these people guessed that he was after a dangerous man, likely a KGB agent, who was also involved in this game.

When he saw the running 'college boy' overtaking him, the blood rushed in pulsating gushes to his temples. Glenn followed him at a distance of twenty steps. The man reached the street and rushed along it to the right. He suddenly stopped close to a Ford car, looked back, and jumped into it. In the same instant, the car dashed off and disappeared in the traffic. A few seconds later, Brad joined Glenn, catching his breath.

"I've lost the bloody jerk," he said with anger, and cleared his throat.

"He's not a jerk. Not a college boy either. Don't worry though," Glenn gave him a friendly hug. "I saw the license plate of the car that picked him up. Let's go back and meet Jeff. By the way, did you see anything suspicious during their meeting?"

"That guy gave Miguel a small package under the table."

"Good job, Brad. Here is Jeff. I will find out the address of the car owner. Be on high alert."

Chapter 14

It took little effort for Sergio to follow Bertha from the hotel to her house. She was a good, responsible driver, obeying the road signs and traffic rules. Her immaculate Mercedes was easy to detect even from far away. After her address was known, the spy activity on Kurt began.

Kurt followed his daily routine with remarkable diligence. Every day, he drove to work at the same early morning hour and came back home in time for dinner. In his early fifties, tall, and almost bald, he still retained a commanding posture and exerted a military-type of confidence in all his moves and gestures. Capturing him, though, was virtually impossible. Everywhere he went, he was always accompanied by his driver, a man about twenty-three years old, who was, beyond a doubt, Kurt's bodyguard. His house also had a good security system.

Uncertain what to do next, Tristan called the group for a meeting at Lara's house.

"I want to know everyone's opinion," he said, shifting his eyes from one person to another.

"Perhaps you can tell us your opinion first?" suggested Robert.

"Sure. Kurt came to Argentina with truckloads of money. No doubt he is a rich man. He donates a lot to *Der Weg*. I talked to *Der Weg* people. Some of them whispered that Kurt had, and still has, money in foreign banks. Got it?"

Nobody made a comment. Tristan continued.

"Perhaps we would have to kill his chauffeur before getting him, but it would take time to prepare for such a thing. Another tactic is to stay a bit longer on-guard and wait for a chance. I am sure that no one, neither the local police, nor the Germans, would identify us. That means that we can stay safely in Argentina as long as we wish."

"How long do you think we should wait for our chance?" Sergio asked.

"Three weeks. After that, I will call it quits and off we go. Let's meet in Italy and then decide how to deal with the Swiss accounts before everyone goes his way."

"Lara?" Tristan asked, looking at her with raised eyebrows.

"I think we should forget about Kurt. Greed is always bad guidance. I suggest getting out of here now. Two to three days max."

"And you?" Tristan asked Robert.

"I tend to think that Lara is right. Besides, as I said before, I have a nasty feeling that I was followed after the meeting with Miguel. I didn't notice anyone; it was just intuition, but still—"

"For sure you shook off the tail," Tristan remarked. "They were not able to follow you to the car, were they? It would have taken a miracle."

Robert shrugged. "You never know," he mumbled.

"Comrades." Tristan began his speech in an unusually pompous manner. "Just think about this. A high-ranking SS officer will be in our hands. If my memory does not fail me, about four to six million Russian POW soldiers died in Germany. How many of them did this damn Kurt interrogate? How many of them were tortured? I don't care much about Jews, or Gypsies, or Poles, or whoever. Not good, but who cares. You know, I had a friend who died there. I saw people who we saved at the end of the war. Risk? Of course. Our job suggests a high risk—"

"It is not our job anymore," Lara interrupted him. "There are many like him here, whom you would love to talk to. One more, one less, does not matter anymore. I am firmly for moving out of here."

The group's heated discussion continued until late in the evening. No final decision was made, but the sentiment of the majority was to move out of Argentina.

The next morning, Robert woke up as a different man. He was relaxed, happy, and without any desire for adventure or risk. The tension of the last few months was gone, and with it the habit of planning and arranging for worst-case scenarios.

Smiling, he dialed Bertha's number. Her gentle voice was like a melody to his ear.

"Can we meet today, Bertha?"

"Oh, you. Somehow I knew that you would call. I would love to, but this time let's meet at Café Tortoni."

"Why?" Robert was disappointed. "Not in the hotel?"

"No, darling, I—"

"Let's go to my apartment. It is not the luxury you're used to, but cozy enough—"

"No, no, my lovely boy. It's not that. I could do it with you even on a gravel road," she laughed. "It's not that. Just to remind you, I am still young. Got the idea?"

"I see. Still, let's go to my place. I want to inspect you personally to make sure that you don't lie."

"Actually," she said through laughter, "you will have this chance sooner than you may think. There is going to be a special occasion."

"What is it?"

"I will tell you details when we meet. So, Café Tortoni at two o'clock?"

"Alright. I'll be there."

He went out. For a few hours he walked on the streets, trying to notice a shadow behind him. For sure there was none. Then the rain started, forcing him to take an early refuge in Café Tortoni. Bertha came in at exactly two o'clock.

"I like the way you look today," she said, taking a chair across the table. "Slept well?"

"Yes. What about you?"

"I haven't heard any compliments from you yet."

"Oh. You look beautiful. What happened? Did you sleep well?"

"Rascal. No, I didn't. You made my fantasy twenty years younger, which interferes with the sleeping pattern. Plus, I spend longer hours in front of the mirror. It takes labour and time to look beautiful."

"If you were twenty years younger now, would you make a decision adequate to your new age?"

"You mean, a stupid decision?" she asked.

"Sort of."

"What is it you want me to decide?"

"Can we go to Europe together?"

Bertha smiled, giving him a squinty-eyed glance.

"How long have you been thinking about this?" she asked.

"The last month."

"The answer is 'no'. But I will kiss you all over for your offer."

"We'll see. And when we'll meet?" he asked.

"That is what I wanted to talk to you about. What are your plans for the next two days?"

"Nothing. Just work as usual, but I can be flexible."

"Good." She paused. "Then I have two pieces of good news for you."

"Tell me about them."

"The first one is that today is the last day of my discomfort. Tomorrow we can meet in a hotel."

"Lovely. What is the second one?"

"It is even better." She paused again, emphasizing the importance of what was coming: "Kurt is going on one of his refreshing business trips. You know what I mean. To his pussy in Tigre. He leaves the day after tomorrow and comes back in two days. He likes that city. He says that it is so safe that people do not lock the doors at night there. For sure, no one is going to disturb his rendezvous. Well … I don't see any joy on your face. Aren't you happy about having two full days with me?"

"Oh. Of course I am," Robert assured her with almost natural enthusiasm. Tristan will be ecstatic, he thought. This is the chance he was hoping for. Millions of dollars! It was worth the risk, which in this case was not that great. Tristan would torture him, for sure, but hopefully not for long, as every second counted now.

"Call me the day after tomorrow at eleven," she said. "We will stay together till late evening, and have dinner."

"Lovely," Robert said with a smile. "I am looking forward to having you then."

Bertha sipped her coffee and lit a cigarette.

"I am trying to limit my smoking. Cannot stop it altogether, particularly so after I have met you. Smoking mixes well with all kind of pleasures. To quit, you have to have either very strong willpower, or a serious health risk. Even Kurt, with all his tremendous guts, was not able to stop smoking until his heart attack. He said that it turned out to be a very easy thing to do."

"Your husband had a heart attack?"

"Yes. Funny, he stopped smoking to live longer, but did not stop visiting his little Spanish cunt in Tigre!" She chuckled. "This hot, young broad will take him to the grave sooner than smoking."

"You wouldn't be upset, would you?"

She gave him a weird look.

"I didn't say that."

"He must be a very brave man to travel that far alone," Robert said. "If he really was an SS officer, Israelis might be after him."

"He knows that," she said, taking the coffee cup in

her well-maintained hands. "There are two body guards in his car. He always takes them when he travels outside Buenos Aires, no matter what the purpose of his trip is. But hey, a vigorous quickie could stop his heart in an instant. Don't you think so?"

A note of jealousy rang in her voice.

"It stopped mine a few times with you. It was not a quickie though. I endured pretty well. Didn't I?"

"Rascal." She slapped his hand. "There was nothing wrong with your heart. I felt its beat with my chest."

"Get your cute little pussy ready for merciless abuse."

"I accept the challenge."

Her eyes sparkled. She laughed and gave him a happy, hot glance. Robert smiled in response. She does not guess, he thought, that she will neither see him nor her husband ever again, no matter how well or sour this last deal goes. But I like her so much ...

After giving Bertha a last goodbye kiss on the cheek, he went to a bar in San Telmo and called Lara from the public telephone. Tristan answered the call.

"Interesting news, Tristan," he said. "Kurt goes to his twat in Tigre the day after tomorrow."

He heard Tristan clearing his throat.

"Sure?"

"This is information from the source. Couldn't be any better."

"Nice. I will call you later tonight."

Robert took a seat by the window and ordered a draft beer. Being alone among the crowd rendered him more privacy than solitude in his apartment. In a public place, the second soul of his dual personality did not disturb him much. This was particularly important now that the gruesome decision had been made, since its implications were impossible to predict. However, a few points were crystal clear. He had signed the death sentence over Bertha's husband. Whether Kurt was good or bad had not been part of his consideration. He had just betrayed a woman who was infatuated with him. He had used her trust to do so. His motive was money, not revenge, or any other moral or political reasons. His government also had no moral or legal issues to settle with Kurt. It had sent the team on a purely criminal mission from the beginning. Back then though, it had been the choice of the KGB; now, however, since their group had decided to betray their country and defect, they were going to be committing murder and robbery by their own personal choice.

The people around him were bustling with drinking, talking, and laughing. Many were engaged in heated political discussions, and for a good reason; the country was in economical and political turmoil. It seemed, though, that everyone had come here to relax and have a good time, free of moral burdens and critical life decisions.

It was dark by the time Robert got home. He did not turn the light on. It was more comfortable in the darkness. He lay on his bed fully dressed, and began smoking.

As he expected, Tristan called.

"If indeed Kurt leaves for Tigre the day after tomorrow, we would have to follow him."

"I agree."

"If you can, study the map of the city. You are the best of us at this."

"I know the city."

"Genius." Tristan was sincere. His memory, although not bad for an average person, was much inferior to Robert's.

"One last thing. Take all your passports, documents, and necessary belongings with you. None of us comes back. Finito la commedia."

"Very good."

"Like it?" asked Tristan with a smile in his voice.

"Very much so."

Tristan chuckled and disconnected. Robert was again alone in the dark, with his cigarette and his thoughts. He badly wanted some company, but there was nobody in Buenos Aires whom he could talk to this evening. Was there? Yes, there was! How could he forget him!

He dialed the number. A familiar voice greeted him with the usual 'Hola.'

"Hi Claus."

"My friend!" Claus' voice rose with delight. "I thought you forgot about me. How are you? Are you still after Nazis? Have you contacted Wiesenthal Center?"

"I am still after them, Claus. Actually, I want to ask you about someone I found myself. His name is Kurt Jeager. Does it ring a bell?"

Claus delayed his response for a few moments.

"Yes, it does. As a matter of fact, I was trying to contact him back then, but got a stern warning to forget about him. After our last meeting with you I found his name, and a few others, in my archive. Frankly, I did not intend to give them to you."

"Why?"

"Well … I will answer this question a bit later. Do you mind if I ask you my question first?"

"Sure, go ahead. I have plenty of time tonight."

"How are you doing with those, whose names I gave to you? I guess there was little success, if any, as there was no news in the papers."

"You are almost right, Claus. But still, I thank you for your help. Do you have any other question?"

"Actually, I don't have any. But I would love to exchange some of my thoughts with you. I know that the last thing young people want is to listen to the unsolicited advice of the older generation, but this issue bothers me all the time."

"I will tell you when it gets too boring," Robert said. "I am curious to hear your unsolicited advice."

"Forget about Nazis, Robert. The war is over, and there is no need to start it again. At present, there is peace, or a truce, if you will, between them and the rest of the world. You disturb the truce, and you start a war with new casualties."

"But they are criminals!" exclaimed Robert.

"Hold on, hold on." Claus was in a rush to get out his point of view. In an apologetic tone, he said, "Please, listen to my reasoning. I know that it is a very hard choice, but most countries and people did it. Russia, Europe and America de-facto stopped their hunt for them. With their tremendous combined resources they would be able to do a lot, but instead they do nothing. Why should you? You are an intelligent young man with a good future. You want to jeopardize it? Remember the old Roman proverb? He who lives by sword, dies by it. In my opinion, it is not worth it."

"So, you think that it is better to let them live in peace than to punish them for their crimes?"

Robert heard a deep sigh of sorrow on the other end of the line.

"I know that it is a very hard decision. Anyone even remotely involved in the tragedy of the Second World War has to make it for himself. I am also a victim of Hitler's regime. I would love to take them all to justice. You know how many of them we would have to punish? At the end of the war, there were several hundred thousand SS troops. You know how many collaborators were in other countries? Hundreds of thousands. You think that all of them were evil individuals? You are wrong, my young friend. This is a part of humanity. These people will do good or bad things for whoever rules them."

"I can't accept your reasoning, Claus. I agree, though, that it is impossible to punish them all."

"Do you wish to get together tonight for a cup of coffee?" Claus suggested.

"No, sorry. I have to go early to bed tonight."

"Well. Perhaps you would be kind enough to let me know if you get some results from your activity?"

"I promise that. Good night, Claus."

Chapter 15

Early in the morning, on the day when Kurt was supposed to leave on his pleasure trip, the entire group assembled in Lara's house. On Tristan's command, everyone took a rucksack with minimum belongings and all documents and passports that could be used on the routes to Europe. After this deal, no one would return to his or her home in Buenos Aires. Lara looked a bit upset. She wasn't throwing any of her usual fond glances at Tristan. There might have been a row between them last night, Robert reasoned. As if confirming his guess, Tristan said, "Come on, Lara. Don't be so grumpy. Make some coffee for us."

Lara sighed.

"Come to your senses, guys," she said. "I suggest calling it off. I have a gut feeling that the risk is too high. Not worth it. We already have enough money."

"I can't die in peace knowing that this SS rat enjoys life with the fortune he got from other people. It is not only money that matters. Risk? Sure. It is a part of our profession." He looked at Lara. "Well, you know, if I see that the risk is too high, I will call it off. Never too late. What do you think, guys?"

"Sounds good to me," Robert said, hesitant to take sides.

"I think it is a good solution." Sergio, as Robert guessed, was in favor of the deal. "I suggest going to his house now and waiting. You never know what may happen. What if Kurt decides to go early?"

"Let me call his wife," Robert said. "She might give a hint.

He dialed. Bertha's low, melodic voice was calm and gentle.

"Hola."

"Can we meet soon?" Robert asked and glanced at his watch. The time was nine o'clock in the morning.

"Are you crazy, my sweet boy? No, not now. In the afternoon. Kurt is still at home in his pajamas."

"Are you sure that he goes today for Tigre?"

"Absolutely. Two of his bodyguards are coming soon. It is just a matter of two to three hours, and then they will be gone. May I call you then?"

"Sure. By all means."

Robert placed the receiver on the cradle and looked at the anxious faces of his comrades.

"She said that he is taking two bodyguards. He's leaving in two hours or so."

"You see?" said Lara, but she did not get any response from the men. She sighed, "Well, whatever. The issue is closed."

"Let's sit a minute before going, as the Russian tradition demands. After all, this is our last day in Argentina," Tristan said, taking a chair.

They sat a minute in silence, then jumped up, picked up their rucksacks and rushed to the car. Half an hour later, they were parked one block away from the white Mercedes. After about two long hours of waiting, the Mercedes moved ahead.

"If there are indeed two bodyguards with him, what we are going to do with them?"

Lara, it seemed, still hoped that the men would come to their senses.

"Depends," Tristan responded. "If his pussy lives in a house, we may try to sneak in. I don't believe that his bodyguards would be in the house listening to their boss roaring in pleasure."

Sergio laughed. Robert chuckled as well.

"Nice," Lara said disapprovingly.

"Most likely, they won't be around too late, and will go to a hotel," Tristan continued. "If worse comes to worst, we will kill them. One by one."

"Do you know, Robert, where we are now?" Sergio asked.

"Yes. I think we go to the highway."

Tristan touched Sergio's shoulder, "Can you watch the cars behind us?"

"Yes, I can. I will notice a shadow, don't worry."

"I can also look through the side window for anything suspicious," Robert said.

"What if those in the Mercedes notice us?" Lara asked.

"Unlikely," Tristan said. "If they are young, as Robert said … However, you never know. We'll see."

Robert took a mental note that Tristan did not mention his intention to call it off, if it becomes too risky.

"They aren't going exactly to Tigre," Robert said, turning back and looking in Tristan's eyes for emphasis. Tristan raised his eyebrows, waiting for an explanation.

"What do you mean?" Lara asked.

"This is the Acceso Oeste highway. For sure the direction is for Moreno. I think they are going there. Not a small spot either, there's a web of streets there, but there's plenty of farmland and even forests outside of it in the south." Turning to Sergio, he added, "It might be useful, you know—"

"In what sense?" Sergio gave him a weird glance. Robert shrugged.

"I can't tell. You never know."

"We shall rely on our living map, which we call Robert." Tristan let out a short laugh.

"I know little about the streets of Moreno," Robert

warned. “We will have to use all our six senses to get out of there, in case of troubles.”

“So be it,” Tristan said.

Robert mentioned that the resident had called and asked to meet with the communists. This triggered a wave of indignation.

“Enough of this communist shit for me,” Lara said.

“Communists have nothing to do with it,” Tristan said. “But the resident has to understand that it is not our business. He is not our boss.”

“He will understand it soon,” Sergio said. “We won’t have any bosses. Shit, I’d love to send a goodbye letter to our brass in the Center. I will.”

Meaningless small talk went on for half an hour. It seemed that everyone was in a careless mood, but Robert knew well how stressful and alert everyone was. Dealing with a former SS and two trained bodyguards was not a joke.

“Here is Moreno,” Robert declared. “Now, if traffic does not help us, we might either lose them, or be noticed.”

The Mercedes made a few turns. On one of the streets, no cars remained between them.

“If this bloody car turns, don’t follow it,” Tristan warned. “We will find it later, we have plenty of time.”

The Mercedes suddenly pulled in front of a medium size house. Sergio kept driving ahead and made a left turn at the intersection.

“Good,” Tristan sighed with relief. “Now we know the pussy’s address. Let’s find a bar or a restaurant here. We all need the washroom and some beer. Here’s a good place, Sergio. Robert, you go first.”

Sergio stopped. Robert left the car and went to the bar. The Ford moved on and disappeared around the block.

Robert lingered a few moments at the entrance. Large windows gave sufficient light to observe the place. Only four tables were taken in a spacious hall, with two visitors at each. The semi-circular bar stand took a central spot. One man sat there. When he entered, everyone sitting at the tables turned his way, and followed his walk to the washroom with their eyes. The man at the bar stand continued talking to the barman. Nothing unusual so far.

When out of the washroom, Robert came up to the bar stand, took a stool, and ordered a draft. The taste of the first sip was very agreeable. He cast a stealing glance at the man to his left. Something in him was not to Robert's liking, but he dismissed his feeling. It was unthinkable to suggest that some people in the bar were waiting for their arrival.

Lara came in, went to the washroom, and then sat at the table. They did not speak, did not even exchange glances, although in this circumstance, it seemed superfluous. When Tristan came in, Robert left the bar. Sergio was outside, lingering by the entrance.

"Go two blocks to the left," he said, "then turn right and go straight, until you see our car. Do you have a spare key?"

"Yes. I'd rather walk around the block where Kurt stopped," Robert said. "See you soon."

To his luck, not many pedestrians were in the street. One of them, a woman in her fifties, was walking a small dog. If there is a dog in the house, Robert thought, we will have to abort the operation. Kurt, in all likelihood, is armed.

After circling the block, Robert came to the conclusion that the shortest and safest way to the back door of the house would be from the parallel street. They would have to cross only two wooden fences to get to the backyard.

After him, Tristan and Sergio observed the place. Their main interest was the two bodyguards. Changing guard in the Mercedes, they patrolled the street once in a while, and, it seemed, felt fairly safe and bored with their duties.

Tristan gathered everyone in the car at ten o'clock. They sat there for two hours. At midnight, Tristan glanced at his watch, turned to Lara and began giving her last instructions. Lara smirked. She did not need any. She already knew her role down to the tiniest details. This was Tristan's habit, though. He wanted to make sure that no room for misunderstanding remained in his subordinate's mind.

"Have your Beretta ready. Stay here for about fifteen minutes, key in the ignition lock. If you don't hear any noise or notice anything suspicious, come in to join us."

"Good luck, boys," she said matter-of-factly. "See you there soon."

This woman has no nerves, Robert thought. Danger has no impact on her.

They came to the parallel street, climbed over two fences, and reached the spacious backyard of the two-story house. Sergio approached its backdoor, while Tristan and Robert took positions at the corners of the house with loaded guns, and stood there for a minute, listening to the deafening silence of the night. The sound of a shot, Robert thought, would reverberate through the whole quiet, sleeping city. Then it would really become a mess.

The full moon shone from the clear sky, casting weird shadows on the ground. In its yellow semi-darkness, Sergio moved like a weightless ghost, with no audible sound. He touched the handle of the door and pushed it. The door creaked, but remained firmly in its place. Sergio stopped dead in his tracks, leaning his ear to the door. A few moments later, he began working on the lock. In spite of all his effort, the tools produced tiny scratching sounds. Then there was a click, which made him freeze again for a few moments. He leaned on the door. It opened smoothly on its well-oiled hinges. Sergio went in, and Tristan and

Robert followed. Moving with noiseless steps, they briefly inspected the first floor. Its stone floor did not squeak, as a wooden one would have done. It was damn dark inside though; only intuition and a tiny rustle from the ghostly shadows of his friends gave Robert some indication of where they were. They all met at the bottom of the staircase.

"Now, let's go upstairs quietly," Tristan whispered. "From the top, move fast. Robert and I will go to the bedroom. You, Sergio, take a quick peek on the second floor and come to us. Go."

Robert ascended two flights of stairs. Solidly built, they did not squeak. Tristan joined him and paused for a moment.

"Go," commanded Tristan in a rough voice and broke into the bedroom. He turned on his flashlight and directed its beam onto the bed. Its light revealed a woman's face; her long hair was in disarray, and her large eyes were filled with fear. The man beside her jumped upright with a nervous jerk and shoved his hand under the pillow. He was too late. Robert had already removed his gun from its hiding spot and pressed its barrel at his nose.

"Be quiet, son of a bitch," he growled. "And behave, if you wish to survive with your broad."

Kurt peered into the darkness beyond the bright flashlight, but could see nothing there. His stare was hard, saturated with hatred and defiance. Robert noticed Sergio's silhouette at the threshold of the room.

"All clear on the second floor," he announced.

"Take care of the broad and meet Lara on the first floor," Tristan commanded. "When she comes, take the keys and wait for us there."

Sergio turned the woman face down and began tying her hands behind her back with duct tape. Robert did the same with Kurt.

"Please, don't kill me," the woman babbled. "I will

do anything you want. Please."

Sergio taped her mouth, and led her out of the bedroom.

"We won't harm you," Robert heard him saying on the way down. "Don't worry. Just be quiet."

Tristan scanned the room with his light. It was spacious; a love seat stood by the large bay window. Heavy curtains undoubtedly blocked any light from outside and inside. There was an antique armchair, into which Robert pushed Kurt. He taped Kurt's legs and torso to it and observed his job carefully. After all, Kurt was a trained military man, for whom risk was, or had been, as natural as it was for them.

"Now, we can talk comfortably," Tristan said. He settled on the bed, blinding Kurt with his powerful flashlight. Kurt blinked a few times and said, "Jewish assholes."

"It is an offense to us," Tristan said, speaking in German. "We are Germans, as you are."

Kurt strained his eyes, trying to see Tristan's face. Realizing the futility of his efforts, he looked down, to escape the blinding beam, and said in a low voice, "Germans, doing a dirty job for Jews."

Robert responded to it, also in German.

"No. We are doing this job for ourselves. It is not dirtier than the job you did during the war. But we are not going to kidnap you, or hurt you. Cooperate with us, and you survive."

"What do you want, then?" Kurt asked, raising his head. Hope blinked in his pale eyes.

"We want to know your Swiss account numbers," Tristan said. "After you tell them to us, we will take you to a good place and hold you there for a few days. If the accounts are okay, you will be free to go. If not, I promise you a nice hell on earth, until you really go to hell. Fair deal?"

After a short pause, Kurt said, "No problem. I can give you my accounts."

"Good." Tristan shut off his flashlight and the room plunged into total darkness. "If you have any fantasy for a happy escape, drop it, Kurt. Your bodyguards are no longer in this town. Our people are around this house. No hope, Kurt. We knew that you are a resourceful guy, and decided to think in advance for you."

He turned his flashlight on again. Kurt squinted his eyes.

"So," Tristan continued. "We talked about your account numbers. You kindly agreed to cooperate with us. Go ahead."

Robert heard some noise on the ground floor, and then quick steps climbing the staircase.

"I'm here," Lara said from the threshold. "Shall we start?"

"Hold on," Tristan said. "Our friend Kurt has agreed to cooperate." Then he asked Kurt, "Didn't you, Kurt? Did I understand you right?"

"How can I be sure that you won't cheat me?" he asked.

"There is no way. You have to trust us. Sorry, there is no other way."

"Fuck yourselves, assholes," Kurt said. "Kill me, I don't care."

Really a hard nut, Robert thought. Bertha was right. The guy had guts, no doubt about that.

There was a metallic click in the darkness. Robert recognized it. It was the sound of the blade of Tristan's knife jumping out of its handle.

"Wait, Tristan," Lara said, searching for something in her small bag. "Mind you, if he really has a serious heart condition, he might die on you. Let's loose his tongue first."

She appeared behind Kurt with a syringe in her

hand.

"What are you doing, dirty twat?" asked Kurt. The expression of defiance began fading on his face. His eyes danced in powerless fury.

"You will regret your dirty words soon." Lara's tone was calm and mentoring, as if she was talking to a misbehaving child. She gave him a shot. "You must show respect to a lady." She returned the syringe to her bag. "In five minutes, you will be a different, much nicer man. Then we will talk."

"What was it?" asked Robert. "Rastormozka?"

"Yes. I gave him a double dose. There is a certain risk in it, but—"

"It's fine," Tristan said. "Doesn't make sense to spend too much time on this shithead. Right, Kurt? Are you a shithead?"

Kurt said nothing. His face was changing by the second. He now looked exhausted to the very last drop of energy.

"It began working sooner than I expected," Lara said.

"Kurt. You hear me?" Tristan asked. Kurt gave him a tired, weird look, but again said nothing.

"Okay. I will cheer you up and give you an incentive to disclose your accounts. Robert, turn on your flashlight."

Robert did as Tristan said. Tristan came to Kurt, tore a piece from the duct tape and sealed Kurt's mouth. Then, in slow motion, he made a deep cut with his knife on Kurt's bare chest, from his left shoulder down to lower ribs. Kurt began shaking in pain, but only a feeble, muffled scream escaped through his nose, as his mouth was taped. Tristan kept cutting. This time he drew a perpendicular bleeding line across the chest. Robert understood now that Tristan was drawing a swastika with his knife. It was revolting and completely unnecessary.

"Could you stop it?" Robert hissed. "This is not the time and place to square war accounts. And mind you, he could die on you."

"Right," Tristan agreed, and took the tape off Kurt's mouth. Kurt groaned, apparently unable to speak. His breathing was heavy. He began coughing.

"Indeed, Tristan, stop it," Lara said with concern in her voice. "Let's finish this."

"Will you talk, Kurt?" Tristan asked. "My friends want to finish our session. Will you?"

"I have only three accounts left in the Swiss banks," Kurt said through his coughing. It was obvious that his will was paralyzed, as well as his ability to sustain any stress. He spelled out his account numbers and associated names in almost a whisper. Robert repeated them aloud.

"That's all?" asked Tristan.

"I swear. Please let me lay down. I am dying."

Tristan taped his mouth again and finished drawing the bloody swastika on his chest. Kurt became soft, his head hung down. He was either unconscious, or dead. Tristan stuck his knife deep into his chest, in the center of swastika.

"I don't need this knife anymore. It is my personal present to Kurt. Now, out. Quickly." Tristan pointed the flashlight at the door. When they reached the ground floor, Robert flashed the beam at Kurt's woman. She was tied to an easy chair, mouth taped. He turned his light off and followed Tristan towards the back door.

It was still dark outside, perhaps even darker than it had been at midnight because the moon had rolled down and lost its brightness. However, the approaching dawn could be detected in the east. The air, saturated with the fragrance of dew, was invigorating. Robert felt a tremendous influx of energy, boosted by the feeling of relief and the thought that the mission was over. Now, they were all free people, with money, and without a need to work.

Heading back to the car, Tristan took a short cut, which was a grave mistake. Instead of returning to the parallel street, he jumped over the fence of the house, which stood on the same street where the Mercedes and their Ford were. When they were close to their car, a gunshot tore the sacred, peaceful silence of the early morning. Tristan returned the shot, aiming in the direction that the sound came from.

Sergio was waiting for them with the engine running. Robert took the front passenger seat, and Tristan and Lara settled at the rear. Sergio pressed the gas pedal and the car jumped forward like a mad horse gathering speed.

"It was a damn good shot," Tristan said, gasping. "Missed me by a hair's breadth. Now, don't go to Buenos Aires, Sergio. Take a turn south, preferably on the paved road. Robert, you know the map, don't you? Take control."

Chapter 16

At eight o'clock in the morning, Glenn was brewing coffee for Brad and Jeff in his apartment. His guests were neatly dressed, as Argentinean custom suggests, this time wearing formal suites, but with no ties. They looked refreshed and full of energy.

"I talked to Eduardo yesterday morning over the phone," he began his story. "I asked how long it would take to let me know the address and other particulars about the driver if I gave him a license plate of a car. He said next week I'd know all."

Glenn paused, pouring coffee from the Turkish jar into the cups. As a hospitable host, he asked, "Anything else, gentlemen?"

"I prefer beer, if you have one," Brad said.

"Of course. The local one."

"Will do."

Brad opened the offered bottle and took a sip from it. The first smile of the morning smoothed his forehead.

"I gave him the license plate number and told him I needed the information in an hour. He gurgled at the other end, poor devil."

Jeff chuckled. Brad brought the bottle to his lips for another swig. "You kicked his ass?" he asked.

"In a diplomatic way. I promised to be grateful and generous. It took him longer than I expected, but by the late evening he called and gave me the address of the car owner. She is a forty-six years old; bought this car a few months ago. That's what I know so far. My guess is that this is her stolen identity. We will find it out soon, but I don't want Eduardo's involvement at this time."

"Makes sense," Jeff agreed. "Let's go and have a look at the place."

"Of course." Glenn nodded in agreement. "We shall not waste time, but be very careful. I am sure these guys are on high alert and might disappear at the slightest suspicion."

"Shall I install a bug in this car?" Jeff asked.

"Yes. Tonight."

A small transmitter was invented in the CIA. Attached to the bottom of a car with its magnetic pads, it sends signals within a radius of about five kilometers. The attached indicator of the following car turns on when the signal is received. If the light is out, then the distance is greater than the technical capacity of the receiver. It helped a lot on long and straight roads, allowing a vehicle to follow at a distance with no chance of being noticed. If, however, the followed car made a turn onto another road, then tracing it became a guessing game. If the signal was gone, it was usually too late to do something about it. As Jeff was an expert in communication gadgets, Glenn turned to him.

"Install radio equipment on your car and mine. Brad's car does not need it, as he will drive my car. I will always be with him, in case I have to follow someone by foot. Install the bug in their car, and the signal-receiving indicator in both our cars."

"Let me do the radio first," Jeff said. "It might take a few hours, considering travel back and forth. At night, I will install the bug."

***

The place where the Ford was parked was convenient to start the shadowing. The one-way street, one of many in Buenos Aires and other cities of Argentina, would prevent the target from making a sharp u-turn and rushing in the opposite direction. Therefore, it could only make a legitimate turn, and even then it would likely find itself on a one-way street. The trick for Glenn was not to be noticed on these turns, and yet continue the chase. For this, at least two cars were needed.

Jeff parked on the same street where the Ford stood, at a distance far enough for hiding, but where Jeff could still see it. Glenn and Brad pulled in further back, behind the corner on the intersecting one-way street. Glenn hoped that their targets were really active. A prolonged shadowing for many days was not possible. If this was to be the case, the task would have to be taken over by Eduardo, which was not ideal, but better than nothing. As if reading his thoughts, Brad asked, "What if they don't do anything for days? We can't sit like that forever."

"I thought about that," Glenn admitted. "It is very unlikely, Brad. These people are not less busy than we are; they are probably even more so. I am positive that they are very active. They are—"

"Here!" Brad uttered in excitement, pointing his finger to the blinking bug receiver. "They're moving!"

He turned the ignition key and pulled the shift into first gear. The radio came alive with Jeff's voice. "The Ford is moving. I'm following it."

"Got it," Glenn said. "Tell me the name of each side street you pass."

"Okay." The radio clicked, produced a hissing sound, and then began working again. Jeff read the street names and commented on traffic, which sometimes obscured his view. Then he made a few turns after the target.

"Are you sure that they didn't notice you?" Glenn asked.

"Quite sure," Jeff said. "There are always a few cars

in front of me, and one of them went the same way for quite a while."

"Coincidence?" asked Glenn.

"For sure. Glenn, I think they're following a large white Mercedes."

"Serious?"

"Almost sure about that."

"Catch its license plate number, if you could."

"Hey, it made a right turn. It was after the steep curve, so I didn't see it from afar. I have to pass on – you follow them, okay?"

"Okay. I see the turn. I will tell you what streets we are passing, and you figure out how to catch up with us."

Brad turned to the right after the curve. A block away, Glenn saw the Ford, and a few cars in front of it. They all slowed down, approaching the stop sign.

"Easy," Glenn murmured. "Keep the distance."

"I know, I know," Brad said. "Do my best. I see the Mercedes."

The radio cracked and Jeff's voice cut through the static.

"I am on the parallel street."

The Mercedes turned left to a busy street, giving Jeff a chance to tail it. The Mercedes struggled through the crazy traffic, and finally stopped in front of a three-story building.

"I am behind you." Jeff reported.

"Pass it."

Glenn turned to Brad.

"Stop the car."

Brad immediately hit the brakes. Glenn stepped out and said, "Follow the Ford with Jeff."

He lingered on a pedestrian walk, pretending to be busy with lighting a cigarette. It was indeed a challenge because of the wind.

A tall, balding man in a gray, long, and very

expensive raincoat got out of the Mercedes and entered through a door, above which was the sign, *Jaeger Construccion*. Glenn approached the car, took notice of its license plate, and caught a glimpse of the driver: large ears, thick neck, and shortly cropped blond hair. The car was already moving on, but did not go too far. It made a right turn at the end of the block. Glenn walked to where the car had turned, and found himself in a large parking lot. The chauffeur – Glenn recognized him at once by the hairdo and big ears – was on his way out. He walked back and entered the building where his master had gone before. Five minutes later, Glenn was there as well. In the nicely decorated lobby, he was met by a receptionist, a young and very serious female.

"Pardon, señora, could you tell me who is the company president?" he asked.

"Certainly, señor. Kurt Jeager. How may I help you?"

"I need to meet with him. Is he here?"

"Yes, he came in just a few minutes ago. Do you wish me to contact him?"

"Not right now. I'd prefer your giving me his telephone number."

"Here it is."

"That's nice of you. Have a wonderful day."

He went out, caught a taxi, got home, and called Eduardo. The policeman was not at his place, so Glenn had to leave a message for him to call back.

Then the telephone rang.

"I am calling from the public phone." This was Brad. "The Ford came back."

"Good. Come to my place. Together with Jeff."

They arrived in less than an hour. Glenn offered brandy to Jeff and beer to Brad. Both were pleased with his hospitality.

"It beats me," Glenn began, rubbing his chin.The

president of the *Jeager Construccion* company was in the Mercedes. His name is Kurt Jeager. His chauffeur is a young guy, about twenty-two years old; he seems in the top physical shape and likely doubles as Kurt's bodyguard."

Jeff scratched his head.

"What the hell is going on?" He raised his eyebrows and held them high for a whole minute. "If the Ford guys are Soviets, I would understand their connections with the local communists. Why then do they take time to follow Kurt? He is German, isn't he?"

"I'm sure he is," Glenn agreed.

"I wonder," Brad joined the discussion, "if they have a dual task: kill the former Nazis and support the communists." With a sharp gesture, he raised both hands, as if in surrender. "Mind you, this is just a stupid guess, but nothing better comes to my mind."

"Impossible." Glenn lit a cigarette and opened the balcony door to let the fresh air in. "Soviets wouldn't waste money on revenge. Never did since the end of the war. There is something else. If… if…"

He stopped talking and let out a cloud of smoke from his cigarette. Jeff and Brad took to drinking, waiting for him to continue.

"You said 'if'," Jeff reminded him.

"Yes. If he is a former SS …"

"So what?" Brad asked.

"Then you, Brad, might not be far off the mark. You know that a few former SS have disappeared in the last few months. If Kurt is also an SS man, then…, then perhaps the Ford people – let me call them this way – might have a link to that. Now they are after Kurt. Stupid, I agree, as neither Russians nor Israelis would hunt these people anywhere in the world, and particularly not in Argentina. Well—"

The phone rang, interrupting his pondering.

"Hola," he said. "Oh, Eduardo. Thank you for

calling. Listen, I need your help and, as always, on very short notice. I have a license plate number for a Mercedes, and the name of its likely owner. Kurt Jeager. Does it ring the bell?"

"Kurt Jeager," repeated Eduardo at the other end of the line. "Sounds vaguely familiar, but I can't tell you anything at this moment. What exactly are you after?"

"I'd like to confirm his car ownership, his address, and whatever else you might come across about him. Can we meet tonight?"

"Sorry, no. The thing is—"

"I know that it takes time, but believe me, Eduardo, time is running out for me."

"Please, listen to me." Eduardo sounded serious in his insistence. "I don't have time today. Can't meet you even if I had everything ready for you. Radical groups, left and right, grow like grass in spring. Some of them armed. Yesterday, they kidnapped a police officer near Cordoba. The best I can do is to meet you tomorrow, at about six. I will give your request the highest priority."

Obviously, further pushing was useless. It was the first time that Eduardo had been that firm.

"Where do you wish to meet?" Glenn asked.

"There is a small café at the corner of the building block where my office is."

"You sure? Not in some better place?"

"I'd love to, but I have no time. I will have about half an hour, even less. I also will tell you some news concerning you personally."

Glenn placed the receiver back and sighed.

"Tomorrow," he said in a low voice, casting his eyes down on the butt of his cigarette. When Brad cleared his throat, Glenn raised his head, returning to the reality of his apartment.

"Let's do it this way. We won't watch them from after midnight till early morning hours. We can't do everything. We will try to trace them from morning till about ten or eleven in the evening. If nothing happens in two to three days, I will ask Eduardo for help. You, Jeff, follow the Mercedes today on its way back home, just in case. Don't push hard — the main thing is not being noticed. Look for anything suspicious. That's all for today, gentlemen."

When they left, Glenn called Lollita. She did not pick up the phone. Glenn knew that she rented an apartment with a roommate somewhere in Montserrat, but she had never given him her exact address. Not a big deal to find it, but what good would it do? In his rare moments of free time, he missed her badly.

Glenn took to cleaning and lubricating his pistol and automatic rifle. Jeff called later in the evening and reported that nothing deserving attention had happened while following the Mercedes. It had returned back from where it was in the morning, and nobody had shadowed it. Its driver apparently had little or no experience in this kind of matter.

***

The spacious, but low-class café, busy as it was, had a few vacant tables. At one of them, in the corner by the window, sat Eduardo, drinking coffee.

"How long have you been waiting for me?" Glenn asked, taking his chair. From his place, he could see an endless flow of pedestrians through the window, bustling about under the yellow lights of the street lamps.

"Not much. A few minutes, actually. You are very punctual, as always."

It seemed that Eduardo was not in his usual jovial mood. He looked tired.

"Any news?" Glenn asked, sliding an envelope with money to Eduardo. The policeman took the gift, slid it into an inside pocket, and pulled a cigarette from his pack. He seemed unimpressed, which was unusual.

"Your guess was correct, Glenn. The Mercedes belongs to Kurt Jeager. He is a businessman, president, and the major shareholder of *Jeager Construccion*."

"Is he German?"

"I expected this sort of question." Eduardo smiled, proud of his smarts. He took a draw from his cigarette and let out a huge cloud of smoke.

"Yes, he is. He came here in 1950. As a matter of fact, his name happened to be in my archives. He was a former SS member who came here with his real name. In the early fifties, he established his construction company. This company is known for its high quality work. Jeager, it seems, is a good engineer and manager. I can give you his home address."

"Fine. Anything else?"

"Yes. Our government established a police unit, whose purpose is to fight armed rebels. I have sent information about your skills and experience through the official channels. They contacted your bosses in the CIA. They want your help."

"How did you explain my presence here?" Glenn asked.

"I told them the truth. You work here for an import-export company, don't you?" He chuckled. "This was enough for them to understand everything. But they have decided to use your skills in a few operations. Particularly important is that you can lead the unit to the place where the rebels are. After that, I believe, you would have to leave the country."

"We'll see," Glenn said, sounding uncommitted. "In a few days, I may ask you for more serious help. I need to shadow someone with cars. Do you have good people to do the job?"

Eduardo shook his head.

"We are very busy now. Let me find out what I can

do for you."

"Thank you, Eduardo. I will contact you in about three days."

"One more thing. Early next week, I will put you in touch with the unit commander."

Eduardo rose to his feet, shook hands with Glenn, and left. There was not even a trace of a smile on his face.

***

Glenn and Brad had been sitting in the car since eight o'clock in the morning. Luckily, there was a small café close by where they could use the washroom. Every so often, Jeff turned on his radio and exchanged a few remarks with them.

"I hate doing nothing," Brad grumbled, lowering the window. He put a cigarette in his mouth, lit it with a click of his lighter, and took a deep draw. Letting the smoke out, he continued: "Our only task is to stare at the empty street, where nothing happens, and expect that something will happen, but we have no idea what it will really be."

"At least we can smoke," Glenn said. "Sometimes you can't even do that."

"True," Brad agreed. "I've had some assignments like that. There was no one to talk to."

"Every job has its boring moments," Glenn reasoned in a philosophical manner, as if it was he, not Brad, who was the older one. "It's even worse before army combat. All the preparations for it sometimes drag on and on. When all is set, and a few hours, or even worse, days, remain before the scheduled time, you just pray for something to happen. You can do nothing but chat with fellow soldiers. However, there is nothing to chat about, because before the battle you have no future. You never know if you'll live much longer after the first shot is fired.

Some people don't talk at all, as they are too deep in thoughts about death. And then, after the first blast, the hell explodes, and you are in the middle of it."

"I've never been in a battle," Brad said, "but I took part in a shoot-out during some clandestine actions. Similar thing, I'd say. There is one option though, which I wish to explore, just as a devil's advocate."

"What is it?" Glenn asked.

"What if you ask Eduardo to arrest them? He could take them either all at once, when they are in their homes, or one by one, whoever happened to be on the street."

Glenn chuckled.

"You can't take them all, when they are together. They will fight, and likely die fighting. Should you arrest one of them, all the others would disappear. Mind you, if my guess is correct, they are KGB agents. As such, they are supported by a large Soviet spy network here, planted many years back. Even in the best case scenario, if we capture these guys, we lose the Soviet network."

"Still …" Brad seemed unconvinced.

"Another thing is, I don't believe in the Argentinean police. Eduardo and his people won't do a good job. No chance. It's one thing to deal with amateur rebels, and quite another to deal with professional spies. "

Brad lit another cigarette.

"There is nothing better in the world than Marlboro," he said, drawing on his cigarette. Glenn ignored his remark.

Suddenly, Brad tossed the half-finished cigarette through the open window.

"Look," he pointed his finger at the blinking indicator. "They're moving."

He turned the ignition key and shifted the transmission into first gear. Glenn cast a brief glance at his watch. The time was almost ten o'clock.

"Where are you, Jeff?" Glenn asked over the radio.

After the cracks of initial static, Jeff's voice emerged.

"I'm here. They are on the move."

"Anything happening?"

"Not that I've noticed. Here, they made a left turn. No one is between us. I have to pass this one and catch up with you later."

"Got it," Glenn responded.

After the turn, Glenn saw the Ford in front, with a few cars between them. It turned right. He told Jeff where they were, and Jeff was quick to react. At one point, he was again between the Ford and Glenn's car.

"I have to pass again," Jeff said. "They made another left turn."

Brad sped up. This street was much busier than the previous one, which made it necessary to shorten the distance. The blinking lamp was still indicating that the car was in the receiver's range.

"I missed the street name," Brad said. "Did you notice it?"

"Yes, I did. It seems to me that the Ford is going to Kurt's house." Glenn leaned forward, "It beats me. Puzzle after puzzle."

"Perhaps we are close to solving it," Brad responded philosophically. "After all, now we know for sure that they are after Kurt."

Radio static cracked and cleared. Jeff's voice emerged.

"They are moving toward Kurt's house. Where are you?"

Glenn told him the street name.

"They might stop in the vicinity of Kurt's house. Pass them and stay somewhere farther on. We will be behind."

"Here, this is his street," Jeff reported. "The Mercedes is there. Its chauffeur and another guy are in it. The Ford stopped two blocks behind. I am passing both."

"Got it," Glenn said. "I can't see the Ford from here, but I will notice it when it starts moving."

The radio fell silent. Brad, as usual in the idle time, took to smoking. "Waiting game again," he said.

"Something is going to happen," Glenn said. "I feel it in my guts."

"That's why you took your rifle?" Brad asked.

"Yes. And the pistol."

"You think that a shoot-out is in the making?"

"Very much so. I wish we had more people today."

An hour passed in idle waiting. Jeff reported all the car and pedestrian movements worth attention. Nothing really important or suspicious had happened. And then …

"Glenn, Glenn, do you hear me?" Jeff screamed. "The Mercedes is moving. Three people are inside it. Now the Ford is passing by as well. There are four inside it, one of them is a woman, I didn't notice much more."

Brad was already steering the car when Glenn responded, "We are moving after you, Jeff. Report every street you pass. What? Yes, we are not far behind."

It was not very hard to follow them, as the Mercedes chose the longest and widest streets. But soon it began making turns.

"Not good," Brad said.

"Where are you?" Jeff asked through the static. "This bloody street is one way and has no end. I …" His voice was drowned in the noise.

"Christ," Brad grumbled. "The last thing we need is to lose Jeff. Oh, look, Glenn. They turned onto the highway."

"Yes. Avenida de Mayo."

Indeed, the Ford was heading there. Glenn could see it from the distance, although quite a few cars were in between them.

"Here," Glenn said. "Perito Moreno. Hell, where are they going?"

"We lost Jeff," Brad said. "No chance for him to find us. You'd better remove your rifle from the case."

"When time permits," Glenn agreed. He leaned forward, watching traffic. "You're right, we did lose Jeff. Now, we are at the mercy of luck and a good guesswork. As long as the Ford is on the highway, they have no chance of noticing us."

"I wanna smoke," Brad said.

"Me too. I think we are in for a long drive on the highway." He pulled two cigarettes from his pack and gave one to Brad. They smoked in silence for a while. Glenn noticed that Perito Moreno became Acceso Oeste. The Ford kept moving ahead at a steady speed.

"You know what?" Glenn said. "Something very interesting is going on here."

"What's that?"

"They have a great deal of skill in shadowing." Glenn lit another cigarette in feverish excitement. "They are following the Mercedes at a considerable distance. We are dealing with real professionals."

"Pity that Jeff is not with us. Something is definitely cooking."

They drove in silence until they reached Moreno. Brad shortened the distance between the cars. On one of the Moreno streets, the Mercedes stopped by a medium-sized, nice-looking house, surrounded by fence and plenty of trees and bushes. The Ford passed by, and so did Brad.

"Don't follow the Ford," Glenn said. "For sure they will stop somewhere not far from here. Let's find a bar or hotel with a washroom. I'd rather watch the Mercedes than the Ford. It will be around for sure."

There happened to be a bar not far away.

"Drop me off here, and park in the neck of these woods. Don't come inside until I come out."

"I'll be waiting for you around the block," Brad said.

Glenn left the car, pushed the heavy door open, and went in the bar. Only a few visitors were inside. It was too early for the nightlife, which begins at a much later hour in Argentina. Glenn went directly to the men's room. Relieved, he came to the bar stand. He ordered a draft, although he had no intention of drinking much of it. He watched the door. Two men went out, but nobody came in. A few minutes passed, and then a new customer came in. Glenn's heart began beating at a runner's pace. This was the man he had followed after the meeting with Miguel. The man also went to the washroom, and then took a place at the bar close to Glenn. Another visitor came in. This time it was a pretty blonde. Without even glancing around the bar, she went into the ladies' room. Glenn took a small sip of his beer to wet his dry mouth.

Soon, the beauty came back from the ladies' room, sat at a table nearby, and asked for the local Yerba tea.

A few other customers came in, all of them unremarkable and seeming like locals. Glenn watched them all discreetly, particularly those who visited the washroom. None of them went there right after coming in, but a few did after having a drink.

Glenn paid for his beer and went out. Brad was waiting for him around the block.

"Let's find another place with a washroom," Glenn said, suppressing his excitement. "I think they are all here."

"What makes you think so?" Brad looked at him with a mix of surprise and admiration. He took his driver's seat in the car and drove away.

"Remember the guy who met Miguel?" Glenn asked.

"Kidding?" Brad's brows crawled up. "Is he there?"

"Yes, I recognized him. He might remember your face, as you were in the café when he met Miguel. There is a pretty blonde, too. For sure she belongs to this group. It beats me though, what she is doing. A puzzle, isn't it?"

Brad parked close to a small hotel and went in, leaving Glenn in the car.

A few minutes later, Glenn saw two young men enter the hotel. One of them was the chauffeur of the Mercedes. Glenn recognized him at once.

Soon, Brad came back. He gave Glenn an inquisitive glance. "Any news?"

"Yes. I saw two young guys go in there. You must've seen them inside."

"That's right. Who are they?"

"The one with the cropped hair is Kurt's chauffeur. Both of them, I am sure, are his bodyguards."

"Where do you suggest we park?" Brad asked, navigating the car through the maze of small local streets.

"Let's park not far from the place where the Mercedes is. It could be a long waiting game. Dusk is approaching, which may help us."

The Mercedes however, was not there. It arrived an hour later, but no one came out of it. The Ford was nowhere to be seen.

"Shall we look around for the Ford?" Brad asked.

"Let's wait. I'm sure that these guys are after Kurt. Kurt though, I have no doubt, is in the house."

They opened the windows and began smoking.

"I'm lost," Glenn admitted. "I was sure that these guys had Soviet connections. I even suspected them being Soviet agents. It seems that I was wrong. What are they doing in this dilapidated city? Nothing happens here."

"Maybe you are not far off the mark," Brad suggested. "As Eduardo said, some of the SS men have disappeared lately. Somebody was responsible for it."

"I thought about that as well," Glenn said. "But the more I consider it, the less probable it seems to me. As I said before, all countries stopped chasing war criminals after the Nuremberg Trials. It is costly and not productive. The only exception was Eichman, but the Israelis wouldn't dare to do something like that again."

"Why?" asked Brad. "They are very vigilant."

"They are. But they had a lot of international complications with Eichman, particularly with Argentina. It would be insane for them to get involved in such a mess again. Mind you, they are pragmatic people. They do not have enough money and manpower to chase even the top echelon of war criminals. Even the Soviets and Americans combined could not do this. There were too many of them. No, Brad, this is something else. The strange thing is, these guys are very well trained, top-notch professionals. They could be either from the Soviet Union or Israel. Or even from America, as crazy as that sounds. Can't think of anything else. Damn it! What a puzzle."

As Glenn expected, the receiver blinked, indicating that the Ford was in their proximity. At the far end of the street, before the stop sign, he saw the taillights of the car, parking at the roadside.

"Shall I sneak out and follow them?" Brad whispered.

"No. Let's wait."

Glenn removed the pistol from its holster and looked around. The street was quiet, like a cemetery. It seemed that people had just abandoned this town, leaving their houses to the mercy of providence. The moon, with its mystical light, enhanced this impression, showing only dim, illusory silhouettes of objects along the street. There was no wind to disturb even a single leaf on the trees, no sound, and no movement of people or cars. A few hours passed in dead silence. Brad got drowsy. His head dropped, but he jerked it up again sharply, and looked guiltily at Glenn.

"Where are they?" asked Brad. "Damn it, if I understand anything."

"It seems to me that something is happening in this house," Glenn mumbled. "I think I saw a glimpse of a flashlight."

"We can't go in there, can we?" Brad said. "After all, it is the task of Kurt's security guys."

"Here," Glenn whispered. "I see someone patrolling around the house. Damn sure that it is one of Kurt's bodyguards."

The sound of shot hit Glenn's ears like a cannon ball. Brad shook, but in a split second he had turned the engine on and shifted into first gear. Glenn saw someone rushing to the Mercedes, then heard the sound of another shot. The tail lights of the Ford and the Mercedes flicked on, and they both jumped ahead with screeching tires.

"Shit," Glenn cursed. "Now the Mercedes is after the Ford. Damn it."

They quickly reached the place where the Ford had been parked, but neither the Ford nor the Mercedes were in sight.

"I'll go to the main road," Brad suggested. Not waiting for Glenn's command, he turned to the left and accelerated the car far beyond the safe speed. The tires protested on the next turn, the car skidded, threatening to twist and roll over, and then stabilized and rushed ahead. On the long stretch of the next road, Glenn caught a glimpse of the taillights of a moving car.

"I'll catch up with them," Brad said. "We just need a couple of turns or steep curves of the road for help."

"We are after the Mercedes," Glenn said. "The lights are not the Ford's."

"Why are they rushing like crazy?" asked Brad. "There must be a reason for racing at a hundred miles per hour on such a bumpy road at night."

"True. Keep going."

When they passed the next curve, Glenn saw the taillights of another car, rushing along in front of the one they were following.

"That's the Ford," Glenn shouted in excitement. He

reached back, grabbed his rifle and released the security latch. "I'm almost sure I will have to use it."

There was again a long stretch of a road, on which all three cars rushed at a maddening speed. The distance between all the cars was shrinking. Brad cursed as his car jumped over potholes, clanging with all its loose parts. He turned on the high beams. In their bright lights, Glenn saw a hand with a gun, sticking out of the window of the passenger side of the Mercedes. Two gunshots were fired. Then, from the rear passenger window of the first car appeared the upper-half of a man holding a gun. No doubt it was a well-trained military man who knew how to shoot from a car. Glenn was familiar with this technique as well. One has to stay with his feet on the floor of the car, and stick his whole torso out of the open window. This way, one can take aim with deadly accuracy, holding the gun in both hands. And Glenn did it as well. When his head, shoulders, and chest were already outside, he aimed at the man shooting at the Mercedes. At the same moment, Glenn shot at him. The man quickly disappeared inside his car, but Glenn was almost sure that his bullet had hit him. In the same second, he realized that the Mercedes driver was either killed, or mortally wounded. His car skidded, jumped in the air, landed, turned over, and stopped on its roof. In spite of all Brad's efforts, their car smashed into it. Shards of glass flew in all directions and the hood popped up. An excellent driver, Brad had significantly reduced their speed, but not sufficient enough to avoid a collision.

"Out!" Brad shouted. Using all his strength, he opened the jammed door at his side and crawled out of the car. Glenn managed to do the same even faster, as his door was not seriously damaged.

"Let's keep a distance from here," Glenn commanded, limping away. "If the cars do not explode from the fire, we might attempt to do something for those who are trapped inside. If they are alive, which I doubt."

They stopped a few hundred meters from the collision place, watching the flames. Glenn looked at Brad; red spots of blood were all over his clothes.

"Are you hurt?" Glenn asked.

"Nah." Brad wiped off the sweat and blood from his face with his sleeve. "It is from the broken glass. We lost them, Glenn, didn't we? Sorry about that."

"It seems so. But it's not your fault. You did an excellent job, Brad."

"Maybe we will catch them in Buenos Aires?"

"No. We lost them forever. Now, we have to find out what they were doing here and in Buenos Aires. The puzzle is still to be solved."

Chapter 17

"Full speed," growled Tristan, closing the door as the car was already accelerating. He touched Robert's shoulder. "Is there any good place around here to change the car?"

"Plenty," Robert said. "There are a lot of small towns around here. Let's drive till dawn. Then we'll be out of reach and in better shape."

"Good. We shall come back to Buenos Aires from a different entry point. The whole world is ours, guys!"

Sergio made a few sharp turns at a speed of 55 miles per hour. On short, narrow streets it was almost suicidal. The car skidded, slid off its tracks, but soon stabilized, seemingly defying the law of gravity and inertia. On the longer stretch of the road, Sergio changed to the highest gear. The motor roared. The arm of the speedometer quickly slid up to 100 miles per hour. The impact of the tires hitting potholes and imperfections in the road was terrible. It seemed to Robert that all the joints of their car would break on impact after the next jump, sending its parts flying in all directions.

"We are in deep shit," Sergio said, looking in the rear-view window. "Germans are after us."

Robert knew it before Sergio said it. The long distance lights of the car behind them lit the interior through the rear window.

"Pretty quick, aren't they?" Tristan said. His voice rang with the bells of a merry mood. It seemed that he was unperturbed, as usual. For Robert, it was a clear signal that a gun battle was inevitable.

Sergio made another sharp turn at the first crossing, which threw Robert onto him.

"Easy," Tristan said, laughing. "You won't be able to shake off this tail. Their car is much better than ours." His voice was shaking because of the numerous potholes. "Their driver is very good, too. We have to kill him. There is no other way out of this."

Robert turned around.

"Look, look!" he shouted. "There's another car behind them. We have two cars after us."

Tristan and Lara stared through the rear window.

"How do you know that the other car is after us as well?" Lara asked. "Could be some early morning traveler."

"No." Tristan sounded firm in his objection. "It's running at a crazy speed, so it must have an excellent engine. I can't see the car, but I can tell you for sure that it is a good one, and so is its driver. He knows what he is doing."

Sergio made another gut-wrenching turn. Both pursuers did the same. The distance between all three cars was diminishing by the second.

"Everyone, have your pistols ready," Tristan commanded. "Don't shoot until I say so."

In the swath of the last car's powerful headlights, Robert saw an arm with a gun outside the passenger window of the Mercedes. The gun fired. The shot tore through the air. The bullet cracked the rear and front windows of their car.

"Shut off all lights and take your foot off the gas," Tristan said. "Don't touch the brake."

Tristan had already opened the window on his side.

He slid his torso through it, with the gun in both hands.

It made sense, Robert silently agreed. With all lights, including the brake ones, off, their car would be visible only if it appeared in the lights of the following cars. A few turns may help a lot, but driving at such speed with no front lights would be a challenge.

When Tristan was positioned with his body outside the window, he fired. A split second after, a shot was fired from the last car. Robert heard the sound of it, and saw a small flame, typical for a gun. Robert guessed that whoever had fired it had used the same tactics as Tristan.

A quick succession of uncontrollable events occurred after that. The Mercedes behind them skidded, twisted, hit something on the road edge with its front bumper, then jumped in the air, blocking the distant lights of the last car for a moment. It landed on its roof, across the road. The last car was not able to stop in time. The distance was too short, and the speed was too high. It crashed into the second car, and the road plunged into darkness.

Robert noticed that the gun slipped out of Tristan's hands and fell onto the road. Tristan crawled back into his seat; his breathing was loud and heavy.

"Tristan!" Lara screamed. "Tristan. Are you wounded?"

Sergio turned on all lights, including the interior ones. Robert saw Lara leaning over Tristan.

"Sergio!" she cried. "Stop now. I need my rucksack. Stop and open the trunk."

"No, no," Tristan said in a loud whisper. "Sergio, listen to my command. Don't stop. Don't stop."

"Don't listen to him," Lara yelled. "Stop. Now."

"I will stop soon," Sergio shouted back. "Let me find a clearing in the forest to hide in. We can't cure him on the road side."

They drove about five minutes, not speaking, listening to Tristan's breathing. He made a few attempts to speak, but failed.

"Here," Robert said, pointing his finger in the direction of a small side road to the right.

Sergio hit the brakes, made the turn, stopped about hundred meters from the main road, and turned the engine off.

"Lara, Lara," Tristan pleaded. "You do not need your medical bag. The game is over for me. Leave me here. Go south out of here as fast as you can. And then—"

He stopped speaking and closed his eyes. Lara leaned over him, narrowing her eyes. All of a sudden her habitually deadpan face twisted in a weeping grimace and tears rolled down her cheeks in small streams.

"Petya, Petyenka," she screamed between shuddering sobs, kissing his hand. "Petya, don't go, my darling! Please, don't go. Oh, God, please, help me. Help us."

Lara was calling Tristan by his original, Russian name. Robert understood why. The game for Tristan was indeed over. It made sense to bid him his last farewell using the name he was called by in his childhood. As a registered nurse and KGB operative, Lara knew death very well. People of her occupation asked God for help only when there was no hope.

What happened next made Robert, for a brief few moments, believe in miracles. Tristan raised his head and looked at everyone with a mix of pain and smile on his lips. Then he fixed his unmoving, clear stare on Lara.

"I love you," he wheezed. "Remember, what poet Sergey Esenin said? 'Destined parting promises a date ahead.' Then even death won't do us part."

The miracle faded. His head fell back. Lara burst into fresh tears as she looked into the open, solemn eyes of her dead lover.

A thought crossed Robert's mind that Petr, nicknamed Tristan, died as he lived: without fear, and believing in his luck and good future. He took his destiny in the scheme of Providence, without protest and regret. After all, his star had been very kind to him for so long.

Lara was shaking with sobs. Robert touched her shoulder.

"We have to move on, Lara," he said. "There is no time for anything."

She straightened up, wiped her tears, and nodded.

"Let's go," she said in a firm voice, with no trace of emotion remaining in it.

"Take your things with you," Sergio said. He got out of the car, opened the trunk, and took out his rucksack. Lara and Robert did the same and began helping him in silence, as if in a well-rehearsed pantomime. Robert unscrewed the lid of the gas tank. Sergio brought a plastic bucket and a long rubber pipe from the trunk. He plunged one end of it into the gas tank, and took the other end in his mouth and started to suck the air in. The gasoline began flowing from the tank to the bucket, spreading around its tart odor. Robert removed all the passports and other identification papers from Tristan's pockets, and threw them on the front seat. When Sergio started pouring the contents of the bucket on Tristan and all over the inside the car, Lara stood with her back to them, looking the other way, toward the road.

"Go guys, go," Sergio prompted them. Robert and Lara began walking back to the road. Sergio threw the burning match inside the car, and it instantly went ablaze. He ran away from the raging flames and caught up with Lara and Robert.

"Let's give him our last respects," he suggested. They stopped walking and turned around to watch the roaring fire for a few seconds.

"Goodbye, Tristan," Sergio said solemnly.

"Goodbye, Tristan," echoed Lara and Robert.

And then Lara added, "Goodbye, my love."

They rushed to the road, where the dawn of a new day was taking possession of the space. When a medium-sized pickup truck appeared on the distant curve of the road, Robert and Sergio hid behind trees. Lara took a stand and raised her hand, seductively leaning on her hip. The truck stopped. Its driver leaned over to the open passenger window.

"Where do you wish to go, beauty?" he shouted over the noise of the motor.

"Just a few kilometers," she shouted back.

"Come on in." He opened the door. When Lara was climbing into her seat, Robert and Sergio rushed to the car. Sergio jumped over the board in the box and Robert took a place in the cabin beside Lara.

"Hey, hey," protested the driver. "I'm only taking the lady."

Robert gave him a fistful of money. The driver smiled, hid the money inside his pocket, and shifted into first gear.

"What were you doing here this early?" the driver asked.

"We are tourists," Robert said. "Hitchhiking all over the country. Lovely place."

"You look like locals," the driver said, giving him a squinting, incredulous look.

Robert supported the conversation as much as he could, hoping that the driver's questions would eventually end. They didn't, but Lara came to his rescue.

"Are you married?" she asked the driver. This maneuver did marvels. The driver began talking about his family, friends, and all his past victories over the weaker sex.

"Did you break many hearts?" he asked Lara with a chuckle. Lara ignored his question.

"What do you think about your government?" she asked instead. Here, she hit the jackpot. The driver, bubbling with excitement, began talking politics, often taking his hands off the steering wheel to gesticulate emphatically. When the pickup truck started to pass by a small town, Sergio hit the roof of the cabin a few times.

"Stop here," Robert demanded.

"You do not wish to go any further?" The driver asked with a great deal of disappointment in his voice. Robert gave him another few pesos.

"Stop here. Thanks. It was really nice of you."

Sergio jumped onto the ground. Lara stepped down and closed the door with a bang. The driver waved his hand and left.

Sergio knew well what he was doing. He removed a small box of tools from his rucksack, came to the first shabby car parked on the roadside, and quickly unlocked the door. It took him less than two minutes to open the hood and turn the engine on. As usual, Robert settled in the front passenger seat. Lara sat behind him.

"I know little about this place," Robert said. "It will be a guessing game to get to Buenos Aires."

"We do not need to go there," Lara said. "Let's get out of this country today, boys."

"I'm going to stay a couple of days here," Sergio said.

"What about you, Robert?" she asked.

"I need a day or two. I'm too tired to start a long journey right now."

"I can understand Sergio," she said. "He has Rebecca here. Right, Sergio?"

"Right," he said. "I want to take her with me. Where do you suggest we meet, Robert?"

"In Italy. You will find me in one of the cafés around the Coliseum. I will be there from four to six every day. Then and there we will decide how to deal with our money in the Swiss banks."

"I will start moving north, to Uruguay, today," Lara

said.

When they reached the suburbs of Buenos Aires, Robert asked Sergio to stop the car near a motel.

"See you in Italy," he said. Lara stepped out of the car to embrace him.

"See you," she said, and then shook with uncontrolled sobs. Robert could not find any words of consolation for her. He clenched his teeth as tears streamed down his face.

"He liked you," she mumbled through her weeping. "He said that you were the most human among us."

"I had a great deal of respect for him," Robert whispered.

"Wish you luck, Robert."

She wiped her tears and returned to her seat. Robert stood a few moments, watching the car merge into traffic. "End of the Robert Chavez story," he said to himself. When he went into the reception area of the motel, he produced another forged passport, issued in the name of Julio Rodrigez.

Once in his room, Robert took a shower and went to bed. When he woke up it was dark inside. He turned the night table lamp on and dialed Bertha's number. In his inner vision, he saw the voluptuous hills and valleys of her warm body, smelled the fragrance of her French perfume, and heard her submissive moan of joy and her hot whisper in his ear: 'Oh, my sweet devil. My dear boy.' But now, he just wanted to hear her voice, nothing else. Nobody picked up the phone. No doubt she already knew about the death of her husband.

Then he called Claus.

"Hola," Claus answered the call after the first ring.

"Hola, Claus. This is Robert."

"Oh, my friend." Claus's voice was cheerful and full of good humor. "Thanks for calling. You wish to tell me some news?"

"Yes. As I promised. Remember our talk about Kurt Jaeger?"

"Of course I do. What about him?"

"He is dead."

"Dead?" Claus exclaimed in surprise. "How do you know?"

"Because I killed him."

He placed the phone back on its cradle. As far as Robert was concerned, the conversation was over. The journey to Italy for Julio Rodrigez had begun.

Chapter 18

For two weeks, Glenn had been training a special police unit assembled to fight armed left-wing rebels. During this time, he had made friends with Bolivar, the commander of the unit, who respected Glenn for his knowledge and experience. When the unit was more or less prepared, he declared to Glenn, "Tomorrow we will take off."

The same day, Eduardo called and said that they needed to talk. As usual, the meeting place was a good restaurant. Eduardo came late and took a chair across the table. His face remained solemn during the small talk while the wine was being served. After the main dish arrived, he stopped talking altogether.

"Something is bothering you." Glenn pronounced it as a statement, as a fact that could not be denied. Eduardo delayed his response, chewing his meat with the blank expression of a man deep in thought. It seemed that he had lost his ability to smile as a result of something, which had happened in his life a few weeks ago. Before responding to Glenn's remark, he swallowed his mouthful and washed it down with wine.

"Frankly, I am lost," he admitted, cutting another piece from his steak. A good appetite was the only feature that remained from his jovial temperament. "We found a corpse in the burned Ford. The man was killed by your bullet, which is already not a secret. Ballistic expertise confirmed that it was fired from your rifle, which was found in your car. One of Kurt's bodyguards, whom you saved, told us the story from his point of view. Police bosses understand that we should not be very hard on you in the investigation. That will keep you out of trouble for a little while, but your days in Argentina are numbered."

"It is not my future that concerns you the most, does it?"

"Right." Eduardo raised his eyes. His stare was heavy, conveying a sense of worry and grim.

"The death of Kurt Jeager stirred the entire German community, and particularly its influential people. We are under pressure now, as our bosses, and some influential people in the government, demand from us an explanation of why a few Germans have disappeared lately. It is true that the police have adopted this practice against radical leftists. The government is okay with this. But when wealthy people who support the government, and right-wing activists, disappear, both the government and the Germans go berserk. The government even suspected us, the police. Stupid. They said, 'Either find the perpetrators, or else you are the suspects.' The point is that the kidnappings, or murders, were done by professionals, and likely by locals, who knew the people and the ways to get them."

"The government does not believe the police?" Glenn asked.

"You can offer all sorts of explanations and hypotheses, but the fact is that so far the police are the only suspects. But Kurt's death was evidence that showed that the police were not involved in the case. There is another piece of circumstantial evidence though, that it was not police who did it. A few weeks ago, a policeman disappeared. He was last seen in Puerto Madero. None of the radical groups claimed responsibility." Eduardo stared Glenn in the eyes. Glenn did not blink.

"We must solve these puzzles at any cost," Eduardo continued, returning his attention to his plate. "We must find those who kidnapped the Germans and the policeman. In all likelihood, they are the same who killed Kurt Jeager."

"I am doing my best," Glenn said.

"I know, I know. You risked your life. But you should've done it with our police. We will discuss this unpleasant issue later, after you help us to crush the communist rebels in the north."

After Eduardo finished his steak, his voice became softer, "When communists disappear, the government looks the other way. But when wealthy, respectable people disappear, it becomes a completely different story."

Glenn twisted his lips into a wry smile. Eduardo noticed it and leaned forward, assuming an air of confidentiality.

"I know what you think, Glenn. Yes, from our government's point of view, they are respectable, useful and law-abiding citizens. The war was over a long time ago. These people are no longer SS members. They are businessmen, professionals, taxpayers, you name it. That's what they are in Argentina. They have no intention to cause chaos, disorder, and crime, as communists do."

"You do not have to explain this paradox to me, Eduardo," Glenn said. "My whole mission here is to fight communists."

"When do you go north?" Eduardo asked.

"Tomorrow."

"Wish you luck. Hope to see you soon in one piece," Eduardo said. A trace of a smile at last appeared on his face. "Try to capture a few prisoners. Maybe they will provide a clue to what happened with the policeman at Puerto Madero."

***

The long column of trucks and armored vehicles began rolling northwest before dawn. In the leading Jeep were the driver, Glenn, and Bolivar, the unit commander. Serious, alert, and eager to impose strict discipline on the soldiers, Bolivar nonetheless indulged from time to time in a swig or two from his flask. “Brandy,” he explained curtly with a cursory glance, offering it to Glenn. Glenn refused. He strongly disapproved of drinking on duty, but he abstained from commenting. After all, he was supposed to help them, not discipline them.

The paved road beyond Buenos Aires merged into a gravel surface and then into a bumpy dirt road, with endless potholes, deep, long dents made by tires, and unexpected turns and twists. Many hours of continuous jolting pushed Glenn’s guts up to his throat. Luckily, there was no rain. The forest on both sides of the Jeep grew lower and denser. In some places, he could see small lakes and marshes in the clearings between the trees, and then again the walls of the dark forest would rise to the right and left of the vehicle.

At night, they set up a camp near a small lake with marshy shores. The soldiers were all in a good mood. They cooked primitive meals, drank the local Yerba tea through a metallic pipe called a bombilla, and exchanged rough, salty jokes of homosexual nature. Roars of laughter burst out now and then, followed by the usual drone of meaningless blabber and the rattle of utensils.

Before retiring to sleep, Glenn accepted Bolivar’s generous offer of his flask. The hot, local liquid of poor quality, which Bolivar had promoted to the ranks of ‘brandy,’ raised his mood and warmed his chest. After Bolivar crawled inside the tent, Glenn lit a cigarette and went to the lakeshore. The night, as black as onyx, gripped the forest. There was no moon and no stars in the cloudy sky. Glenn turned on his powerful flashlight and directed its beam at the lake. Reflecting off of the eyes of the numerous alligators that were resting under the lake surface, the light sprang back as if it had hit tiny, scattered mirrors. The beasts did not blink, and did not move; their open eyes remained raised above the surface of the quiet water like the small periscopes of submarines.

The next afternoon, the column reached a small village where indigenous people lived in primitive huts, with no conveniences, no modern technology, and no decent food or clothing. They did not seem to be unhappy though. One of them, for a small reward, agreed to show Bolivar where the guerilla had gone two nights ago. They were alarmed, he said. Someone had warned them that the government was after them. The native smiled when he received some money for the betrayal of the people who were ostensibly fighting for his sake. He took a place in the front jeep, together with Bolivar and Glenn, and gave them directions.

They passed a few lakes, on which floating islands drifted. The roots of trees, bushes, and lianas interwove into a tight mass, in some places a few meters deep, providing numerous birds and other species with a safe place in the forest. For a human, walking or even hiding in there would be impossible. There was no room for a person to even take a step.

The native brought them to the place from where, on his accounts, the rebels had gone into hiding. Bolivar gave the command to stop and jumped out of the Jeep, stretching his legs.

“I studied the map of Corrientes quite a bit,” Glenn said. “Americans produced one, pretty accurate. If this local guy does not lie, which is unlikely I think, then they didn’t go too far. Lakes and marshes would have limited their maneuvers. My assessment is that there are more than two hundred people there. Many of them are trained, smart fighters – don’t underestimate them.”

He peered into the forest; although it was very dense, the trees were thinner than in the jungle of Bolivia, allowing for observation at a far greater distance. But this would work both ways, he concluded, and the enemy would likely have the marginal advantage of noticing the advancing troops before they themselves were noticed. He decided to send a few groups ahead for reconnaissance, while the bulk of their force would follow at some distance. When location and distribution of the guerilla's force were understood, the tactics of the battle would be defined and refined, depending on circumstances.

Bolivar agreed with his considerations and sent a few small groups ahead, with two or three soldiers in each, spread out from one another at a distance of about three hundred meters. The major force moved behind them at a greater distance, ready to drop on the ground at the first sounds of shots, and then return the fire.

Bolivar was close by, and more serious than ever, perhaps because he did not have even a single drop of alcohol inside him.

"Coordination is the most important factor in fighting," Glenn repeated to him, well aware that it irritated the commander. "Sometimes you have more casualties from 'friendly fire' than from the enemy. I suggest, Bolivar, not to take prisoners. What are we supposed to do with them?"

His concern was Miguel and Flavio. They might spill the beans, which would add a heavy weight to his troubles.

Bolivar nodded and gestured back at the radio operator, who followed his steps.

"If they split into several groups, do not fight all of them at once," Glenn kept instructing him. "Let us finish them one by one, I will tell you in what sequence. Okay?"

This instruction was not taken lightly. Bolivar gave him a fierce look of anger, which expressed better than words his thought, "Are you taking me for a fool?"

He was not a fool, of course, but Glenn knew too well that soldiers with no experience in real action were not easy to handle the first time. Seemingly smart during training, they often behaved like a herd of raging bulls, or worse, a flock of scared sheep, when the bullets start flying and the ground started shaking with explosions.

The unit was well-equipped with automatic rifles and light, portable artillery, and had a good supply of ammunition. The rebels were doomed, Glenn concluded, no matter how bad the luck would turn out for the troops during combat.

Half an hour later, the dry rattle of the first shots reverberated and quickly grew into the deafening roar of guns. Bolivar proved to be good at making his own decisions, but he nonetheless followed Glenn's instructions as a disciplined soldier.

Although violent death was a part of his job description and a factor in his daily life, Glenn still was unable to extinguish his burning fear of it before going into battle. However, when the first shot was fired, he forgot about it, as he had always done in the past. His thoughts we preoccupied with actions, decisions, and commands, as if death did not exist.

"They are split in two groups," Glenn shouted to Bolivar. "The one closer to us is smaller. Let's finish them first."

These rebels were obviously well-trained, Glenn noticed. He was not facing the chaotic shots of daring revolutionary wannabes, but of disciplined, dedicated fighters, with the determination to win or die. A few soldiers fell, either wounded, or dead. So be it. In modern war, the level of technology, skills, armament, and communication defined its outcome, not the courage or dedication of the fighters. His foe was poorly equipped.

Bolivar gave the command to surround the rebels and lock them inside the horseshoe-like arrangement of his troops, its open part being marshes and the lake. After this task was completed, the real meat-grinding began with hand-held grenade launchers and heavy machine guns.

The fighting ground, however, was still large; the rebels began retreating to the marshes, leaving their wounded and dead behind. Advancing with the troops, Glenn encountered the first bodies of the guerillas, some of which were not dead yet, and were trying in vain to hold onto their rifles.

There was no one who surrendered or pleaded for mercy. They were very brave, believing that they were dying for the right cause. A thought occurred to Glenn that he might soon see Miguel or Barjardo, perhaps even alive. He did not like the idea, but what the hell? In his profession, you do not leave a place for sentiments in your soul. They are going to be dead soon one way or another. The real important thing was that the enemy's hardest defense was crushed; the rest would just be technicalities of war.

A few meters to the left, he took notice of a small, lifeless body, lying face down in the mud. For no reason at all, just following some weird instinct, Glenn turned it over. What he saw made him utter a cry of horror. It was Lollita, dressed in a camouflage outfit, with blood and mud covering her face almost beyond recognition. Glenn fell on her in despair, then lifted her off the ground, and looked at her face. With no hope in his voice he murmured, "Lollita, Lollita. Do you hear me?" In her open, glassy eyes he read her silent answer: "I am dead, Glenn. I love you."

He let her lifeless body drop in the mud and looked around. Bolivar was behind him, on the left side. Glenn hurried to the right with quick steps, trying to hold in his grief as long as he could. When nobody was in sight, he embraced a thin tree and shuddered in a silent, desperate attempt to suppress his violent sobs. Nothing helped. Something inside his chest and stomach was shaking him like the worst fit of malaria, with no end in sight. He squeezed the tree tighter, as if asking Mother Nature for mercy. It worked; his sobs subsided, then stopped. He wiped away his tears and returned in almost normal shape to where the soldiers were. The first person he met with was Bolivar.

"You have your flask with you?" he asked the commander. Bolivar gave it to him without saying a word. Glenn drank almost all of its contents and gave it back to Bolivar.

"Did you know her?" Bolivar half whispered.

"Sort of," Glenn said. "Everything is under control?"

"The left group, the larger one, retreated farther away into the marshes. It is too late today to chase them. Never mind though, at night they will be eaten alive by mosquitoes. Tomorrow, we will finish those who remain."

Glenn went back to the armored cars and sat there till dusk, not interfering with the actions of the military unit. Then Bolivar returned from the forest and offered him his spare flask, filled to the brim.

"Any POW?" Glenn asked.

"Nah. We killed everyone," Bolivar said. "You were right. Too much work and trouble bringing them back to Buenos Aires." He smiled and took the flask from Glenn. Indulging in a huge swig, he explained his eligibility for quenching his thirst: "I deserve it."

"What did you do with the corpses?" asked Glenn. "Left them where they were?"

"Nah. We threw them to the alligators. The simplest mode of disposal."

Glenn nodded and yanked the flask from Bolivar's hands.

"We did a good job, Glenn," Bolivar said, hugging him with his heavy hand.

"We certainly did," Glenn said. His brain was no longer able to absorb the outside world. I wish I were killed before seeing her, he thought.

Chapter 19

The import-export company where Glenn held his fictitious job allocated a few rooms for American intelligence operatives. Glenn visited his office now and then, as he kept his files and records there. It was a reliable place; the security was tight, and all measures of precaution were undertaken to prevent break-ins or access to the sensitive material. Glenn came there three days after the communist rebels were finished, and took to arranging his papers. He was almost sure that this was his last day in this company.

After clearing his desk, he leaned back and stared at the large picture on the wall. In it, a dark-skinned gaucho – the Argentinean version of the American cowboy – sat on a horse and held the end of a lasso in his right hand. The loop was about to land on a bull's neck. Glenn recalled that before coming to Argentina, he had wanted to travel a bit to the pampas, the Argentinean prairies, and see the rural life and this singular exotic place with his own eyes. Regretfully, there was no time for it.

The door to his office opened and Jeff poked his head in.

"Max is here," he said in a low voice. He moved back and closed the door. Soon after, their boss, Max Robinson, showed up, all smiles and bubbling with energy.

"How are you?" he asked, taking Glenn's hand in his tight grip, which was supposed to convey his good mood and friendly disposition.

"Good." Glenn got out two cigars from his top drawer. "Want one? Cubans. You won't get them in the States."

"Sure," Max said, grabbing a cigar. After the short ritual of cutting and lighting it, he said, "You have to move out of Argentina. A new assignment is waiting for you."

Glenn expected it. He also knew that his past accomplishments did not diminish the significance of his failure with the Soviet agents.

"I regret that we did not capture Soviet spies. We were pretty close to it."

"We will get them eventually. They support communists, and communists will spill the beans."

"We won't capture those who kidnapped the Germans. I'm sure they are gone."

"You are right," agreed Max. "Now it will be completely in the hands of the local police. We will support them no matter what they do."

"They do nasty things."

"True. Enough about them. Do you have a girl that you wish to marry?"

"No. Why?"

"Because your next assignment is not for a married man."

"I understand. Where is it?"

"Paraguay."

Glenn looked him in the eye and paused.

"So what? Marriage is the best arrangement for people of our profession," he said, and chuckled.

"Why so?" The boss asked, anticipating a joke.

"I recall what Oscar Wilde said about it."

"What?"

"The one charm of marriage is that it makes a life of deception absolutely necessary for both parties."

The boss laughed.

"C'mon, Glenn. I know that you were a very educated kid before you joined our force. Well, back to serious matters. Paraguay."

"There are some former SS members there. Are you after them?"

"No. Not them." Max frowned.

"Why not them? We can get them. After all, they are still active and considered criminals."

"They support forces that are against communists and all sorts of leftists. And they are no longer SS members. And many of them cooperate with us."

A trace of displeasure twisted his lips.

"Have we forgiven them?" insisted Glenn.

"Glenn, Glenn," his boss' voice shifted to the tone of a gentle, fatherly reprimand.

He lingered a few moments before giving Glenn an answer, an acidic smile forming on his lips. "Morality issues are not a part of our job. We are behind the scenes of a huge theater called geopolitics. There are many innocent casualties of it, and morals, regretfully, almost always is one of them. On the global scheme, communism is the primary culprit, and we fight against it. This ideology has no morals. Can an earnest man fight a dishonest one and win, if everything else is equal? We welcome the cooperation of anyone, as our foe is powerful. Look at Cuba! Look at the troubles in Argentina and other Latin American countries. Can we afford not to have alliances?"

"Okay. I will take a short vacation and think about my new assignment."

"You will get instructions in the States. Wish you luck, Glenn."

Max rose to his feet and left the room, still holding the burning Cuban cigar.

END